THE OBESITY CONSPIRACY

MARK SARNEY

CHAPTER 1

I F YOU WANT TO UNDERSTAND why we have an obesity epidemic, watch me make lusty mouth-love to this chocolate-covered fry cake. Why would I do that when I know better? I was away from home and short on time. The fry cake was free and ready to eat at my hotel's continental breakfast spread. Outside the hotel was a food desert: no grocery store for miles, but plenty of fast food restaurants. And the fry cake's taste, ah, that buttery sweetness reminds me of sitting in a bakery with my father on Saturday mornings.

Ironically, I'm a nutrition expert who was about to go on national TV to lecture one of America's most obese towns about how to eat better. And no, I'm not overweight.

Yes, I am a hypocrite. I savored every bite of the fry cake's crunchy outside, the sweet chocolate frosting, and the dense, dry cake inside. I also understood that I was ingesting a ton of sugar, carbs, and saturated fat.

But I didn't feel conflicted. I was knowingly duped by all the factors that conspired to make this town one of the most obese in an obese country. When in Rome, right?

Half an hour later, I was walking to the makeup trailer of the inspirational reality TV show *We Will*, when that donut turned into a cement brick in my stomach. I knew this was coming. I climbed the steps to the trailer and went inside, prepared to tough out a sugar coma and have my appearance critiqued.

I opened the door and the bright lights inside blasted away the gloom of an overcast early morning. "I'm Elaine Cassano."

"Yes, hi, I'm Anne," said the makeup artist, a blond woman in her forties. "Have a seat and let's take a look at you." She stood behind the chair and I watched her in the mirror as she did a silent evaluation.

By the way, if you think I'm reporting on the weight and obesity status of everyone in this story, you'll be disappointed.

She fluffed my hair. "I love your springy, black curls. I'm just going to apply the standard touches for filming in high-def."

She got to work and bustled around every side of my head. "The call sheet says that you're a nutrition expert. Did you know the crew has a weight loss challenge too?" She grinned. "I smuggled in a stash of healthy food to cover the entire twelve-week shoot."

Well, that was one way to deal with a food desert. I suppose I could have done the same.

She explained that she and the other crew of *We Will* were part of a challenge segment to see how the production crew fared eating on location. Craft service would offer only local food so the crew would eat like the locals.

"Well, the high calorie burn of the production schedule should help mitigate some of the weight gain from eating local. But with little time to eat, convenience, long shooting schedules and lousy quality have the makings of a nutritional disaster for the crew. Especially for women our age."

She gave me a look. I was being too blunt, again.

"That's why I smuggled in my own stuff," she said.

A high-strung production assistant stepped in the trailer. "Dr. Elaine Cassano, right? I'm Rich, no pun intended, haha. Are you excited to be on TV today?" he asked without looking up from his tablet. He was rail-thin and deeply tan, with a mop of styled hair. He reeked of cigarettes.

"Where's Melanie?" I asked. Melanie was the one who'd contacted my agency's press office about having a government expert on their show.

Rich didn't look up. "Industrial accident at a food processing plant that she wanted to check out. Then she's off to Memphis to talk to the free liposuction tour people about stopping here."

He poked at his tablet. "Elaine, you have two scenes today: the interview with RJ at nine and the town hall at one. You went through the practice interview with Melanie yesterday, right? Good. This is a two-camera setup in a doctor's office over at the medical building, a news interview. Are you a medical doctor or an academic?"

"Academic. My PhD is in Systems Biology."

Rich scribbled a note on his tablet. "And you work for the government, right?"

"Human nutrition research at the Agricultural Research Service," I said. That was actually my last job, before I was sent to the public relations shop. But it's what a non-Fed would understand.

"Great, that's what I have. Now, for the town hall, you're giving a presentation about the causes of the obesity epidemic and then Q&A." He looked up. "Is this a presentation you've given before to Joe Six-Pack?"

"Several times." It had been my job for over a year now. Since Congress had forced ARS to form a 'truth squad' to educate people about the obesity epidemic. My bluntness had landed me there, my boss claimed, because I would be an asset in that context. But the real reason was so I would no longer antagonize certain folks back in Human Nutrition.

Rich scowled. "It's not dry and scientific, right? We don't want the crowd asleep. If it doesn't work, we'll just have to cut it, okay?"

"It's for a layman audience. Bottom line: There are no silver bullets or smoking guns. The end is a peppy 'You can take control' call to action."

Rich nodded. "Fantastic. This is for the season premiere. The town hall is unscripted; I'll warn you that some local people are already unhappy about the show being here. You got the season's synopsis, right?"

I nodded. *We Will* was several reality TV shows wrapped into one. It chose a different improvement theme each year and then helped the community that made the best case for needing that type of change. Last season had been reducing crime in a Detroit neighborhood. I had watched it religiously, as had my mother. I have a soft spot for reality TV.

This season focused on physical fitness. It included a weight loss contest, a healthy cooking segment, improving the town's food choices by revamping grocery stores and starting a farmer's market, and an engineering competition to make the town more walkable.

Rich continued, "Melanie says that you're a real straight shooter, which is perfect. We really need you to explain why people become obese. Don't sugarcoat it, haha. I'll see you on set, Dr. Cassano. You'll do great."

RJ Newcastle is everywhere these days, hosting radio and TV shows, and emceeing national concerts and parades. You can tell by that smile of his that he likes people. Half the reason I wanted this assignment was to meet him.

When he shook my hand and turned his charm in my direction, I smiled my stupid, gaping fangirl grin that makes my cheeks hurt after a few seconds. Truth was, I wanted to jump in his lap and run my hands over his lean, brown, shaved head. For starters. I told myself I should think of adipose and lipids. I'd already had my moment of weakness with that fry cake.

RJ and I did the interview standing at a nursing station in a doctor's office. The director made me don a white lab coat and wanted to capture the breezy, confident look of those erectile dysfunction ads where the patient has a wonderful but silent interaction with his doctor. Standing implied action and importance, and it looked as though I were taking a break between seeing patients, even though I reminded him that I'm a scientist, not a medical doctor. But that's television.

While the crew finished prepping the scene, RJ and I chatted about things that I'll never remember. The director came over and explained that the interview would be featured in the first episode to put context around the challenge. RJ would record voice-overs that restated my technical points to explain the rationale behind various challenges.

"If the crowd rips your head off at the town hall, we'll have a nice juxtaposition with a quiet interview here," RJ added with that smile.

We took our positions, and the cameras started rolling. RJ thanked me for coming. "Elaine, could you tell us a bit about yourself?"

"I have a PhD in Systems Biology and work at the Agricultural Department doing nutrition research."

"What does Systems Biology have to do with obesity?"

I smiled. "Good question. Systems Biology is the big picture of biology: how various components in an organism act as a whole. For example, how does the human body process energy? That is a key question in studying obesity. How many calories do we burn standing versus sitting? Does it depend on what we ate and when, our mental workload, stress, and other factors?"

"And now you work on a truth squad. What is that?"

"Congress was alarmed that people didn't have accurate information about nutrition and obesity. Most scientific research is highly technical and inaccessible to the general public. So, Congress mandated that several agencies reach out and inform the public about the obesity epidemic."

RJ stared at me for a second with a frown. He said, "So, tell me the truth, Dr. Cassano: How fat are we?"

"A third of American adults are overweight. That means one out of three have a body mass index over 25 and less than 30. Another 40% of adults are obese, which means they have a body mass index of 30 or greater. Together, this means that seven out of ten Americans weigh too much."

"We have never been a skinny country, though," RJ countered.

I nodded. "But we've been skinnier. Over the last fifty years, the proportion of overweight adults hasn't increased much but the proportion of obese adults has exploded. In the early 1960s, 13% were obese. It was 23% in the 1980s, 30% in 2000, 40% in 2010, and over 45% today."

At that point, the director stopped us and set us up to walk down the hall slowly for the next question.

"What, exactly, is making so many of us fat, Doctor?"

"We take in more calories than we use. Our bodies store the extra energy as fat tissue. Too much food, too little exercise. There are no shortcuts. And it's not a matter of just exercising more; if you eat three thousand calories of junk food per day, exercising for half an hour won't burn it off. We need to eat less."

"That's a tough order to follow." RJ shook his head sadly. "So what happens if we don't?"

"Obesity feeds heart disease, stroke, diabetes, cancer, hypertension, infertility, sleep apnea, and a host of other diseases and disorders. Joints can't handle the physical strain and give out. It can be especially devastating for children and teens. We're only just starting to learn about the long-term effects of obesity on young bodies."

When Melanie had first contacted me about participating, she'd said each episode would begin with one of these damning factoids about obesity, followed by a simple, black-on-white message: "We Will Beat It."

The next question was filmed back at the nursing station. "How did this rapid increase in obesity happen?"

"The truth is, we're not sure, RJ. There are many culprits that we think have combined to make this epidemic take place, in a little over a generation."

RJ scowled. "Come on, doctor, there have to be specific causes."

This was a tricky question. Whatever I ticked off could be pointed at as the only cause by an enterprising journalist searching for a storyline heavy on drama but light on facts. "Exercising too little, eating too much, more sedentary jobs, environmental pollution, video games, computers, cable TV, the Internet, the explosion in romance novel reading, bigger dinner plates, lower food prices, 'food deserts', eliminating gym classes for kids, more junk food, more takeout, more snacking, a drop in smoking, medications that alleviate obesity-related diseases, the Food Network, antibiotic overuse, growth hormones in food, kids not playing outside, the car, the subway, suburbia, exurbia, lack of medical care, artificial sweeteners, cultural attitudes about food, agricultural subsidies, social pressure to indulge, lack of social pressure to stay fit, long commutes, false advertising, the school lunch program, the aging of society, the decline of manual labor, global warming, food additives, changing clothes sizes, escalators, food subsidies, lack of willpower, security concerns, and food addiction."

"How many of those factors are really to blame?"

I shrugged. "No one knows. Many of those factors feed on one another. In basic scientific terms, we consume more calories than we burn, and that leads to buildup of fatty tissue. We're building up more fatty tissue than we used to. There are many systematic factors at work."

"What would you tell someone in America who wants to lose weight, to stop being obese?"

"Eat less. Exercise more. Your body is a finely tuned energy processor."

"You're saying that personal responsibility comes first?"

I turned my mouth into a thin line. As a fed, I couldn't answer that question. I could only deflect it. "If you wait for the world to change before you save your own life, you'll just die sooner."

"If your child were becoming obese, what would you do?"

I stopped cold. I thought of my son Charlie. I couldn't help it. What could I say? Charlie was heavy for a ten-year-old and the heartbreaking truth was there was nothing I could do about it. Losing custody greatly limited a parent's reach.

A lump formed in my throat. I opened my mouth and nothing came out. My eyes began to fill and once I start crying, my eyes are bloodshot for a good hour.

"I'm sorry; hit the wrong chord, there." RJ smiled reassuringly at me and touched me lightly on the elbow. "Take a second and we'll go again."

The director motioned to keep rolling and I tried to gather my wits. I swallowed and cracked my knuckles.

RJ said, "If a parent asks you what to do to prevent their kids from becoming obese, what would you say?"

I rolled out the stock answer. "There is a social aspect to obesity. As with smoking, parental actions can send powerful signals to a child about what is acceptable and even admirable. How a parent eats and exercises teaches the children how to do the same."

"Dr. Cassano, what do you think about our effort? Can this town make itself more fit?"

"I hope so. I really do. But probably not."

"That's pretty pessimistic," RJ replied skeptically.

"Unless attitudes about eating and exercising change, people will revert back to what's easier, cheaper, and familiar. This is a very tough epidemic to fight. I do wish them the best."

When Melanie had interviewed me, she deemed me the show's Doubting Thomas, the pessimistic government bureaucrat whom the town would prove wrong. It would give the residents something to rally against. I was happy to play the villain if it pushed them to be healthier.

The director had us walk again, for a hall-strolling shot.

"What else should we do?" RJ asked.

"Make sure every house has a mirror and a scale. Regular checkups. Raise the price of soda and junk food, and add a takeout tax. Subsidize farm stands that sell fruits and vegetables. Have a dinner plate amnesty where people turn in their oversized dinner plates for smaller ones. You need to build up a critical mass of changes in lifestyle and health to counter all the factors that have fed the obesity epidemic."

"You know that we'll work twice as hard now to prove you wrong," RJ said with that sly grin of his.

"I hope you do," I replied. "I really hope you do."

"Thanks so much for talking with us today, Dr. Cassano. I have one more question for you. What did you eat for breakfast this morning?"

I didn't answer RJ's question. For lunch, I'd had a turkey sub from craft service and stripped out the Swiss cheese. I'd only eaten half of it while Rich drove me to the town hall in a golf cart.

As I went backstage to check that my presentation would work on the projector, RJ went onstage to warm up the audience. That turkey sub did the backstroke in my stomach with languid strokes, bumping into the fry cake, probably. There was one of those long pauses as they made the final preparations for filming, and then RJ called me up on stage.

RJ gave me a generous introduction to the audience, who filled the seats and stood in the aisles. When I appeared, he gave me a kiss on the cheek and a full body hug, like we were old friends. I was grinning like a jackal when I took the podium and hoped that he had transferred some of the crowd's goodwill to me. One look at the audience stomped that hope into the ground.

I began with a dramatic rendition of the rise of obesity across the nation, complete with the CDC charts showing each state becoming more obese over a few decades. I covered a lot of the same ground that I had in the interview with RJ, but with graphics to back it up.

I've done this presentation a dozen times for a variety of audiences. Most of the audience listened intently, nodding their heads at some points and shaking them in disappointed shock at others.

As production assistants hustled around with microphones for questions, the first question went to the mayor. She was a portly woman in her sixties with a gracious smile. She thanked me for being here, thanked the network for providing so many resources to help the town. "We're not the most obese town in America," she noted, "but we entered this contest because we know we have a lot of work to do. Do you think this will work and make us fit?"

"No, it won't," I said. The crowd sucked in their breath and I let them hang in suspense for a second. "It's only a good start. After the show leaves, it will be up to all of you. Can you eat healthier and eat less, exercise more? Will you help your friend, your neighbor, and your child when they are struggling?"

The mayor's face clouded and she sat down. No key to the city for me.

A meek Hispanic woman in the back held the microphone awkwardly as she asked, "But when my kids want that bag of Doritos, or there's a birthday party and they have cake, or all their friends bring their stupid video games to school, what I can do? This is beyond our control." Heads bobbed in agreement.

I wanted to tell her to just say no. But I couldn't be the Dr. Phil of nutrition or the Suzie Orman of obesity and tell people to take control of their lives. "Your kids' lives are at stake. Take charge, make a pact with other parents about snacks, video games, birthday cake."

Next question. "Isn't this really because of genetics?"

I shook my head. "The epidemic happened in just about thirty years. There would have to have been a massive environmental change that mutated our genes, but we haven't seen any evidence of it."

An old woman stood up, hunched over but with her eyes burning. She grabbed the microphone like it was a billy club. "I'll tell you the real problem. There's no personal responsibility any more. Gluttony is a sin, and fat people have no one to blame but themselves. If you're fat, it's only because you eat too much. End of discussion!" She sat back down and folded her arms, waiting defiantly for my response.

I gripped the podium with both hands until the veins in my hands popped. "Every time I give this talk, every time, someone fat-shames. It's either jokes or outright insults like that last comment. It's rude, it's counterproductive, and it's not true. Next question."

The woman started yelling back at me, but she had given up the microphone. I pretended not to hear her. "Next question." I pointed at the next person I saw standing with a microphone.

Another angry, scowling woman stood up. "Look, I'm getting sick and tired of you people marching in here and telling us how to live our lives. Telling us not to speak our minds. You think you're perfect? I work for a living. I raise my kids and pay my taxes. Who the hell do you think you are? What do you say to that, you skinny little bitch?"

The crowd gasped and there was a smattering of giggles and applause. I suddenly noticed security guards in dark t-shirts fidgeting at the exits.

"No one's called me skinny in years, thank you, dear! Actually, I could lose a few pounds. I speak before I think sometimes, which is why I have a script to stick to. But the bottom line is that obesity is a disease. It will shorten our lifespans if we all don't work together to fight it."

An older man stood up with a microphone. "How can the epidemic be caused by everything and nothing at the same time? I don't believe it."

"I'm sorry sir. Are you having trouble believing that there is one cause, or that there is an epidemic at all?" I asked, straining to not sound condescending.

"All of it. It's just scientists cooking the books again, like you do with global warming and smoking. No one mentions the ozone hole, anymore, do they?"

I waited for the next questioner, but then realized that the audience wanted me to respond. I cleared my throat. "Scientists are committed to finding the truth. As a scientist I have to say that you are flat-out wrong in not believing in scientific evidence. Science is why the roof above us doesn't cave in, and these television cameras can record sound and video. You may not like what the evidence shows—I certainly don't—but we can't ignore it."

The old guy dismissed me with a hand wave. "There's more things on this Earth than science can tell us. When I was a young man, things happened that no science can explain. Angels walk the earth. And so does the devil."

A smile snuck up the side of my mouth. "I can't disagree with you. I'm half Italian, and my Italian grandmother swore to her dying day that she had once fought off a Romanian striogi when she was in Bucharest. A striogio is like a vampire, she told me, but this one didn't bite. She was warning me about going out at night by myself when I had just started high school. Now, I love my grandmother very much, but I don't believe she fought an undead man when she was in her twenties."

He sat back down.

Another man stood up and the assistant handed him a microphone. He was wearing a business suit and had a gracious smile. "Maybe being a bit bigger has happened because we are richer. Medical care can allow us to live with it. So, what's the big deal?"

"It's not just a bit bigger," I replied. "This is a monstrous explosion in being dangerously overweight. I don't think we want people to get knees replaced before they are fifty. Or to have Type II diabetes in middle school. Obesity will kill you faster, kill your children faster, and it's avoidable."

A short woman with a head of white hair was next. "This is nothing but a conspiracy!" she yelled. "Bunch of fitness freaks and liberal hippie farmers, trying to pick the pockets of working people. Buy lettuce for under a buck in a grocery store but its five bucks if it's organic. Pretty soon, everything will be organic and ten times the price! They raised our taxes when we were starving to stop hunger. Now they want to tax our soda because we're fat and we never see a red cent from it. It's another unconstitutional Washington scam, paid for by our tax dollars!"

A few others in the crowd hooted their approval. I saw a sheriff's deputy step in the back door with Melanie. The crowd might be rougher than they'd expected.

I shrugged. "The government paid for me to come out here in hopes that a couple of you will not cost taxpayers millions in dollars of health care expenses. And yes, we want everyone in the country to live longer, healthier lives."

The questioner had her arms folded, but now asked a follow up. "Fine, but what's the government doing to help us?"

I tried answering that with the USDA Food Pyramid and some simple, old-fashioned advice. I explained that several government agencies—including NIH, CDC, FDA and my shop, the Agricultural Research Service—were scrambling to provide answers. To make sure food additives were safe, to better count calorie consumption and document Americans' eating patterns. The presentation and the outreach were part of the effort to help.

But my answers sounded lame even to me. The crowd went quiet in the wake of the awkwardness and I could feel the stage lights burning my skin.

A very large woman stood up, her brow furrowed, looking intently at me. Someone quietly passed her a microphone. "My name is Jeannie Miller. I've made some mistakes in my life. But I got right when I found Jesus. Yes, I did. But the one thing I can't fix is my size, you know." Tears ran down her cheek, but she kept on talking. "I tried everything. Diets, counseling, calorie counting, exercise. I've prayed and prayed. Nothing works. My sister says I should see a doctor, because she knows someone who was like me who had that surgery. But I can't afford that. And my kids are getting big now, too, and it... I'm sorry. I'm sorry for getting this upset, but it scares me to death, you know?

"I was so happy that we won the contest because I knew I could get help. Thank you for coming to talk to us. Thanks to the TV people for coming here and spending money to make us healthier. I want to know if there is anything you can tell me that can help me and my family."

A moment passed as I tried to figure out what the hell to tell this woman. The cameras all swung to my face. Jeannie stared at me, the tears running down her face.

What could I say? Most of my colleagues studied specific molecules, single cells, or chemical reactions occurring in one organ. I studied the big picture: how the entire body works. And it was an amazing system, very adaptive. If you pushed it in a healthier direction, it would help you become healthier. If Jeannie took the courage she'd shown here, and was relentless in becoming healthier, her body would come to her aid. But I was no Oprah. So, I shrugged and said, "Just don't ever give up."

Jeannie Miller nodded appreciatively but I saw heads shaking in disappointment. Okay, I'm not a motivational speaker.

RJ came back on stage and announced that we were out of time. He thanked me, shook some hands with some of the audience and then Rich hurried him off stage. I detached the mike and left it on the podium; my bit was done here and it was time to get home. I had a lot to do before the weekend and hoped to catch an earlier flight. I had Charlie this weekend and that was the only thing that mattered.

I had my hand on my rolling carry on bag, ready to make a quick exit, when I turned and saw Melanie and the sheriff's deputy headed for me. I couldn't think of any laws that I might have broken here unless possession of trashy romance novels was illegal. But Melanie looked serious.

"Elaine, the deputy would like a word with you."

CHAPTER 2

M ELANIE GAVE ME A PAT on the shoulder and said everything was fine as I climbed into the front seat of the sheriff's car. The deputy admitted that he didn't know what was going on either, other than he had been dispatched to bring me to the station.

He drove me to the sheriff's office, a single-story brick building on the other side of town. The sheriff and an assistant district attorney introduced themselves. I am so terrible with names, especially in an uncertain situation, that I instantly forgot them. Tom something and Linda or Lynn something else. The sheriff was ex-military, ramrod straight, decently fit, with a patient look on his face. The DA was a blond woman with big, blue eyes and about my age.

"Dr. Cassano, we have a strange situation," the sheriff said, offering me a seat. "And we're hoping you can help us. The TV producer said you were a scientific expert on obesity. Is that right?"

"Yes." I'd even written papers about applying systems theory to biology and chemistry and nutrition science, once upon a time, before I was exiled to the Truth Squad.

He consulted a folder. "According to an assault victim, Tyler Donaldson, just after lunch break at the warehouse, the assailants, his friends, cornered him and beat him senseless. The night guard stopped them and said all four assailants were in a blind rage and yelling incoherently, like they were sleepwalking. He had to club two of them to make them stop."

I nodded, biting back a retort that this had nothing to do with me.

"The attackers claim to have no memory of what they did. The last any of them remember was being in the break room. They weren't drunk or high when they were arrested—we tested. But they are pretty big guys, if you know what I mean." He nodded at the DA. I noticed the nameplate on his desk said Crowley. Tom Crowley.

"Are they obese or just overweight?" I asked, as if that made any difference to whether they had beaten up someone.

"Um, obese. The defendants are pretty big, you know, and the victim is skinny," the sheriff said.

I shrugged. "They're also all men. Frankly, that's a better predictor than body fat percentage, but it also doesn't explain why they would attack their friend."

"Would that in any way cause them to attack their friend? Or cause memory loss?" the DA asked.

I shook my head, trying not to smile. These people were serious. "I can't think of any way that obesity could drive people to be violent. Even some kind of hypoglycemic episode or a diabetic coma would be highly unlikely to cause this behavior. And four people, having the same kind of episode at the same time, while together, and focused on the same person? No."

They both stared at me, as if trying to figure out how to press me. I looked from one to another. "But you're taking this seriously. Has someone claimed this before?" An obesity-induced insanity defense would make other insanity defenses seem highly reasonable by comparison.

The sheriff squirmed a bit but the DA said, "Just weird stuff, hard to explain. Overweight folks involved in altercations and not having any memory of it. We're just trying to figure out what happened. Is there a medication that obese folks take that could cause this?"

I raised an eyebrow. "Psychiatric drugs, anti-depression medications, there are some possibilities. Ambien can have some odd sleepwalking side effects. Illegal narcotics too: speed, LSD, PCP. The old standby, alcohol. But you said they tested negative for anything like that."

"They were clean for alcohol. They were perfectly normal by the time we responded to the scene. They only reported hypertension and blood pressure meds. One is on a mild anti-depressant. These guys aren't the type to go to the doctor very much."

I shrugged. "They could be lying about that, I guess. Four people don't lose their short-term memory and go on a rampage together because of individual prescriptions. They didn't attack one another and just ganged up on one guy? Okay, that makes it weirder. And their toxicology tests were clean?"

The sheriff nodded. "We'll know soon, but I'd be surprised if they weren't. All the others in the past were clean."

I looked from him to the DA and back. "The simplest explanation is that they wanted to beat this guy and thought of this excuse when they got caught."

The DA said. "But the defendants are not trying to talk their way out of it. They're close to the victim. They're more worried about Tyler's health and their relationship with him than they are about jail time. One of them is the godfather of Tyler's kids."

"Is there a possibility that an environmental contaminant could be responsible? They do work at a food processing factory," the sheriff asked. He shrugged sheepishly when I didn't respond. "In the warehouse, though. I took a look around. Pallets of pre-wrapped cartons of cereal boxes and fruit juices. Not much different than a Sam's Club. Cardboard dust is your biggest contaminant. But, you know, I want to cover all possibilities."

I shook my head. "No, that makes no sense."

The DA looked at me again. "I'd like you to watch some of the questioning of the suspects. Their lawyer is ready. If you'll excuse me, I have to make sure we're ready for the interview." She stood and left.

I turned to Sheriff Crowley. "Uh, I have a flight to catch back to DC at six and I still have to check out of my hotel." Wonderful government travel software guaranteed overpaying for flights that only flew at inconvenient times.

"We'll get you to the airport in time. There's one more thing," the sheriff said. He opened a drawer and pulled out an evidence bag that contained three bags of chips. "I bought a couple of these chips from the same vending machine they used. I think you should run some tests on them, just to rule out some possibilities."

"Possibilities, okay." I tucked them into my purse. "I can't promise I can get anyone to test them. My agency could refuse without the company's permission, or at least a complaint filed."

The sheriff shrugged. "I bought them from the machine myself. No one else touched them."

He knew something, but before I could ask him, it was time to interview the defendants.

The DA and I went to a small viewing room down the hall from the interview room, connected by a closed circuit TV. A deputy brought a suspect in. His name was Charlie Metts. Five-eight. He weighed about two-fifty. He breathed noisily through his nose and had floppy brown hair hanging over a likable face.

The sheriff entered the room and sat across from Charlie and his attorney. While they went through introductions and Miranda rights, the DA handed me a file on Charlie. No criminal history, softball coach, lived in this town all his life. No medications other than blood pressure and over the counter pain meds for his bad knee.

"Tell us what happened, Charlie," the sheriff said.

"Okay, once more for the home audience," Charlie said and nodded at the camera. "We ate lunch in the break room. We're the only guys on the night shift this week. We were settin' around, talking about whether we should fix Jeremy's old deck or build a new one. Tyler knows lumber pretty good and Bobby digs post holes in his sleep. Anyway, I remember standing up to get back to work. Next thing I know, someone is pounding me on the back and I turn around and it's the guard. And we're in the warehouse. And Tyler's lying on the floor bleeding and yelling."

Charlie shook his head. "You have to understand, Tyler's a brother to all of us. When Bobby and Donna had a miscarriage two years ago, Tyler and Sue, man, they were there for them, day and night. My truck broke down last winter, dead battery, Tyler came all the way out to my place, during the storm, to get me to work. He's a twitchy guy, but funnier than hell. We would never hurt him. Now Jeremy, he needs a good thrashing about once every ten years, with the mouth on him. Just doesn't know when to shut up. But Tyler, he's a rock."

"Was there any drinking last night? Any one with a flask for a long night shift?" the sheriff asked.

Charlie shook his head. "No way, sir. We're operating fork trucks and heavy machinery out there. Alcohol makes me sleepy, the last thing you need on the night shift. I always have a Diet Coke on break to keep me sharp."

"Any prescription medications or supplements beyond the blood pressure pills?"

Charlie shook his head.

"What about meth or smoking some weed?"

"No, sir, nothing like that."

"What did you have to eat last night on break?"

He folded his hands. "Well, my wife packs me these small meals. Last night it was meatloaf, two rolls, green beans, and a banana. Never fills me up. So we take turns buying dessert from the vending machine each night. One person pays. Whoever paid the night before chooses for everyone. Bobby picked the Fiesta chips they had in there. Too spicy for me, but better than nothing."

I looked down at my purse. All three bags were Fiesta chips.

The sheriff asked, "Charlie, were there any strange smells or odors in the warehouse last night?"

Charlie shrugged. "No. Nothing that I remember."

The sheriff opened a file. "Tyler has a broken wrist, two cracked ribs, a black eye and bumps and bruises all over. According to him, after lunch you all went back to work, but Bobby and Jeremy started teasing him. He said you looked pissed off and Mike was ignoring everyone. But Jeremy got more belligerent. You all tracked Tyler down to the corner of the warehouse and Mike threw the first punch, just out of nowhere. Tyler says you all looked furious. That ring any bells?"

Charlie shook his head. "No. I mean, if I heard someone did that to Ty, hell, I'd go kick their ass."

"The guys each offered to help support Tyler while he's recuperating," Charlie's lawyer added.

The sheriff shrugged. "Help me understand how this happened. Because right now it's looking like you and your pals tried beating him to a pulp for the fun of it."

Charlie laughed helplessly. "That's crazy."

The sheriff leaned forward in his dull gray chair. "That's all I have unless you say different. Was it joshing around that got out of control? Was there some kind of fight club or wrestling you guys did, with no one around? Maybe last night it got out of control."

Charlie shook his head, sniffled. "No sir. We don't do things like that. Maybe a fork truck race when we have two trailers to fill at once. Nothing physical though."

The sheriff nodded. "The guard says he heard Tyler screaming. He found the four of you kicking him on the ground. All four of you, no exceptions. Tyler and the guard yelled at you all to stop, but no one listened. He pulled you away from Tyler and you just stood there, panting. Why were you doing that?"

"I don't know, I don't know! The only thing I remember is Old Willy—that's the guard—yelling at me. It must have snapped me out of it."

The questioning continued, but it covered the same ground in different ways. The DA turned to me, "What do you think?"

"There's nothing about nutrition or obesity here that could explain this. I don't know why I'm here. Unless you want to tell me about the other incidents."

The DA huffed and puffed and finally caved. "Nothing that we can prosecute. A bar fight here, a tangle over a parking spot there. The victims were normal weight or skinny. The perps were overweight or obese and don't remember doing anything. Even under hypnosis. No alcohol, no drugs. This is the first time that the victim and the perps were close. The only thing that all the perps have in common is being obese and working at the food plant."

I shook my head. "Obesity does not turn you into Dr. Jekyll and Mr. Hyde. It doesn't alter your brain chemistry in half an hour and then stop. I would test that factory."

The DA folded her arms. "I've asked, but I doubt the company would ever let us. I'll have to charge these guys. I might plead it out to reduce the charges. But even if they beat it, the arrest and the charges will probably cost them their jobs."

The sheriff escorted me back to his office while the DA talked with Charlie's lawyer. The other assailants had been interviewed earlier today and were back in the county lockup. He sat in his chair, rubbing his face while I skimmed the transcripts from the other interviews. I kind of felt like a detective and had the odd feeling that I was on another TV show.

I handed the file back. "There's no known connection between obesity and what happened."

The sheriff nodded. "I know. I appreciate you taking the time to help us out. We knew it was a long shot anyway, but…"

"Sheriff?" A deputy said on the intercom. "We have a lawyer out here looking for the DA."

The sheriff scowled. "Send him in here." The sheriff looked at my purse. "Do you think you can get those tested?"

"I will. Here's my card." The sheriff shook my hand and I stood to leave.

"Sheriff?" said a voice from behind me. "Am I interrupting?"

I turned around. The lawyer was a thin man in his early sixties wearing a ludicrously expensive suit. His hair was a thin mat of gray above cold blue eyes. In a single look he regarded me as nothing more than an angle to work, a walking and breathing set of arguments, money, and property to navigate. He reminded me of Bob's lawyer from the custody case. I disliked this guy immensely.

"John Stitcher. I represent Flawless Foods." He wore a thinly disguised scowl of impatience and was bouncing on the balls of his feet.

When I introduced myself, Mr. Stitcher brightened when I mentioned the Truth Squad. "USDA? That's terrific. There are so many misconceptions out there, and people trust government information. What brings you here?"

"The attack in the warehouse," I said reflexively, and instantly regretted it. I readjusted the strap of my purse and tried to remember that lawyers exploited statements as easily as their lungs converted oxygen to noise pollution and money.

Stitcher turned to the sheriff. "Just because it happened at a food industry facility does not mean anything."

"Take it easy," the sheriff said. "The perps are heavy guys is why. We just wanted to consult an expert to confirm that their weight would not affect their mental state. In case the defendants' attorneys try to use the Twinkie defense."

Stitcher smirked. "The Twinkie defense is a media creation from the Harvey Milk murder trial. Dan White's legal team never claimed that low blood sugar impaired his reasoning."

The sheriff hand-waved aside the legal hair-splitting. "The thing is, no one understands why this happened yet. Including the defendants. The fact that they are all heavy and the victim is not was another issue we wanted to run down. Dr. Cassano has helped us rule that out. We want to be ready in case they claim they ate, drank or breathed something that turned them into violent zombies."

"Zombies?" Stitcher shook his head. "The undead that eat brains or whatnot? Dr. Cassano, is there any food or drink that the FDA has found that produces violent monsters?"

I wasn't going to be his puppet. "Red Dye #5 can cause hyperactivity in children. But not short term memory loss or violent behavior," I said. "Alcohol can spur violent behavior and memory blackouts too, but these men were sober."

Stitcher grinned as if I had just backed him up.

"So what brings you by, Counselor?" The sheriff asked. I could tell he didn't like Mr. Stitcher, either.

"The DA's office asked if you could inspect the warehouse again." Stitcher shrugged. "This is a working warehouse; my client runs a just-in-time distribution system. The schedule has been trashed by the incident and they are scrambling to recover without a night shift. The warehouse will miss its performance goals for the year. My client may be looking to downsize. That's the reality. And since Tyler isn't pressing charges, there's no need to continue the investigation."

"He isn't? He's still in the hospital from getting pounded near to death," the sheriff said.

Stitcher smiled thinly. "I just spoke with him. He will be released today. He is banged up all to shit and gone, I'm not going to sugarcoat that. My client will compensate him and pay his medical bills, plus a lump sum for any Workman's Comp payments he would be due. But Tyler doesn't want his friends jailed. He wants to put this all behind him and move forward. Hopefully I can convince the DA to have the state drop the charges as well. Do you know how much longer she'll be?"

"She's still interviewing one of the defendants," the sheriff said, in a tone that lacked any friendliness.

"Which is a waste of everyone's time if the charges are dropped, isn't it? Could you let the DA know that, Sheriff Crowley?"

The sheriff shooed us out of the office to a waiting area out front, and told a deputy to check on a ride for me, scowled at Stitcher, and then headed back to the interview room.

"Your client is going to fire all of those guys, isn't he?" I said.

Stitcher raised an eyebrow. "No, they're good workers and the company wants them back on the job ASAP. They really are busting their asses at that warehouse. As you must know, the food business is fucking booming these days."

"I don't think the sheriff appreciates the profanity, by the way," I noted. "Did you see all the churches on Main Street?"

He looked at me. "A straight shooter with science credentials to back it up. Have you thought about lobbying? Do you live near a big city?" His phone rang. We both looked down at it. He picked it up and began thumbing the keypad. "Eh, just more assholes with messes to clean up. I'll break their legs later." He kept texting. "I'm serious, Dr. Cassano. Most of the food industry's lobbyists are salesmen, lawyers, or attractive former Hill staffers with contacts but who don't know shit about the science. You're legit, and your style is just perfect. Unvarnished truth—you couldn't fucking lie if you tried, could you?"

I glared at him. "I know industry lobbyists. I would be fired in under a week." How come emergency rooms and police stations had the slowest service when they seemed the least busy?

"I'm sure you would never be asked to do anything you're uncomfortable with."

"You don't understand, Mr. Stitcher. I'm committed to the truth all the time, not just when it's easy or convenient. I can rub people the wrong way, especially when I think they're shading the truth."

Stitcher grinned, revealing very worn teeth. "Well, here's my card anyway. I operate out of DC, unless someone royally fucks up out here in the Heartland. Call me when you want to stop making dog food money and get something done for a change."

The card was a watermarked cream color with gilt writing in a swirly, Gothic font. His law firm was named after himself. Maybe he had a hard time working with others as well. I filed it deep in my purse, to be thrown out or forgotten until I bought a new purse on my dog food salary.

A deputy finally appeared to take me to the airport. It wasn't until I was on a plane an hour later that it occurred to me that I didn't know what Stitcher meant when he'd mentioned a fuckup in the Heartland.

CHAPTER 3

I GOT HOME LATE THAT NIGHT. It was pouring rain on the whole ride back from Reagan National Airport and I arrived drenched and tired at my deserted house. I live in a townhouse complex in Bowie, Maryland, close enough to Beltsville to keep the work commute short and far enough away from my previous employer to not remind me of the bad old times.

I slept in the next morning, since I had taken the day off. The house needed a thorough cleaning and organizing before my son Charlie came for the weekend. I had a mountain of laundry to do, dry cleaning to send out, and groceries to buy. I ran the errands first so I could settle in and focus on the house before Charlie arrived.

Charlie is ten years old, a quiet and thoughtful kid. He notices everything and makes observations that just floor me. There has been many a day on the job that the only thing that got me through, and held my tongue in check, was worrying about how being jailed for beating a colleague with extreme righteousness would affect my son's life.

Charlie lives in two worlds. One world is here, with me, where things are modest but genuine. Where we visit my mother in Tacoma Park so she can fawn over him. His other world belongs to his father Bob, a cufflinked lobbyist for the food industry, and it exists in Northern Virginia and Philadelphia, where Bob's family is from. Bob and I never married. Hell, we never even dated. A one-night-stand at a food science conference was how Charlie sprang to life. This was back when Bob was still working on his food science credentials and before he sold his soul. We tried to build a relationship but it became clear that the only thing we had in common were strong libidos and working in food and nutrition. And after Bob failed to be there for Charlie early on, I was repulsed by the idea of ever screwing him again.

I had custody of Charlie for the first five years of his life. Bob was busy climbing ladders, and as he put it, children weren't that interesting to him. My own career was circling the bottom of the toilet for reasons that had nothing to do with being a single mother, so I focused my energy on Charlie. Looking back, those five years were probably the best time of my life.

Then Bob settled down some and became more interested. Long story short, Bob became rich and connected enough to wrench custody away. He showed the court how he had a big house in NVA, and a pharmaceutical sales rep fiancée, (a former Duke cheerleader with no ass), who he claimed would parent my little tyke.

And his lawyers attacked my parenting skills, and me personally, in ways I'll never forgive or forget. All that mattered to Bob was that he wanted to be with his boy and I was in the way. They even took away my visitation rights. By the time it was over, the best thing left in my life was my ever-shittier job.

Charlie had finally convinced Bob last year to let him visit me on the weekends. Bob couldn't say no. As much as it horrified me that it fell to the kid to figure out how keep me in his life, I was so damn proud of him for manipulating his father.

Anyway, weekend visits with Charlie were what I lived for now.

In the last five years, Charlie had grown to be a good-natured ten-year-old. He was quiet, serious, and a big fan of sports, comic books and Pokémon. My biggest worry was his health, because he had gained too much weight and was sick a lot. Bob had become overweight in the last decade, too, and was now pushing into obese territory. There was little I could do about either one.

My solitude of dusting, laundry, vacuuming, and straightening was broken up early in the afternoon by a call from my supervisor. George was a nice guy whom I could only fault for being overly gung-ho about the Truth Squad. He was the type to take whatever directive had been thrown his way and make the best of it, whether he personally believed in it or not. Typical for a member of the government's Senior Executive Service.

"How was the trip?" he asked. I summarized the interview and the town hall.

"When does the episode air? Did they get your credentials correct?"

He was worried that the Truth Squad wouldn't get its fifteen seconds of fame. When he brought me the assignment, he had mentioned that being featured on a popular reality TV show would be a major bullet point in his performance appraisal and mine.

"George, they wouldn't tell me. But even if it all ends up on the cutting room floor, the important thing is that the show gave us a captive audience in one of the more obese towns in America. If they cut my segment, it wasn't a waste of taxpayer money to send me there."

"I suppose," he replied.

Maybe it was a misbegotten sense of sympathy for his performance appraisal that made me add, "The *We Will* producer referred the sheriff to me to consult on an assault case." I told him about the assault and its weird circumstances.

"Haha, maybe they misunderstood what kind of truth squad we are," he joked. "What do you make of all that?"

"The sheriff asked me to test samples of the food the assailants ate. I think we should do some poking around on this. They've had a number of incidents of obese folks attacking normal-sized people and don't have an explanation as to why."

George was silent for a second. Uh oh. I could see the future of the Truth Squad flash before his eyes, even over the phone. But I bit my tongue. You have no idea what an Olympian feat this was for me.

"Explain again why you think we need to get involved?" he said.

"First of all, it's really odd: obese people attacking skinny people, and having no memory of it. The sheriff gave me the food samples and asked me to have them tested. He thinks something more is going on here. So I think we test the food just to convince them that junk food doesn't make people violent."

"Second, um, remember the media storm when that obese man beat a DUI charge by claiming that his obesity made the tests inaccurate? There may be an opportunity here." Third, I didn't say aloud, *I met a crazy food industry lawyer who was cleaning up a mess and acted like he was there to cover something up.*

George sighed. "Give your samples to one of the labs. But keep this quiet. We are an education/outreach unit, we don't do investigations. This is for our own edification. To uh, expand the nutrient database."

He was referring to the Nutrient Data Laboratory, which updates a variety of databases of food components. It was one of the six laboratories that made up the Human Nutrition Research Center at BARC, USDA's facility in Beltsville, Maryland.

My old pal Jim Knox at Nutrient Data would probably be happy to help me out. For some reason this made me excited. Was it because it was time spent away from press releases and giving speeches to high school health classes? "Have a good weekend, boss."

It was the first time in a long time I was looking forward to work on Monday. And that was even with having Charlie over and the heartbreak of saying goodbye to him on Sunday.

Friday night rolled in with light showers, so I was already expecting Bob to be late bringing Charlie over. Beltway traffic could be a killer any day of the week, but heading north out of Virginia into Maryland on a Friday was worse. A rainy Friday was the worst. The news was reporting accidents all over. I made myself a couple of tacos, ate, and waited.

I tried calling Bob when he was ninety minutes late but he didn't pick up. He was probably driving and getting close. I'll be honest—doubt was creeping in. If he canceled Charlie's visit at the last minute, again, I would go nuts. He had played this game a couple of times since Charlie had forced the visitation issue. Bad traffic, late work, and his own family obligations had become the usual suspects.

But this time was different. Bob and I had talked about this at length. We had agreed that I would give Charlie his own cell phone this weekend. A rite of passage for the pre-teen set these days, I guess. Someone at work had told me that if you gave your kid a phone before ten, you were a spineless irresponsible fool, but if you didn't give the kid a phone by the age of twelve, you were a reckless parent unconcerned with your child's safety.

Bob and I may have both been feeling a bit guilty given Charlie's fractured upbringing and decided that age ten was right. Charlie was a responsible kid and more importantly had not been clamoring for one. It would let me stay in much closer touch with him. Bob would pay for the phone plan and I had already bought the phone. I was giving it to Charlie this weekend, after he showed me his latest report card, which Bob assured me looked quite good.

Two hours late and the phone rang. It was Bob's cell.

"Please don't hate me, El," he said amid a lot of background clatter. Charlie wasn't coming. My heart stabbed itself and then fell over into an abyss. "Daddy scored tickets at the last minute to the 'Sixers game. It's the playoffs and he wanted Charlie to see it."

"What the hell?" was all I could utter. My brain froze as anger, despair and shock all collided on the way out like the Three Stooges squeezing through a doorway. It all boiled down to one white-hot thought: I hate it when grown men call their fathers 'daddy.'

Bob murmured, "I'm really sorry. I know it's been a while and I'll make it up to you."

"Couldn't you have told your father no? That Charlie had other plans?"

"I can't do that" Bob said, "not since Daddy broke his hip last year. I don't know how much time he has left and if he wants to see his grandson, I can't kick him down the calendar."

His 'daddy' had been in poor health since before Charlie was born and had been knocking on death's door since I lost custody. The rich old fuck somehow made wondrous things happen for Charlie on *my* weekends.

"I haven't seen my son in over a month now, Bob. We had this worked out, the three of us. Remember the parenting plan, the visitation agreement? It's what Charlie wanted, it's what he *insisted* on." The tears came on suddenly, hot and fierce, and my damn voice was quivering. Some women hate crying in front of men, and think it's a sign of weakness, especially when they're mad. It doesn't bother me; emotional response is how humans are wired and being ashamed of it is as silly as feeling bad about having two feet. On the other hand, I cursed my own weakness.

"I'm really sorry, El. I don't want to hurt you. You're a good mom. But this was really not my decision. It was out of my control." He was using his bullshit lobbyist tone on me. Phony people never realize how easy it is to tell when they are being gratuitously phony. I could not believe this piece of shit was allowed to raise my son.

"Don't you dare try to tell me that Charlie made this decision. Don't you dare. Did he even know about this weekend? Or did you tell him that I was okay with this? Why don't you put him on the phone?"

I could hear nothing but people roaming around food concessions. It was halftime at the game, which I had just found on TV. The fucker hadn't even bothered to call me beforehand.

"Look, you're upset right now," Bob said, adding thinly-sliced anger to his voice. He had lied to Charlie about something. I knew this because Charlie had told me that his dad got defensive when Charlie caught him in a lie. Charlie was six at the time he realized this, God love him.

"Don't hang up on me, or the next call will come from my attorney. In fact," I said, the anger having won out over shock and despair, "maybe it's time to revisit the custody arrangement."

"Hey, I'm doing my best, but things happen. Let's not forget that you don't have visitation rights. I'm doing this because Charlie wants to, not because I have to."

"It's time to revisit that," I said.

Bob laughed. "You're serious? Do you want to go through that again? Do you think anything will change? It would hurt you *and* Charlie. The last time he was too young to understand much, but now he'll see it all unfold. Do you want to do that to him?"

I gripped the phone. "What's changed is that I won't be blindsided by your wolf pack of lawyers. This time you don't have a stay-at-home fiancée. What happened to Missy, huh Bob? So you're single-parenting just like I am, and how does that work with a lobbyist's schedule? I think I'll have a much better chance this time around."

I could sense him fuming. "I can't believe you would put all of us through that again because of a stupid basketball game. Jesus. I—"

"Just a basketball game? So, are you bringing him back down here tomorrow? You going to drop him off on your way back?"

More silence and then a loud buzzer in the distance. Finally, he said, "No. Daddy would be offended if we left right after. Look, I have to get back."

"Yes, because the game is back on. I can see that on TV." *You could have invited me to come along, dickwad*, I thought. The only thing that mattered to me was being with Charlie. I didn't care how, or where, or when, or who else was there. A cold, silvery anger poured through me and decisions became as clear as glass. "I can't live like this. I need Charlie in my life. I'm reopening the custody case."

"Jesus," Bob said. He was walking through the tunnels of the Sixers stadium and his voice echoed strangely. "This will be hell for you, Elaine, absolute hell. Worse than last time. I hate that you want to force this."

"I'll settle for primary custody, and you and your daddy can get every other weekend and half the holidays."

He hung up on me.

The doorbell rang half an hour later. It was Ma in a rain jacket, holding a plastic-wrapped platter of cookies.

"Where's my grandson?" she said, stepping past me, looking for him. My mother was taller than me and thinner. She had sandy-blonde curly hair and nervous blue eyes that made people wonder if I was really her daughter.

I closed the door behind her. "Bob skipped out. Again." I stood there, in my robe, staring at the floor so I could avoid the pitiful look I knew would be in her eyes.

Ma turned around and looked at me with a blank expression until I met her gaze. I blinked back tears and looked back down.

"Oh, dear." She doffed the rain jacket and gave me a big hug.

I wiped my eyes. "I tried calling you but you must have been driving already. I'm sorry you came out here in this terrible weather."

Ma pulled her phone out of her purse and stabbed its buttons a few times. "I had it on vibrate in my purse. I'm sorry. I would have come over anyway, if I had known. Even with the backup on Route 3." Ma hung up her coat. "How are you doing?"

"Angry," I said. I then began ranting about Bob, starting with "That son of a bitch" and continuing downhill from there. Ma was used to these outbursts from me, but had never become comfortable with them. She was from your standard WASP background and profane outbursts were politely frowned upon. She had struggled with how to deal with Pop's family, a hotheaded band of Italians who expressed every feeling at maximum intensity but then cooled off quickly.

She made me sit down, like she did when I was a kid. She thought that sitting down took the fire out of people, which of course was wrong, but since it made her feel better, I always ended up sitting.

"I'm really sorry, honey. You're both in such a tough spot." She sat next to me. She had never understood why Bob and I hadn't moved closer to one another, or ideally, got married. Bob had seemed so pleasant to her, from when they met after Charlie's birth and every crossing of their paths since. "What will you do now?"

I folded my hands together. "Sue for custody. I can't live without Charlie in my life. The last five years have been a living hell." I choked back a sob as I thought about the still-boxed cell phone sitting on Charlie's bed upstairs. "A living hell I didn't deserve. I'm not letting that asshole screw up my life anymore. Or getting his slimy hooks further into my son."

Ma regarded me with a calm eye. She always was my cool-headed sounding board. "That may not be a good idea."

I sighed and waved my hand in lazy circles. "Okay, talk me out of it."

"Well," Ma said, "there's the expense and the uncertainty for Charlie." She peered at me uncomfortably. "And it was emotionally wrenching the last time. Something happened, I don't know what. But you were devastated even before the ruling."

I had never explained to her exactly how Bob had won. I hadn't told her about the deposition or the hearing. The mystery had rankled her to no end. Charlie was her only grandchild and she had nearly lost him for unknown reasons.

Ma unwrapped the cookies in the kitchen. "It doesn't make sense. A single mother loses custody of her boy even though she is a fully employed PhD. scientist, owns her own home, has no criminal record, and treats him well. Everyone tells me that you must have had the worst lawyer of all time or there's something else going on. Abuse, mental competence, drug addiction, *something*."

"Ma, I really am not up to talking about this now, okay?"

"I'm worried that if you try again, it may get worse."

I shook my head. "Bob has been making more and more excuses for skipping my weekends. This weekend it's because of a basketball playoff game. He's blocking Charlie's wishes with logistical excuses. Charlie's disappointed but Bob keeps substituting something even cooler than seeing me."

She nodded. "I know, I know. Charlie is ten now and it won't be long before he starts finding his own excuses. In time, you're going to lose him one way or another just like every other mother."

My father was whom I had inherited the irresistible urge to spout the truth at the worst time. Ma, she's the sweetest person I know, and lacks any kind of the self confidence my father had, but her hesitant mumblings often are a barbed spear of truth flung right into your chest.

Ma handed me a cookie. It was the soft, chewy pumpkin kind that Charlie loved. "I'm sorry, dear, but he's more than halfway to being an adult. You've got the next eight years. If you push this custody thing again and lose, you may lose him until he's grown up."

"If I don't, though, Bob will squeeze me out in his idiotic, passive-aggressive way." And Bob knew it, too, I realized. Things had changed. Bob was not married with a family life that a judge wouldn't remove Charlie from. And Charlie was old enough now that he might be able to weigh in on the decision. That was probably what scared Bob the most.

My poor mother looked even more perplexed as she realized that I was about to do exactly what she'd counseled against. "There's really no way you could move closer to Charlie?"

"Commuting from Fairfax to Beltsville would be insane," I said. We had discussed this many times before. She lived in Tacoma Park and worked at an office park nearby. She didn't fight Beltway traffic in Virginia.

"Don't even mention me and Bob having a better relationship," I said, as she was about to bring it up. Telling your mother that, at age twenty-five, you got pregnant from a one-night stand was hard. Failing to convince her that living with or marrying the father of your child was a non-starter had turned out to be harder. Especially since no one else had come around yet.

"Okay," Ma said, wiping crumbs from her hands. "New topic. How is work?"

I laughed. "Are you kidding me? Is this how you're trying to cheer me up?"

She shrugged innocently. "How am I supposed to know if you had a good week or a bad week? You don't tell me anything."

Well, it had been a good week. I told her about the reality TV show. I highlighted meeting RJ, who makes us both swoon a bit. I didn't mention the warehouse assault at Flawless Foods. She was in a good mood, proud of me for having met television stars and being so important as to rate national television exposure. It seemed too wrong to mention something so macabre and odd right now.

When she left an hour later, I felt a tinge of regret. She was just as much affected by the custody situation as I was, but there was even less she could do about it. All of her common sense arguments boiled down to easing the way for both of us to see her grandson more. But she and I both knew that I wouldn't take her advice.

CHAPTER 4

THIS WAS THE FIRST MONDAY in a long time that I was happy to be back at work. The Truth Squad is housed at BARC, the Beltsville Agricultural Research Center, in Beltsville, Maryland. It's a beautiful campus that often gets mistaken for the University of Maryland, which is further south on Route 1. BARC actually extends across a much larger swath than it appears to, including several buildings on rolling fields to the east.

The Truth Squad is located in a temporary holding space of cubes and offices in picturesque Building 4 off Route 1. It's about as far from the labs and other scientists as you can get. To me, it felt like exile.

The Truth Squad staff is a hodgepodge of communications types, a few scientists like me, and a couple of people from the advocacy world. Almost everyone but me is pumped to be on the squad and no one expects to still be there two years from now. For them it's a launch pad; for me it's goddamn Purgatory.

It took a solid two hours to deal with the *pro forma* water cooler talk about my trip to the *We Will* set. Communications people do love to talk and build rapport until you want to slap their bubbly smiles right off their cherubic faces. I had bags of chips burning holes in my work bag.

I needed to deliver them to Jim Knox, a chemist over at Human Nutrition's Nutrient Data Laboratory. He knows food ingredients like other people know their children. His lab studies enzymes, preservatives and various other chemical reactions to update the National Nutrient Data Standard Reference, a database of food ingredients.

He took a liking to me on my first day because I was the only systems biologist in Human Nutrition. Everyone else is a molecule chaser, he told me, focused on minute reactions. I studied the big picture, how the subsystems interacted, how metabolism reacted to nutrient levels, how energy levels interacted with blood pressure. He found it refreshing and was nerdy enough to ignore the interpersonal problems in the office that eventually drove me out.

He told me to bring the chip samples right over. I drove to Building 307-D and it felt like visiting home. Scientists doing real science, not public relations. I missed it more than I had realized, interpersonal problems notwithstanding.

Jim was elbow-deep in something with a small crowd of his staff when I came into the lab. One of the techs was a tall gaunt man with braided hair who was busy sketching something about blackberries on a white board while Jim squinted in deep concentration.

When they were done Jim came over and gave me a solid clap on the shoulder; he was not the hugging type. "Hey, kid, how's the life of an itinerant preacher?"

I harrumphed. "Sucks ass."

Jim guffawed and led me back to his office, a narrow space thickly insulated with stacks of articles, journals, and books. Unlike most scientists, who were stuck far down the rabbit hole of their own niche, Jim was a voracious reader of several different fields of biology, chemistry, and sports medicine.

His bushy eyebrows shot up after I explained how I got the chips. "Well, we don't get forensic requests very often. Once in a while we test for an allergen, but that's about it."

He hefted the red and orange bag. "Fiesta Chips. I've never heard of them."

"Flawless Foods is test-marketing the chips in ten cities and plans a national rollout later this year. They have a few of their own brands," I said.

"Have you tried them? The chips?"

I shook my head. Tasting them had never occurred to me.

"Back in the day, that's how scientists tested the unknown," he said. "Now if we did that, we'd get fired for disobeying OSHA rules."

He photographed the front and back of the chip bag with his phone. He took another photo of the nutrition information panel and the ingredients list.

He brought up the nutrient standard reference database on his computer and a couple of other applications I didn't recognize. As he selected each ingredient, a pulldown appeared that tried to auto-complete the spelling of possible ingredients. There were only so many chemicals under the sun.

He compared Fiesta Chips to other brands. The application matched most of them up to each other, but not all. Jim shrugged. "The ingredients aren't all that different. Corn, salt, sugar, and lots of preservatives and flavor phytochemicals. No rage juice here."

A wave of relief rushed up my spine. I didn't think that one of the lengthy-named ingredients was capable of turning responsible men into rage-fueled monsters. But this incident was so strange that it was good to know science and common sense still held up.

Jim held up the bag. "I can test it for contaminants. But do you have any idea what could cause such a reaction?"

I shook my head. "The memory loss could be from something like an Ambien. But for a group to turn on a friend and become that violent? I don't know of anything like that."

"So, the suspected reactions are violent mood swings, anger, and violence. Wait, you said violence?"

"Yes, they beat their best friend to pulp, but not one another. The authorities fear that the defendants' lawyers will claim the Twinkie Defense because the assailants are obese and the victim is thin. I know, it sounds crazy, but checking out the chips is just due diligence on the sheriff's part."

Jim nodded. "And you want to be told ASAP if we find anything. This was requested by the local sheriff, who clearly doesn't understand biochemistry."

I held up my hands. "Hey, I did the best I could. Does the law enforcement angle make a difference?"

He nodded. "Sure. It makes it a higher priority. Moves it ahead of dissecting the greasy pizza and bad Chinese food we ate for lunch. Okay?"

I stood up and gave the old duffer a hug before he could defend himself. "You're the best, Jim."

When I returned to my cubicle jail, there was a stern voice mail from George telling me to come to his office in less than half an hour.

The Truth Squad stayed busy, it seemed, by searching for engagements to keep us busy. Weight-loss seminars in sleepy hotels, academic conferences, fitness events, press interviews, public service announcements, confabs with friendly advocacy groups and interest groups. Everyone always seemed to be scurrying to make sure their calendar was booked solid. We hadn't raised our profile high enough yet that people sought us out. The reality TV show spot was a real prize that came to me when George pulled my name out of a hat.

The path that had brought me to the Squad was not a pleasant one. I had been moving along the academic track pretty smoothly at another federal agency that shall not be named. I published papers, was involved in interesting projects, and helped evaluate extramural research funding requests.

It was the extramural research that got me into trouble. When it comes to science funding, the federal government has become the big man on campus. The private sector has pretty much withdrawn from basic research, turning universities into grant chasers and lobbyists who twist their elected representatives into shoveling federal funding their way. Most of the money is passed through an agency's scientific unit which has to vet these projects and ensure that the tax money is well spent.

But with so much money comes pressure to give it to the 'right' people. If an application is turned down, managers can get calls from Congress or higher up the food chain in their department. If they resist, grants can become earmarks that bypass any scientific vetting. And sometimes there's some inside dealing by the scientists themselves, chummy colleagues who sign off on each others' projects. When I learned about that at my old agency, I blew the whistle in my typical blunt and honest way. Before long, it was clear that I would have to leave if I wanted to do anything other than generate dirty looks from coworkers and disdain from management.

So, I came to ARS at BARC. They were looking to expand their portfolio in Human Nutrition beyond molecule chasers and people versed in covalent bonds. They hired me, a couple of sociologists and even some psychologists to tackle the obesity epidemic from a couple of more angles. I studied how the entire human body reacted to food intake, obesity, and weight-related disorders; they were squinting at DNA, amino acids, and proteins. But after a few years, the dominant molecule-chaser culture drove most of us odd fish to move on, no hard feelings, until it was just me and them.

As a black sheep with a big mouth, I expressed my frustration by picking apart lazy methodology. It was a pet peeve of mine going back to grad school: Give really smart people amazing tools to answer pressing questions, and grimace as they take the easy road.

Judging from the tone of George's voice mail, I had dug myself a brand new hole. Maybe the dailies had come back from my segments on *We Will* and were awful. Or maybe George had devised a way to get rid of me.

But when I arrived at his office, he gave me a polite smile and told me to follow him. There's a fancy executive conference room that we use for VIPs because it looks out on the rolling lawns and peaceful shade trees. He left me in the conference room and went to sign in and escort a VIP.

The VIP was John Stitcher, Esquire.

The two of them were talking about people they knew when they came in the room. It was George's signature ice-breaking move. I had seen it work several times in the insular world of USDA, the food industry, and health research. But this time, George couldn't find anyone that he and Stitcher had in common.

"Dr. Cassano, so good to see you again," Stitcher said. He shook my hand with a cold, powerful grip. "I was in the area and thought I would stop by and say nice things about you."

I cocked my head to the side. "Why?"

Many people these days don't know how to respond to that simple, one word question. It's a little too direct and confrontational for them.

Stitcher was not one of those people. "To thank you for the work you did on the incident in Grand Forks. The local authorities had a lot of loose ends with that case. And they were getting desperate to tie them up." He turned to George. "But Dr. Cassano—may I call you Elaine?—Elaine was terrific in keeping them focused on scientifically-backed information about obesity, food additives, psychotropic drugs and other medical matters."

I smiled, despite feeling wary. This meeting could actually go well for me. "I simply provided them the standard obesity myths and facts."

He shook his head. "Nonsense. First of all, you actually showed up. You didn't have to and I expect that ARS scientists are rarely called to consult on criminal investigations. You were in town to film an interview, I understand? So, you helped out there and then gave the sheriff and DA wonderful help. I've spoken to them a few times since then and they were so appreciative. You underestimate how much trouble you saved them, Elaine." It occurred to me that he might have been referring to himself when he mentioned the trouble.

George thanked him and made a well-practiced plug for the Squad's mission. He's a real pro. He wove in elements from my assistance on the Grand Forks incident. I had heard it so many times before that I tuned him out.

Stitcher smiled, revealing coffee-stained teeth. "I can't say enough how much the food processing industry loves your work. You provide a comprehensive picture of what affects health in America. The damn granolas, if you'll excuse my language, just want to break the industry's legs. They're using obesity as a Louisville Slugger and ignoring all the other factors."

George made appreciative noises back at him. He was much better at diplomatic bullshitting than Stitcher. Smooth talking didn't come naturally to the lawyer. Or he was out of practice. He seemed much more at ease yelling at people over the phone.

"So, what has happened with the criminal case?" I asked.

Stitcher leaned back in his chair. "The charges were all dropped."

My stomach dropped. "But no one understands why it happened," I added. "Not even the assailants."

Stitcher shrugged. "Which is probably why the DA dropped the charges. Too weird to sell a jury on a guilty verdict. Weird things happen all the time. From my perspective, my client, Flawless Foods, doesn't have its operations hit too hard by having its night shift rot in jail. The accused are relieved and are happily helping out the victim's family. The authorities are back to bagging drunk drivers. Life returns to normal."

I straightened my back. "So, what's the real reason you came over here, Mr. Stitcher?"

George muttered, "Elaine…"

"No, it's okay, George," Stitcher said, waving away his concern. "I love how straightforward she is! You know what she is, George? A throwback to an older era. An era when people spoke their mind and we all weren't walking around like a mob of flesh-and-blood press releases. I admire that. It makes her effective in cutting through the bullshit."

George swallowed audibly at Stitcher's use of profanity, but said nothing.

"The number one reason I came here was to thank you, Elaine. And to let you know that the investigation is closed. The DA said you offered to do whatever you could for them, whether it was to provide information, that kind of thing. And knowing you, that wasn't just a polite platitude, right?"

I could tell George was sucking his breath in. I had shoved confrontation into this amiable chat, aimed right at a connected industry mover-and-shaker, and my boss was ready for an antacid. Which didn't help with ulcers anyway. I knew that.

Stitcher continued, "I didn't think so. So if you were still looking around on your end, I wanted to let you know that doing so is no longer necessary." The words were sweet, but his tone carried a dark warning. And in a sense, a question. He wanted to know if we were doing anything.

It wasn't clear if Stitcher knew about the samples, but he had left the door open for us to mention them. There was no way I would do that.

George held up empty hands. "We're part of the communications shop at ARS. If there are investigations or testing of products made by Flawless Foods, they don't tell us. Keep in mind that we maintain huge databases of food components and update them with the latest and greatest food products out there. It's publicly searchable on the internet. Any issues like that are really FDA territory."

Stitcher nodded cautiously. "Let me stress that the authorities told me and my client repeatedly that they believed my client has gone above and beyond to rectify the situation. We didn't fire the employees, we didn't hamper or hinder the investigation, and we're paying all the victim's medical costs."

"Yes, you've done everything you could to make this go away very quickly and quietly," I said evenly.

"Elaine!" George hissed.

Stitcher smiled a tight grin. "No, she's right. We did want this to go away as soon as possible. It's bad for business. And we want to assist you as much as possible. We can't do that if there are investigations happening that we don't know about." He may have said 'assist,' but it sounded to me like 'stop.'

"From what Elaine told me," George replied, "Flawless has some obese employees who could maybe benefit from more information about obesity. That could cut the amount of lost work time due to illness."

That was George-speak to end the meeting or seek out another speaking engagement for the Squad. And, I had to note, to deflect the conversation away from our poking around those chips. Good boss.

"I would recommend removing any vending machines in the cafeterias and break rooms," I said with mock thoughtfulness. "Or at least stock them with healthier choices. Water rather soda. Fruits rather than snack food."

For just a second, Stitcher's face fell. I had toyed with him and made him angry, but he was too much of a pro to let that feeling run free. Maybe I had just outed myself as knowing about the assailants' claims about the chips. If the sheriff had told him about the samples, I'd probably just made things worse. But I couldn't help myself.

Stitcher kept looking at me. Finally, he looked at George and winked. "Be careful, George, because I may try to steal her. But I've taken up too much of your time. It was good to meet you." Stitcher paused as something occurred to him. "You know whom I think we both know, George? Todd Brambey, over at the Podesta Group. Did presswork at the American Beef Association before that. Served here at Ag back in the last administration, I think."

I don't know much about politics, but that sounded like a veiled threat to me. Stitcher knew people who knew people, and he wanted George and me to know it.

George brightened. "Yes, Todd Brambey. Great ties that guy wears."

"That's Todd," Stitcher said and stood up. "Elaine, thanks again."

CHAPTER 5

I MARCHED INTO THE WARDMAN PARK Marriott Hotel with two goals. One was to touch base with colleagues at the first annual Obesity Research and Nutrition Conference (ORAN). The epidemic had reached such proportions that a plethora of alphabet soup agencies had agreed to cosponsor it. It was large enough to rate the Wardman Park. A great opportunity to wiggle my way back into the research world.

Plop me in a comfy chair in an auditorium with a lively methodology discussion up front and I'm happy. Here things made sense, or they didn't, and I loved sniffing out which type each study was. New insights and techniques burst out of cutting-edge work. Lazy researchers' methodology could be properly stomped on.

My second goal was to call Bob. My new attorney Sandy thought my best shot at gaining visitation rights was to use the threat of petitioning the court for relief to make a new visitation agreement now, before things progressed further. Re-opening the custody situation should be a last resort, she insisted. The circuit court judge would ask if we had attempted to settle this, anyway, and would then send us to the county's Custody and Mediation Program to devise another parenting plan.

But I knew how that would go. Bob would go through the visitation arrangements again but would do nothing to alter the status quo. He would take a couple of judicial slaps on the wrist over visitation and run out the clock until Charlie graduated from high school. He would be more amenable facing the threat of losing custody. Deep down, I knew I had been screwed over when I lost joint custody, and was itching to right that wrong.

I called Bob at the end of a presentation about the effects of depression on weight gain in the Ohio Valley. Bob picked up on the third ring. I told him we had to try talking this out.

"Okay, lets talk right now," he replied.

"Over the phone? Bob, this isn't going to look like a good faith effort to the judge."

"That's all I got," he said.

I looked around the huge, crowded hallway of the Wardman. Where does one go for a private cell conversation any more? I found a corner of an empty meeting room.

"Elaine, it's in your interest to stick to our current arrangement. You can't afford to piss away thousands of dollars that should go to Charlie's college fund. I'll get better about respecting your time with Charlie." Bob had his lobbyist bullshit tone layered on thick.

"That's not acceptable," I replied. "Those are just words. I want action."

"Nothing has changed materially in the last five years. You're not going to win this time, either," Bob said, almost whining.

After we did a few more rounds like this, Bob claimed he had to run. We had ended up where we started and all I had to show for it was missing half of a conference session.

Seething, I slipped into the back of a packed room on international comparisons of obesity incidence, hoping to forget my personal life for twenty-five minutes. International comparisons were interesting because they were natural experiments. The people in two countries had the same physiology, but could have different cultures, climates, lifestyles, incomes, economies, diets, and diseases. The key was to get one's hands on comparable data from each country.

The old story was that as Western culture permeated other countries, obesity and obesity-related diseases followed. The reasons were the same mishmash of interrelated ones that explained domestic obesity. About half the papers were updates of older work with newer data. After a while, you learn who the paper mills are, the ones who regurgitate the same paper three times a year in different packaging and, when they get new data, start the process all over again. They are about as informative as an automotive check-up that confirms your car, which you drove to the shop, works okay.

The hotshot researchers were the ones out on the bleeding edge, looking beyond correlation, trying something new. A Stanford economist presented a paper titled, "Are Western CEOs bad for your waistline?" that compared obesity gains by geography over time in Asia and found that the introduction of Western executives, not the construction of new factories and the later rise of worker incomes, coincided with weight gain. The discussant raised serious questions about the data that sent the presenter scribbling notes furiously. An ambitious Venezuelan researcher had carefully tracked the introduction of microwaveable meals in a poor neighborhood in Caracas and found it preceded a large weight gain by two months. You know it's been a good session when the questions have to be cut off because time runs out and the speakers are mobbed afterward. This was one of those panels.

It's such a spirit-lifter to be among a bunch of pumped-up researchers, dreaming up new ways to resolve questions left hanging, ready to charge off to the hotel bar with pens and napkins in hand. This was what I was meant to do, not telling the public to eat its veggies or arguing on morning call-in shows that obesity was not the result of HBO producing too many interesting television shows.

"Dr. Cassano? Dr. Cassano?"

I turned around in the hallway, not an easy feat with all of the rooms emptying at once. A dark-haired Latino man with a thin mustache and nervous eyes was trying to reach me.

I pulled over to an empty spot next to a poster on adipocyte generation so he could catch up. He stumbled out of the crowd with a high-pitched "excuse me" and came to a stop in front of me.

"Lyle Nunez," he said, pointing at his convention badge. "I admire your work and was hoping you could talk for a moment."

"Sure, but I want to catch the next session. Who are you affiliated with?"

"Oh." He glanced down at his badge, as if he were hoping the answer was there. "I'm an independent health consultant. I don't get to publish much because everything I do is proprietary. Data mining of health data, that kind of thing."

Great. Consultants circled conferences looking for government contract officers who have unsolved problems and unspent cash. This would probably be a one-way interaction not in my favor. "I don't work in extramural funding, anymore," I said.

He looked at me, perplexed for a moment. "Oh. No, I'm not interested in funding. I heard that you had a run-in with John Stitcher."

Things suddenly became really strange. "How do you know that?"

Lyle Nunez looked around. "Look, can we find someplace to talk? I don't like crowds." He chuckled at his own nervousness.

We went to the hotel's spacious lobby, but it was packed with a family reunion checking in, and scientists and clinicians milling about with cell phones stuck to their heads. The hotel bar was empty, though, and we took a booth in the back.

Lyle picked up a sugar packet and stared at it. "Stitcher's the food industry's plumber. Bad things happen, he comes in, the bad things go away. He also has a nasty reputation. My work in the corporate world has given me a backstage pass to some stuff I'd rather not have seen."

"He's a big fan of our Truth Squad," I said for no particular reason. Maybe I wanted Mr. Nervous Nunez here to flinch again.

Instead, his eyes flicked up to meet mine. "Of course. The Truth Squad is a dream come true for him. You're spreading the good corporate word about obesity. And I love how you do it, like how you handled those callers on C-SPAN's *Morning Journal*? But it also squashes the blame game with that line about there being no one cause, no one's fault. Do you really believe that, by the way?"

I laughed. "Of course I do. It's backed by science a mile wide and ten miles deep. Several elements of our lifestyles and our culture have combined to cause the epidemic."

He nodded. "Exactly. And that means you can't blame any single thing for it. Everyone's blameless if everyone is to blame. How convenient and lucky for the food industries."

I sat back against the vinyl bench. "You're a conspiracy nut." It was time to deploy an exit strategy. And keep my contact info away from this guy.

"Dr. Cassano, you're the one of the sharpest researchers here. You're tough on methodology and your degree allows you to see a bigger picture than a single amino acid. What do you think about the current state of obesity research?"

I shrugged while I grabbed my purse to go. "It's probably no better or worse than any other field. Progress is always slower than expected. We're probably moving slower than cancer research, but faster than clean energy. Science often turns up more questions before it produces answers."

He frowned. "Don't you think the research scope is awfully narrow?

The epidemic has unfolded in our lifetimes and yet, the research can barely document it, much less explain it, much less develop any effective remedies. A more cynical person would say that researching obesity has become its own industry, with incentives increasing every single day to never find an answer. Who needs to study how to make a combustible engine these days, right?"

Okay, he had a point; in fact he had made my point from a discussant talk I gave at an NIH conference three years ago. My remarks were poorly received. This guy had done his homework. I put my purse back down on the booth seat. "Yes. But a lot of that comes down to the mindsets of researchers and clinicians focused on microscopic chemical reactions and ameliorating the health effects of the epidemic."

He nodded. "With John Stitcher waiting in the wings in case anyone gets close to the real truth. Tell me, did anyone ever test the air and water in that warehouse in Grand Forks? Anyone do a medical work-up on the attackers or the victim? Test their blood beyond the usual toxicology tests?"

He kept twirling the sugar packet.

I shook my head. "No. So, what *is* going on then? A nationwide effort to fatten and sicken Americans? Is it a terrorist plot? A leftover Soviet campaign that worked all too well? If you have the secret answers, speak up."

Lyle sighed. "I don't know. I need your help figuring it out. I think companies like Flawless have been using their workers as test subjects. I get the sense there's a lot of other odd, dark things happening. I have eyes and ears out there that you don't. But I can't evaluate the science like you can. I don't have access to the government."

Ah. He was digging for a source at USDA. He wanted money, information, or just an ear to jabber at. I grabbed up the conference binder and my purse. "Lyle, it was nice to meet you. But I have a lot of other trouble on my plate and I don't need more. Now, if you don't mind, I need to get a close seat at the adipose panel, because the PowerPoint slides are impossible to see from a distance."

Lyle stood to shake my hand. But he didn't follow me out of the bar, thank God.

CHAPTER 6

LYLE'S POTSHOTS WERE MORE OF an indictment of how academia responds to fast-moving crises than signs of a lurking conspiracy. Any kind of health crisis brought the medical responders in first, then the epidemiologists, the clinical researchers, the biotech firms, and eventually academia.

I kept telling myself this the rest of the afternoon, but it didn't stop my intuition from saying that there was some truth to Lyle's claims. Science funding had become too corporatized, too focused on applied rather than basic research, too focused on marketability and grabbing grants, not plugging gaps in knowledge. Any malaria researcher who was well-practiced at rubbing two nickels together could confirm this. Ironically, though, obesity was the opposite of an underfunded research area waiting for Western, rich, white folks to catch the condition in question before the money gates opened. It was exactly the reverse.

After the conference I retreated to my cubicle in Beltsville and pored through all of the latest research. I categorized it as retread, suspect, or promising. The promising work I divided by field and focus. There was a lot of Holy Grail work searching for the guilty molecule that had caused, or would cure, the obesity epidemic. There was a big effort on treating diabetes and documenting the emerging effects of obesity on child development. In any field, there was a herd mentality: A new finding would cause the field to pile onto a particular subject for a while, to poke, prod, and test the new finding, and vacuum up the money pouring into that area. This was a good thing, part of the magic of how scientific research worked.

Lyle's take on the direction of research didn't fit well: It required a leap of paranoia that just wasn't warranted. With my systems biology background, sure, I was leery of highly isolated chemical reactions causing systemic adipose accumulation, but I didn't see everyone running away from any promising avenues. Even the food industry poured money into work on how to limit and treat obesity.

However, Lyle's questions rattled around my head. There was a mystery about what had happened in that warehouse that analyzing a bag of chips would not resolve. I decided to confront John Stitcher and see if any of Lyle's claims rang true. He did leave me an open invitation, right?

Stitcher's law firm operated out of a swanky Georgetown address, in a row house on a quiet street. Old brick on the outside, classy antique decor inside. His firm occupied the second floor in the back.

His receptionist was a brittle, elderly woman who peered at me over her glasses as she fed sheaves of legal documents into a scanner. She acted like she had been doing this for at least twenty years. "Going digital," she said tonelessly.

After I introduced myself, she wordlessly ushered me into Stitcher's dark office, which contained a desk with two blue, mesh-backed chairs, one on either side. On the desk was a large laptop, screen closed, a tablet, and nothing else. With the drapes closed, the only light came from a number of old-fashioned lamps. No bookshelves, diplomas, or glory wall of photos with the rich and famous. It was nothing like Bob's office on K Street, or any attorney's office I have ever been in.

Stitcher stood by the window, cursing quietly and steadily into his cell phone. The neutral colors helped make his complexion look less gray than it had appeared under the cheap office lighting at BARC and in that sheriff's office in Grand Forks. It was hard to peg him to an age though. Maybe early sixties, but with a sickly look to him, like cancer survivors sometimes have.

His receptionist scooted out of the office, closing the heavy wooden door behind her. Stitcher looked over at me and nodded. I sat in a blue guest chair and waited. Finally, with a string of quiet curses, he hung up and tossed the phone onto his desk. He sat down and rubbed his face.

"Some of my clients are like nervous little puppies, constantly shitting themselves. I'm going to break all their fucking necks some day and run off to Cabo, I swear," he said, but I got the sense he was enjoying himself immensely. "Dr. Cassano, I'm so pleased you stopped by. I hope you have some good news."

I shifted in my seat and smiled a little. My mind darted to the samples being tested. Had he found out about those? I looked around. "This doesn't look like any lawyer's office I've ever seen."

He smiled. "A good lawyer never has to practice law. You discuss; you negotiate. Law is a last resort."

Ouch. How true. "I hear you lean on people for the industry. Kind of like a heavy for the Gastric Mafia."

He grinned. "I perform solution triage. That's just my BATNA—Best Alternative To a Negotiated Agreement. Look it up sometime. I usually get the negotiated agreement and everyone avoids an unpleasant situation."

"Like the mysterious incident in Grand Forks."

He shrugged. "I guess. I don't think about them much when they're fixed. The next crisis doesn't wait for me to finish an after-action report."

That was rich. "Your visit to ARS was another mess to clean up, wasn't it?"

He grinned. "Grand Forks was damage control, not a cover up. Those fat fucks will now kiss that company's ass forever, and no lawsuits or media coverage will happen. Believe you me, you play the cover up card only when absolutely goddamn necessary."

I folded my arms. "But why don't you want the government to look into it, then?"

He waved a hand. "Are you kidding me, Elaine? I know you're testing samples of the Flawless products. You won't find anything, but the regulators from OSHA or someplace will have an excuse to shove another auditor up our asses. I visited your boss to wave you guys off before that happens. But if that doesn't work, then it's one more fucking headache for old Johnny Stitcher. Swell."

I dipped my head. "Does that mean you won't break our legs over this?"

"Of course not. This is a minor headache; it's a paper cut on my client's hand. The industry has a metric fuck-ton of other problems to deal with. The obesity epidemic, for example."

I made a skeptical face, evidently, because he leaned forward. "The epidemic is wrecking our business model. Whenever there's a study or product recall that panics the public we have to trash our production lines to adjust. We field multiple diet versions of every product, which is enormously expensive. Plus, of course, the lawsuits and bad PR."

But the food industry wasn't hurting financially. And their diet products were opportunities for the industry, not costly burdens. He was making the fleas look as big as the dog. I didn't buy a word of it.

His phone vibrated on his desk. He frowned and stabbed the call to voice mail. "We support high-quality medical research on obesity because we are desperate to beat this thing. For sound business and humanitarian reasons. But our research is all over the place, like goddamn alchemy, and our spokespeople are a bunch of ditzy former cheerleaders and frat bros who have no credibility. We need a research director at our think tank who can speak truth to a TV camera."

Slick change of subject, I thought, and then realized what he was saying. "Me? I can't carry water for a corporate messaging machine."

Stitcher leaned back in his chair and smiled. "After seeing Congress and the press bust the balls of Big Tobacco and Big Oil, our CEOs know that everyone sees through their bullshit. Conceding that the other side has a point builds credibility. A straight-talking spokesperson in the food industry is about to become a hot commodity."

I raised an eyebrow. "An astroturf lobbyist?"

"Director of Research at an industry-funded laboratory. Better than the Obesity Truth Squad," Stitcher said, his eyes blazing. "Directing research in the right direction. But without the bureaucratic obstacles, lack of resources, and dog food pay."

I harrumphed. "Industry-funded research is self-serving and has no credibility. It would destroy my reputation. I would just be a highly-paid spokesmodel that everyone dismisses."

He nodded. "That could happen. You'll have to work twice as hard to convince people your research is legit. But your standards are so high that won't be a problem. And it will be your show to run."

I sighed. I had worn out my welcome at ARS. Stitcher was offering me money, staff, resources, and possibly a soapbox. I could go for the biggest bang for the buck, not worry about chasing down grant money if I didn't want to. The possibilities danced in my imagination like happy woodland fairies.

Until some corporate puke, like Bob or Stitcher, decided I had to go defend soda or breakfast cereal as part of a healthy diet. The corporate overlords would want to shade results, rethink a finding they didn't like, rewrite the findings, or revisit their funding. CEOs change, and if the current crop were enlightened, the next crop might not be. I would be forced out quickly.

Plus, Stitcher must expect something in return for dangling this. We were negotiating a deal here. He had only mentioned his contribution. I would have to throw something out there, just to see what he was interested in.

"Let's not play games. What do you want from me in return?" I asked.

Stitcher leaned back. "I'm not playing games, Elaine. We want nothing from you other than to think about the offer."

"What if I discover that, say, diet soda and snack food chemically encourages people to overeat?"

"It's Nixon going to China, which, trust me, was a bigger deal than you think."

He gave me what I'm sure he thought was a warm smile, but it looked more like the leer of a horny construction worker. Everything about that moment felt surreal. I was more convinced than before that Lyle was on to something. I was also intrigued by Stitcher's offer. How those two things could coexist in my head made me feel dizzy.

Then his phone rang again and he sighed. I took the hint and fled.

CHAPTER 7

RETURNING TO WORK DELIVERED A double whammy of reality. George assigned me to man a table at a high school health fair in Frederick County and left a box of brochures and trifolds in my cube. I can't possibly express how depressing that was. The last time I did something like that, some teenage bitch spat a Ho-Ho in my face.

And Bob left me a message. He said that apparently our attorneys didn't think that he and I had tried hard enough to work out our custody problems. He proposed meeting at Union Station in DC today. Convenient for him, but I'd have to take vacation to get down there. Anything for Charlie. I packed up and shut down my computer.

Carol, my cubicle mate, gave me a funny look. "Are you leaving already?"

Carol's a gossip, and dull. She couldn't grasp why pregnant women would be excluded from obesity statistics despite repeated explanations by me and others. But she was a perky communications expert who loved to overshare far and wide. Somehow she must not have overheard me talking to Bob.

I didn't want the whole office to know about the custody case yet. But even lying to her was something I couldn't do. "Yes, have a good night," I said.

Union Station is near the Capitol, and an hour and a half from Beltsville in clogged rush hour traffic. Bob was waiting for me at a food court table by the Chinese place, gnawing on a giant chocolate chip cookie and watching two tired mothers wrestle three toddlers into highchairs.

"How's Charlie?" I said by way of greeting.

"Great. I'm picking him up from school right after this," Bob said.

I nodded at his cookie. "I hope you're feeding Charlie better than that."

Bob took a large bite and chewed noisily. He had told me on several occasions that concerns over fat and sugar were just hand wringing by health freaks. "People tell me you're crusading against the industry."

I laughed. "They do? I'm working a table at a high school health fair in Frederick County this week."

Bob squinted at me. "You're putting me in an awkward spot. I work for these people, you know."

His narcissism had slid into the chair next to him like a third party. I turned, figuratively, to address it. "I seriously doubt anything I'm doing at work can get you into trouble."

He glared at me. "First it was a call from a buddy of mine over at the Podesta Group telling me he heard that you were part of some investigation into the industry in Grand Forks. Then a PR staffer at one of our major clients mentions offhand that your name is getting dropped in lots of exec meetings for some reason. Finally, my boss asked me what the deal is with my girlfriend."

"I'm not your girlfriend," I replied.

He rolled his eyes. "Baby mama. I know. When it's complicated, people say 'girlfriend.' It's easier."

I shrugged. "What do you want from me?"

"For one, can you knock it off, whatever the hell it is that you're doing?"

I explained to him what had happened in Grand Forks and my brief interaction with Stitcher. I stressed how minimal my role is.

But Bob's eyes bugged. "Stitcher? John Stitcher? Christ, he's talked to you? He's reserved for the worst situations. Real weirdo, too. Oh, Elaine, this is real bad."

"I thought we were here to talk about custody, Bob."

"We are. You're undermining my job, my means of support, the stability that I provide that you can't. Just to get a leg up for your weak custody filing."

"I went to Grand Forks to be interviewed by a reality TV show. I never planned for anything else to happen. And I don't see how this could possibly affect your job."

Bob shook his head. "My boss came to my office and closed the door. He's been getting complaints about what you've been doing. Word is getting around the industry about the Grand Forks thing. There's a lot of nervousness, especially with Stitcher involved. They want me to have you drop it. And if I can't do that, what good am I to them?"

I tried to kill the giggle that came up, but failed miserably. "I'm sorry, but how do they think you can do that?"

Bob looked miserable for a full second. "However I can, I don't know."

It was interesting that Stitcher's interaction with me was spooking Stitcher's own clients. Maybe they didn't know what he was up to. But Bob was really nervous. He wasn't lying about the pressure from his boss or others. He was gobbling that cookie like it was his sole source of psychological comfort.

This did give me new leverage. Even if I tried, I seriously doubted that I could affect Bob's little insular world of lobbyists, think tanks, and Hill staff. But the important part was that he thought I could.

"I get primary custody. You can have visitation rights, say every other weekend and half the holidays."

He shook his head, as if I hadn't even reached the outskirts of reasonability. "I can't believe you would do this. You're threatening my career to take Charlie. Hell, you're abusing your position in the government to take my son from me."

"Our son. Dial down the talking points. I'm not abusing anything." I took a deep breath. "Stitcher is thankful that I told them that obesity and junk food doesn't cause violence. I did you all a favor but only because it was the truth. And you know what? I didn't think once about how any of this would affect you. It's not all about you, Bob."

I could just take the job Stitcher outlined and still try to get Charlie. Maybe Stitcher was offering it because industry execs did fear whatever I had stumbled upon. It felt good to maybe not be the pawn for once.

Bob wagged his finger at me. "You think I'll choose my job over my son. Do you realize what you're doing? My job allows me to support Charlie. He needs my job just as much as I do. So you're not just threatening my career, but you're hurting Charlie. You're a total bitch."

"I think we're done here," I said.

He levered himself out of his chair. "I'll see you in court, Doctor."

I watched him walk off. When he disappeared, I called my lawyer, Sandy. It was time to accelerate the prep for the hearing. She sighed heavily but said okay.

Next I emailed Jim Knox about his lab's testing of the Flawless chips that was upsetting so many lawyers on K Street. When the tests came up clean, I would be able to get Stitcher and my conscience off my back and maybe even Bob would be reluctant to make a full court press.

But by the time I got home, Jim emailed that the initial results had been fouled up and they were redoing them. He'd have something tomorrow and asked that I send my other bag of chips to his contact at FDA's Center for Food Safety and Applied Nutrition. CFSAN tested food safety and could identify components, ingredients and tampering. That sounded a bit more serious than I was hoping this would get.

This time, I did think about how it would affect Bob and I smiled.

CHAPTER 8

A WEEK LATER, JIM KNOX ARRANGED a conference call between him, me, and his contact at FDA/CFSAN, a scientist by the name of Barbara Straub. I had sent the second bag of chips to her at Jim's urging a few days earlier.

"Hiya Elaine," Jim began when we were all on the line. "You really gave us a good one this time."

My heart sank. I wanted the tests to come back clean, if only to avoid any more trouble with Bob or encounters with Stitcher. I still hadn't given him an answer on his job offer. "Go on."

Jim said, "At first, we thought we screwed up, because the results made no sense, so we ran it again. I also wanted CFSAN to confirm what we found. But now we've both replicated the results a few times."

"And..."

"Well, the chip looks like your standard junk food corn chip, with spicy seasoning. It's very similar to Doritos, or some other flavored tortilla chip. Ingredients include corn, high fructose syrup, cayenne pepper, the usual suspects.

"But there's an additive not on the ingredient list. It stimulates production of vasopressin and acetylcholine, and suppresses serotonin levels. All of which induces someone to feel irritated, angry, and aggressive. It's like a shot of hormones right to the anterior hypothalamus. Chemical rage."

Dr. Straub added, "Whatever this is, it shouldn't be in food."

Food tampering? Contamination? Plain old falsifying the ingredients? This was screwing with brain chemistry, which was a tricky prospect. There were so many chemicals that could affect mood. Maybe it was a side effect of something else, possibly from a combination of components? There had been some research done that correlated food dyes and preservatives with aggression in children. But nothing in that research approached the magnitude of what had happened in Grand Forks between adults.

Spiking food with anger juice sounded like some misguided experiment run by drunken psychology grad students. I blurted, "It's a bag of rage."

"Actually, its worse," Jim said. "It also appears to react to the amount of adipose tissue in the body. When you told us about the assailants being overweight, we fed the chips to mice of different sizes just to see what would happen. The more adipose tissue, the more violent they became after consuming the chips. Also the more glassy-eyed they appeared. This chemical appears to turn fat tissue into aggression and to induce some kind of trance-like state. It wears off quickly, though."

"Okay," I said, hoping my head would stop spinning. "Okay. Are you saying that Fiesta Chips are sprinkled with angry juice and dusted with Ambien? And that it turns obese people into monsters?"

"It appears so, based on preliminary results," Dr. Straub said. "We found the same thing that Jim and his crew did. Larger body size usually dilutes the effect of a particular dosage, but for this additive it somehow amplifies the effect."

"Is that even possible?" I asked.

"It shouldn't be," she replied. "I ran this by folks in drug testing over here. They were completely stumped and have been pawing over our samples. They say this must be a pharmaceutical-grade chemical but way more advanced than anything they have ever seen. The obese face differences in absorption, distribution, metabolism, and elimination of any drug, depending on whether it infiltrates the adipose tissue. But our drug guys know of nothing that would use adipose to increase the effect like this. They think the additive could be converting the adipose into the aggression-building hormones. No one has ever crafted a drug to do that though. I mean, why the hell would they?"

"I've never seen anything like it either," Jim added. "To me the big question is: What is something like that doing in a bag of chips? What if it goes to some vending machine in a high school? Or at a soccer stadium? Or a bowling alley, for Christ's sake?"

Panic fluttered in my stomach. The sheriff in Grand Forks probably knew much more than he'd let on. "Dr. Straub, aren't these things supposed to be approved by the FDA before they're sold? How does something like this happen?"

Dr. Straub cleared her throat defensively. "Yes, but for a food product like this it is mostly a formality if there are no new ingredients listed. It is not the same as the drug side of the house where clinical trials are required. We could never test every single new food product going to market. These chips are knock-offs of several other brands. We have to rely on the manufacturer to clue us in that something in them is different."

"Like when people begin pummeling one another. Or dying in droves," I retorted.

Dr. Straub sucked in a noisy breath, unsure of what to say.

"I'm sorry, no offense meant," I added quickly. "I just see a heap of trouble on the horizon because of this."

"But Elaine, this is a huge discovery," Jim said. "You may be the reason that these chips don't go out. You may have saved a lot of lives. And, if there is a way to increase the effect of a drug for the obese, that could be a big breakthrough for diabetic medications, blood pressure, you name it."

Well, there was that. "I was only in town filming a segment for a reality TV show. The producer put the sheriff in contact with me. FDA and we have had enough trouble recently with pissing off the industry. I wasn't looking for trouble, honest."

"Yes," Dr. Straub said with a sigh, "We are the new jack-booted government thugs. And I believe you guys at ARS have been called body-shaming nutrition terrorists, right?"

"Only by several Senators and half-a-dozen talk show hosts," Jim said.

"So, what's the next move?" I asked.

"Well," Dr. Straub replied. "We have to open an investigation on our end and do more testing. We'll send inspectors to the facility that produces the chips. If we find this Chemical X in more of the chips, we'll have to start talking recall."

There went my olive branch to Bob. And my custody case. And Stitcher's job offer. George would rip me a new one too. Oh, great.

"And I have to alert management here," Jim said. Oh crap, that meant his boss Jeannie. I had a history with her. "We need to put more people on this. This could be huge. Thanks for bringing us in on this. I hope it doesn't cause you too much trouble, Elaine."

"Come on," I said, feeling a tension headache coming on. "Getting into trouble seems to be my thing."

CHAPTER 9

I KNEW I WAS IN TROUBLE when the director of BARC scheduled a meeting the next day between him, Jeannie, my boss, and I.

I imagined terrible scenarios where Stitcher speed-dialed the Director when the FDA started snooping. But I think he was just as out of the loop as me: Why else would he shrug when he learned that we were testing Flawless' products? His clients probably tried to cover up things from him first.

To make matters worse, Bob called me right before the meeting. I always took Bob's call no matter what; something might have happened to Charlie. Or it could be Charlie using his dad's cell, because of course he hadn't received his own phone from me yet. Out of the corner of my eye, I saw Carol give the eye roll when she could tell it was Bob. She grabbed her purse and headed out.

Bob skipped saying hello. "Have things sunk so far between us, Elaine, that you went and called the motherfucking FDA? Jesus, I never thought you'd play hardball like this."

I tried to laugh off his paranoia. "The Flawless situation actually has nothing to do with you, Bob. All I did was bring back samples from a vending machine in their building because the sheriff requested it. I don't have a dog in this fight. I would make this all go away if it were ethical. It's disrupting our custody disagreement, pissing off everyone here, too; do I really want any of that?"

"BS. I know you. You don't let anything go. You piss on your colleagues' work all the time. You constantly nitpick how I raise Charlie. You're not whistling innocent on this one, Elaine."

I groaned. "Don't be a dumbass. All I did was courier some samples back to the lab. I'm not a lab rat. I don't have it in for the food industry. But from what I hear, your clients really screwed the pooch on this one. Have you heard about the stuff they found in these chips?"

"No, why don't you tell me?"

I winced. "Uh, I guess I can't comment on that."

"See? You're trying to wreck my clients to get to me. And if you're not, then you're too stupid to realize that this is exactly what the result is. I'm catching shit from everyone about this now. It's become a *situation* and I'm on the verge of being kicked off of that account."

"None of this has anything to do with you, or me, or Charlie. Tell your bosses that. I'll see you in court, Bob."

"Why don't you make it about us, before I lose my job? It would be a huge favor to me if you got the FDA to back down." And possibly as a reward have him soften him up about the custody arrangement, he implied.

I considered it for a second, but then thought about how close to unethical territory just having this conversation was. "Goodbye." I hung up.

George called me down for a pre-meeting ahead of meeting with the BARC director. I crammed an energy bar into my mouth and trekked to George's office. Yeah, apparently I was *that* employee who needed detailed coaching before meeting the bigwigs.

"The director's schedule has been trumped by all of this, by the way," George pointed out when he saw me. "All I want you to do is state the facts and stay quiet. Let FDA point the blame finger. It's not our fight."

I nodded eagerly. "I want this to be over, too." I told him how this was complicating my personal life. He blinked in surprise, but I think he believed me. We took the short walk to the Director's suite. It felt like heading to the principal's office: Make small talk with the assistants in the outer office, try not to be intimidated by the grandeur of the executive suite.

We were joined by Dr. Jeannie Raymar, the tall, thin, uptight head of Human Nutrition. She was the one who had pawned me off on George. She looked distinctly unhappy to see me again. She was alone; apparently Jim Knox was not allowed along for this particular ride. I hoped he wasn't in trouble.

The BARC director called us into his office. He was a hefty white political appointee in his fifties named John Basker. His large, square head was completely bald and he wore big, horn-rimmed glasses that made his eyes look that much smaller. He nodded curtly to George and Jeannie, and shook my hand.

I let George and Jeannie get the first words in. Managers always had to talk first to their own boss, even though they weren't the main attraction. I sat still and kept my mouth shut as George explained the context.

John Basker turned to me. "So what happened, Elaine?"

I explained why I was in Grand Forks, what I saw at the sheriff's office and how the sheriff had requested the sample testing. I made a point to mention that he and the DA admitted that there had been several similar incidents.

I began to summarize the conference call between Jim Knox, Dr. Straub and I when Jeannie interrupted. "I already briefed the Director on the testing."

I stared hard at her. "Has anything changed since Dr. Knox and Dr. Straub determined that there were dangerous, unknown compounds in the Fiesta chips that could have serious side effects on people who eat them?"

George gave me a look that was the equivalent of a kick under the table.

"Yes," Jeannie said, "there have been further developments. It's too early for us to say that we've found anything. Certainly too early to call in the FDA and get the manufacturer involved."

What the hell? "Jim Knox was the one who called FDA," I said.

Jeannie refused to look at me. "That's not how I understand it. I've looked at the results myself and agree with Dr. Knox's conclusion that they are inconclusive. More testing is needed."

So that was how it would be. Lyle Nunez would call this a cover-up. Maybe it was, but more likely, Jeannie just wanted to look like she was in control and not lose face with her boss.

Director Basker nodded and then looked at me. "Elaine, I'm sorry that you were put in an awkward position. You were in Grand Forks on a public relations assignment, I understand for our obesity outreach effort? Very good. I am happy they sought your help on this case. And I want to stress that I want everyone to feel comfortable speaking out whenever they come across a health or safety issue."

He was cushioning the blow. I braced myself as he continued.

"But I want to remind you that these kinds of things should be taken through the proper channels, if for no other reason than that management can bring the appropriate resources to bear."

"We understand," George said. He wanted out of this room as quick as possible.

"Dr. Knox will be reminded of the same thing, isn't that right, Jeannie?" Director Basker said.

Jeannie was caught off guard by that. "Uh, yes, he will be."

"Excellent," the director smiled and spread his hands in satisfaction.

"One question, if you don't mind," I said. George tensed under his pinstriped suit coat. "How is the investigation proceeding? Is FDA picking this up, too? They certainly sounded interested. I would like to be kept in the loop."

Jeannie folded her hands and sighed. "This is being taken very seriously. We'll let you know how it turns out." What she meant was that they were leaving me out of the loop.

The Director smiled and dismissed us. A nice guy but not so nice that I didn't feel the reprimand. When I got back to my desk, I emailed Jim and apologized for any trouble I'd got him in. He didn't respond. Even Carol was giving me the silent treatment now. I stared hard at my computer monitor the rest of the day, but I got nothing done.

CHAPTER 10

FRIDAY NIGHT AGAIN AND I was running all over the house, trying to clean, bake, and declutter. Bob had called me two hours ago, just as I left work, to tell me he was bringing Charlie over to stay for the weekend. He mumbled something about working this weekend, no thanks to me. I was so happy to see my boy that I didn't care about the short notice or what caused it.

My townhouse has two modes: Elaine mode and Mom mode. Elaine mode involves unwashed dishes, trashy romance novels and a profusion of journal articles and books. Mom mode consists of made beds, cookies or banana bread on the dining room table, and a different set of TV channels programmed in the remote. I banish all the lazy, self-indulgent Elaine habits to dark corners and basement closets. Doing this always made me feel like a better person. I had been in Elaine mode for too long.

And somewhere in the back of my head, as I rifled through each room, I couldn't help thinking that Bob had just undermined his claim that I wasn't fit to have partial custody. He couldn't claim that he didn't trust me with Charlie, except when he was really busy.

With every flash of headlights around the townhouse complex, my heart jumped. It had been over a month since I'd last seen Charlie. I talked to him on the phone whenever we could connect, but it wasn't the same thing at all. I was afraid he would have grown noticeably since the last time I saw him.

The doorbell rang as I took the pumpkin chocolate chip cookies out of the oven. There was Charlie, with his backpack and his suitcase and a goofy, happy grin on his face. I gave him a big hug that tried to make up for lost time. He was warm and I didn't want to let him go. Neither did he.

When I looked up, Bob was standing there, smiling despite himself, still in his suit. Behind him, his Porsche was still running. He said goodbye to Charlie, gave me an I-told-you-so look, and was back in his car before I'd closed the front door.

Charlie plopped himself down on the couch while I grabbed up cookies and water bottles from the kitchen. When I came back, Charlie looked really tired and a bit glassy-eyed. He noticed me scanning him and said, "Okay, I don't feel so good."

His forehead was warm to the back of my hand.

Bob, that son of a bitch. How could he not tell me this? *The kid gets sick and he dumps him on his mom, huh?* "Does Dad know about this?"

He shook his head, guilty.

"Charlie, you can't keep doing that. You have to tell him when you're not feeling well. Even when he's busy or distracted or if he gets angry or upset. Okay?"

He nodded listlessly, looking away from me. How inconvenient Charlie was to Bob's life was an issue that lurked under the floorboards until it oozed up at a time like this. I had the feeling that Bob had been put out by Charlie's sudden, perfectly typical kid needs for a long time now.

So much for the weekend. I had a fresh deck of Pokémon cards waiting in his bedroom that I had bought the last time he was supposed to stay here. I could see the outline of his three-inch Pokémon card binder in his backpack. Charlie was just a hair shy of being totally obsessed with the game and was psyched an adult would actually throw down with him. Bob kept promising to take him to a tournament but that never seemed to happen.

"I'm sorry, Mom," Charlie said in a small voice.

I wrapped him up in a blanket. "It's not your fault. If you're sick, I'd rather you be here with me than anywhere else. And any time you're here is better than when you're not. Do you want some cookies? I just made your favorite."

He shook his head.

"Okay, mister, what else is wrong and how long have you had it?"

"Sore throat. Tuesday."

"We're going to your doctor's tomorrow morning. You've been miserable like this since Tuesday? Honey, your dad will take you to the doctor if you're sick. It's not safe for you to hide this kind of thing, plus you're making yourself unnecessarily miserable."

I abruptly shut my piehole. I was lecturing a sick kid. I gave him the Pokémon cards, the new cell phone, and cold medicine. He rallied briefly and we watched TV for a while. He volunteered to go to bed by 9:30 and was sound asleep soon after. I planned a trip to the Saturday morning sick hours at the pediatrician. And then I called Bob, not to yell, just to give him an update.

"Now is not a good time," Bob answered.

"Are you still at the office? That's how you answer your work phone?"

He sighed. "Yeah. I was at a fundraiser tonight and the boss wanted to have some after-action reports right after. This Flawless thing is heating up and we have a ton to do now with that pork recall."

I switched subjects quickly. "Did you know Charlie's been sick most of this week? Sore throat, and now a fever. I'm taking him to the doctor tomorrow."

"Dammit. He never said a word to me," Bob replied defensively. I wondered how much attention Bob had been paying this week. He's a rat, but he's a nervous rat, and his hyper-focus on his own hide at work might have blinded him to what Charlie was up to. That would not do during the teen years. "I've told him not to hold out on me."

"I know, I'm not blaming you. But he's afraid of upsetting you with these things. Does he think you'll yell at him? You wouldn't do that, would you?"

Bob sighed. "Of course not. But I won't lie to you Elaine; I'm not happy when he gets sick, or when he tells me he has a report due on Johnny Tremain the next day and we're at a Caps game. He also knows it breaks my heart to see him hurt or unhappy. And he tries to act tougher around me."

"Fathers and sons," I said.

"Yeah. God, I'm sorry this is ruining your weekend with him, Elaine."

"Thank you, I appreciate that. I'm going to take him into the doctor tomorrow. He and I have a lot of Pokémon to catch up on."

Bob laughed. "Better you than me—I can't tell a Stadium from an Arena card. Thanks again for taking him on such short notice *and* when he's sick. I have to get back to work. Later."

Oh God, an almost civil conversation with Bob. He must be in deep trouble.

I went upstairs to watch Charlie sleep. He looked like he was about five years old. That was how old he was the last time he'd slept here every night. I stood there in the doorway and just lived in the moment until I started nodding off.

I let Charlie sleep in. He still had a fever when he woke up but was hungry. When he drowned his waffles in syrup, claiming that it soothed his throat, I bit my tongue. We had to get going and I didn't want to fight with him at the moment.

It was a warm sunny morning, at the point before the trees and shrubs were fully decked in leaves but after the cherry and apple blossoms had fallen. Charlie insisted on wearing a hoodie because he was chilly. We fought through over an hour's worth of traffic to get from Bowie to McLean.

They whisked us into the exam room, anxious to motor through the sick kids and leave to enjoy the weekend. The nurse did the rapid strep test. We waited for the results and the doctor.

My phone rang. It came up as Lyle Nunez's number. I had no idea why he would be calling me on a Saturday morning. I let it go to voice mail and patted Charlie's leg as we small-talked about Pokémon evolutions.

A tall Asian doctor came in. "I'm Dr. Alistair," she said to me.

Charlie beamed. "My mom is a doctor, too."

I turned sheepish. "Hi. PhD in biology."

Dr. Alistair still nodded, impressed, probably for Charlie's benefit, not mine. "Usually, your dad brings you in," she said.

"I'm with Mom this weekend," he replied with no small amount of pride.

The doctor smiled and got the hint. "Good call by your mother, young man, because you do indeed have strep throat. This is the fourth time in the last year."

"Really?" I said. "That's once every month."

Dr. Alistair became uncertain for a second. "Um, yes. Charlie gets sick about once a month with a cold, or the flu, or strep."

"Oh boy." Charlie looked at his sneakers.

"And how are his height and weight?" I asked, trying to read his chart.

Dr. Alistair swiped through Charlie's file on her tablet and turned it around for me to see. "High on the weight side for a boy his age and height. I'll print it out for you."

"Thanks. This sounds like someone has been eating a lot of junk food to me," I said.

Charlie grinned guiltily and turned to Dr. Alistair. "My mom studies nutrition. Do you know how rough that is?"

Dr. Alistair harrumphed. "Sounds like an advantage to me." This doctor and I would get along just fine. She sent off a prescription and wished us well.

When we reentered the waiting room, every adult was staring slack-jawed at CNN's breaking news banner, "*Sesame Street* Murder Caught on Tape." In retrospect, someone probably should have changed the channel, but everyone was too shocked to think clearly.

I watched the TV as we picked up the prescription at the front desk. Every adult in the room was watching or trying to distract young children who were captivated by the Sesame Street characters showing up in video clips that ran as CNN reported the story.

"An incredible story near Philadelphia," the anchor said, "A crowd of parents beat another parent to death at the popular Sesame Place amusement park. In front of their own children. The assault occurred during the parade of Sesame Street characters."

"Now, we have a copy of a video showing the deadly assault. Be warned that these images may be disturbing to some viewers."

Somebody should really turn this off, I thought. But I was frozen in place, as was every other adult in the room.

A shaky, grainy video showed a crowd surrounding someone on the ground, kicking, and punching furiously. The attackers were black and white, short and tall, men and women, and all were mad as hell. They yelled and taunted the victim. Behind them was a sea of strollers parked outside the Elmo's World studio.

A security guard ran into the frame and tried pulling the assailants off. They ignored him and kept pounding away. Three more guards entered the scene, along with two employees and three visitors. After some scuffling, they finally succeeded in breaking it up. As they pulled one of the attackers away, you could see the pure fury on the man's puffy face. The video ended there and CNN started to loop it.

Guess what all the attackers had in common.

The anchor continued, "The twenty-four year old victim, Tina Blanchard, died at a local hospital. We have a live report from Regina Germany, who is on the scene. Regina, I understand that police arrested ten people but what caused this assault is still in question. What in the world happened?"

They cut to an incredibly thin, thirty-something Hispanic woman standing in front of the gates to Sesame Place. "It's really not clear at this point. One witness told me it was an argument over a spot to watch the character parade that comes down the main street here."

The anchor shook his head. "I can't believe it would turn into something so violent. What have you heard about reports that this poor woman was chased and then beaten?"

At that point, the screen split between the reporter and a replay of the tape in slow motion.

"Ms. Blanchard was chased away from the parade route to this stroller parking area. Witnesses say almost a dozen people chased her and surrounded her, and there was no escape."

"Regina, what is the park doing in the aftermath of this tragedy?"

"Park officials declined to be interviewed on camera, but they did tell me that nothing like this has ever happened before. They are reviewing their security procedures and praised the efforts of their security guards, and the employees and customers who intervened. The ten suspects were all arrested and will be arraigned tomorrow."

"Thank you, Regina. An incredibly bizarre and sad story that we will continue to follow."

"Did we ever go to that park?" Charlie asked me.

My mind snapped back to the pediatrician's office. I felt the blood drain out of my face as I realized he had been watching that horrible video clip. "Huh? Oh, yes. When you were six. You asked Elmo why he was so much bigger than he is on TV. He chuckled at you and rubbed your head. You weren't scared of him at all."

Charlie nodded. "I remember climbing on those nets and the bouncy ride thing."

"The moon bounce?"

"Yes, I'm too old for that now," he said. It was one of those declarations that I had learned to just nod at. I used to argue about these premature assertions, like when he was three, standing there in urine-soaked pants, and declared that he was too young to be potty-trained.

I steered him outside and to the car. "There are days when I wish you weren't so old." We began the long trek back to Maryland.

CHAPTER 11

CHARLIE'S FEVER FLARED UP AFTER lunch and he laid on the couch sorting through his Pokémon cards listlessly while I banged dishes into the dishwasher. He could sort those cards for hours. Two years ago, I'd learned not to let him choose my deck, as he set me up with a dysfunctional combo of fire Pokémon with water energy cards and he beat me quite handily. He had laughed himself silly at his own cleverness.

The phone rang just as I was savoring a nice Saturday afternoon moment. It was Lyle Nunez, conspiracy crank. "Did you see the news?"

I cleared my throat. "How about calling me at work, on Monday?"

"Oh, come on. What's a few minutes? How could you not know about this?"

Fever or not, Charlie would perk an ear up if I hung up on Lyle. "Yes, I saw it," I admitted.

"Can you believe this? It's Grand Forks all over again, but this time people died. And it's on the news! This could really break things wide open."

I headed upstairs to the kitchen to be out of Charlie's earshot. If I had to talk crazy conspiracy theories, I'd rather this not factor into the custody case. "You're jumping to conclusions, Lyle. Obese people commit crimes all the time, just like skinny people do."

"Come on. You saw the video, right?" he said, clearly relishing this. "Did you see their faces? They were enraged, all of them, but they were out of it. Just like Grand Forks."

"I don't think some shaky cell phone video can tell that much," I said blithely. But the truth was, I had noticed the same thing. The assailants were like angry automatons that were slightly confused. But would the police or the DA notice or care?

"We'll see. We'll see, Elaine. Because when the news first broke, I called the local police up there, made an anonymous tip. I told them to do a blood test, to look for drug substances. I think they did it. Now we'll be able to see if something is really in their blood. Where it came from."

I shook my head, even though he couldn't see it. "No, we won't. The police aren't going to call you back and keep you updated on their investigation."

"They don't have to: the media is having a circus with this. The networks all have trucks here. They're talking to witnesses, family members of the victim and the suspects, asking lots of questions, trying to figure out what happened. When they can't figure it out, they're just going to keep digging."

"Until there's a car chase filmed in LA or something. Do you have anything else to do this weekend other than watch TV?"

He went sheepish for a second. "Not really." He was outside. I could hear cars driving by.

"Lyle, are you up in Langhorne, Pennsylvania right now?"

He laughed nervously. "You betcha! Came up right after the story broke. I've collected samples of all the food they serve inside the park. And guess what I found? Flawless Fiesta Chips and Flawless Cookies, in limited-calorie packaging! Maybe you can have your labs look at these. I've already called the FDA."

I thought of George, Jeannie, Director Basker, Bob, and Stitcher. Hopefully none of them would find a way to blame this on me. "Oh really? And what, pray tell, did they say?"

"Uh, they will get back to me, but they were interested in hearing the details."

That was because they were already investigating, but they couldn't tell him that. I wasn't sure *I* could tell him that.

Charlie was calling for me from downstairs. He probably assumed I was off the phone by now. I rubbed my head. "I'm very happy for you, but I was reprimanded about this once already by the lab director." I gave him thirty seconds of how that went down, keeping my voice low so Charlie wouldn't hear. "I have other things to do today and you're kind of interrupting them," I said. I had finally gotten a weekend with Charlie, who turned out to be sick, and the idea that I would sacrifice one minute of it for this nonsense enraged me.

Lyle replied, "I know, but just listen to this. I'm getting in pretty good with some of the assistant producers. You know, the TV producers. They'll put up with a public health crusader if it gives them an advantage. But they want a nutrition expert to back me up on this. They want some names. I was going to give them yours. Is that okay?"

"No, any request about that should go to my boss. He will choose someone else, I'm sure. Besides, Lyle, you want academics for this, not a government spokesperson who will never comment publicly on the forensics of a local criminal investigation."

"Good point. Do you have suggestions of who I should call?"

"No, all of that stuff is at work. I'll talk to you later, Lyle."

"I'll keep you posted, Elaine."

I hurried back downstairs, feeling frazzled. There just had to be another incident related to whatever chemical cocktail Jim Knox and Dr. Straub had found in the Fiesta Chips. With an investigation underway plus the media attention, Lyle could be right, this could be busting out into the open. Lyle was in full crank mode and there was nothing else for me to do. At least until Monday morning.

"That was someone from work," I explained as I came back down the stairs. "Someone who hasn't learned how to go home and enjoy the weekend. How are you feeling?"

"Better," he said. I felt his forehead: normal. "I'm hungry."

"I don't doubt it. You barely touched your lunch. I'll go warm it up."

"I don't want soup, Mom," he said.

He went into the kitchen and I followed, curious about what he would choose. He reviewed the cupboards' contents and then took inventory of the pantry. I'll admit that I didn't have the most kid-friendly assortment of food. But it was food that a Human Nutrition scientist wouldn't be ashamed to buy in public.

Charlie stood there in a trance with the fridge open. Other parents told me that falling into a non-responsive stupor in front of an open refrigerator has an onset of around ten years old and continues on until eighteen or even later.

"Earth to Charlie."

He closed the fridge door, annoyed. "There's nothing here."

"What do you want?"

He thought for a second. "A chili dog."

With a sore throat? "Well, kid, I don't have hot dogs. I have the soup you didn't eat half an hour ago. And I can make more garlic bread." It was chicken noodle soup. Sue me—I'm a traditionalist. It was warm on a sore throat and delivered a boatload of fluid to those who wouldn't chug water.

"Come on Mom. I don't feel that good. Do you have any Cokes?"

I felt a food fight coming on, even though neither of us was in the mood. He was sick and I didn't want to fight with him the first time we were together after so long.

I knew Bob's approach to nutrition was abysmal. Charlie's height and weight chart confirmed it: My son was overweight. Not a lot, not obese, but still. I couldn't help but feel ashamed and inadequate. I zipped around the country preaching about the obesity epidemic and here was my son already starting down that road. If I had lacked any resolve to win the custody battle, I had it now in abundance.

I kept an even tone, draining as much negative emotion from the situation as I could. "What do you eat at your dad's house?"

"Good stuff. Coke and apple juice, Pop Tarts, Hot Pockets, hot dogs, Froot Loops. Snacks. I don't know what else," he retorted. He looked at me a second and realized that his annoyed knee-jerk reaction walked him right into my trap. "There are vegetables too. Just not ones, uh, that you have."

I raised an eyebrow. It was my mother's trick when dealing with my hot-mouthed father or me. A questioning look was sometimes worth a thousand words. Especially when it made him confess and you didn't even know what he had done.

"All right," he said. "I'll eat the soup if you make that bread."

I made him a single piece of bread while the soup warmed up. I use a recipe from the internet that involved pouring melted garlic and butter with a dash of salt on the bread and then 'double-baking' it by baking the bread for ten minutes before putting it on the broiler to brown. Not really healthy, hence the single piece. If I make something that tastes good, it has to taste really good but also not appear frequently.

He sat down with the soup and immediately burned his mouth. Then he guzzled half a glass of water to cool it. I watched him go through these machinations with a certain amount of amusement. If he was that hungry, then he was on the mend.

"So was that your boyfriend on the phone?" he asked, as he blew on the chicken noodle soup. "It's okay with me if it was."

I laughed, caught off guard. "No, he is most certainly not my boyfriend. It was a work thing, really."

"Have you had any boyfriends since I was born?"

I shook my head. My answer became more awkward each year he asked. Charlie smiled. "What's wrong with you? You should go out. Dad does."

There wasn't a lot of time to date for a single mom raising a young child. But that wouldn't explain the last five years. The first two, I was in a deep funk after losing custody and was a huge bitch that drove everyone away. Since then, I had been repairing my career, I guess. Truth was that, libido aside, I wasn't interested in a relationship. But how did you tell that to a ten-year-old boy? *All Momma needs is a vibrator and a romance novel, so don't you worry your pretty little head?*

Charlie bit into the bread and smiled with his eyes closed. "My Italian mother makes the best garlic bread."

"My paternal grandmother, God rest her soul, would not agree with you," I said. If old Maria saw my life right now, I couldn't imagine what she would be most outraged by—my cooking, my job, or my bastard child.

"I'm fat," he declared.

I blinked, not knowing how to respond. He was bouncing the idea off me, to see if I agreed. As a mother, I wanted to assure him that he was most certainly not, but to some extent that wasn't true. A child his age would see through false statements just as well as most adults.

"You're a little overweight. I don't like the term 'fat'." I almost winced as I said that first part. It was true, but it sounded like a rationalization.

"God, Mom. Overweight means fat. Don't try to sugarcoat it." He ate another spoonful of soup. "Is that why you want to get custody back? Because Dad let me get fat?"

"Well, not entirely. It's because your father has made it harder and harder for you to see me. The important thing to know is that we both love you and we want what's best for you. Sometimes, our desire to be near you overwhelms that other stuff, though."

"It's not because you think I'm fat?" Charlie said.

I took his hand. "You should say 'overweight.' And no, it's not because of your weight. I would like you to be in better health. You're sick more than you should be. I bet you have a lousy diet and don't get a lot of exercise."

"I've never been on a diet," Charlie said, a bit defensively.

"I meant diet as in the type and amount of food you eat."

"You wouldn't let me get like this, you mean," he said.

"Not if I could help it! But weight gain is a problem for most people in our country."

"I know. I've heard your speech." Charlie thought for a second. "You know, neither of you has asked me who I want to live with."

It was a fair point. It was also an incredibly awkward and in some sense, unfair position to put a child, choosing one parent over another.

"We don't want you to feel forced to choose," I said.

"But then I don't get a say."

I shrugged. I really was afraid to know what his opinion was. "You don't get a say in your bedtime either. You see what I'm saying?"

"That's exactly what Dad said. Clearly, you take better care of me. But, I haven't lived here in five years. All of my friends are at Dad's. And he doesn't make me do chores like you do." He finished the last spoonful of soup. "This bread serving size seemed awfully small."

"How about we go for a long walk instead? Before it rains later."

Charlie soured. "Maybe another game of Pokémon?"

I smiled as I cleaned up his dishes. It felt so good and right to have him home.

CHAPTER 12

COME MONDAY MORNING I WAS curious to hear what Lyle had been up to. I couldn't believe he'd actually trucked up to Langhorne, PA to stalk the media covering the murder.

Most offices on Mondays get started slowly as people recount their weekend adventures and finally slip back into their work. But today, the Truth Squad was a beehive of activity when I arrived at eight. Carol was busy pecking away at some PowerPoint deck and barely said hello. She seemed really tightly wound, which sucked, because I wanted to tell her about my Charlie weekend.

Lyle's messages consisted of: *We need to talk, you need to turn on the TV, come on pick up.* So before I called him back, I hit the news sites.

The so-called 'Sesame Street Murder' had become one of those media events where a strange story breaks during a news lull, strikes a chord, and goes national. The victim turned out to be a skinny blonde babe with a telegenic picture. There also was video of the attack. The local police chief was unprepared for the media spotlight and unpredictable, making his press conferences worthy of live coverage. And floating above it all was the unanswered question: Why did this happen?

The theories offered to explain it were a talk show host's wish list: over-protective parents, the lack of civility, the evil of amusement parks, television, the decline of family values, and—you guessed it—questions "being raised" about whether obesity causes violent behavior. Now I understood why Lyle was so emphatic on the phone. Today's big event in the media circus was the arraignment. To fill airtime, the cable news stations were discussing whether obesity caused monstrosity.

"It's crazy, huh? I have to brief the director this morning about this," Carol said. She was looking over my shoulder at my monitor.

"The Sesame Street thing? We're involved?"

Carol rolled her eyes. "Honey, are you kidding? We've had requests coming in from the media, Congress, the White House, everyone."

Lyle had wanted the obesity angle to get attention and he should be plenty happy now. He was either incredibly lucky or incredibly effective in making that happen. I wondered if the Fiesta Chips or some other food product tainted with rage juice really was involved. I couldn't mention that to Carol, though.

"So, let me guess: our position is that since such a large proportion of the population is obese that it is not that uncommon for obese people to be both victims and perpetrators of violent crime?"

Carol nodded. "You saw the new talking points, right? Why are you looking at me like that? Didn't you see the email from George? The Director wants us on morning shows, radio programs. He sent it to, like, everyone."

I shook my head and Carol realized she had stepped into a puddle of awkward. "Oh, I assumed it went to everyone. Um. He probably doesn't want you hogging up all the airtime," she said with a weak grin. "When does your episode air?"

"I'm not sure," I replied, feeling that old Italian anger bubble up. George was leaving me out of this one because of the sample testing blowup. I shouldn't have cared but I did. I wanted to be out there. "I think they're still editing. You know reality TV. They may have to change footage in Episode One to highlight a drama queen they only discover in Episode Four."

I surfed around for a food contamination angle in the Sesame Street story but there wasn't one. "Has anyone mentioned food contamination as a possible cause?"

"No. How would food poisoning make you kill someone?" Carol looked perplexed. "Other than the cook?"

"Not poisoned, contaminated. Something that could alter the brain chemistry, enrage the person. Like those claims about Red Dye Number 5 increasing aggression in children?"

Carol still looked at me like I was crazy. She'd be a great co-worker at Target or Jo-Ann Fabrics. But she was a science buffoon at a scientific research organization. Whenever I tried to explain something scientific to her, she weirded out and ignored me. But this time, I had the feeling that she thought I was the idiot.

"But it's a dye. It doesn't even have calories," she said matter-of-factly. She collected her PowerPoint slides from the printer and left.

Well, she was right that there was no mention of anything having to do with food. The obesity angle was all hate and prejudice towards the obese. Since joining the Truth Squad I had become enormously sensitive to this dark undercurrent of American society. The more futile the research was in nailing down a cause for obesity, the harder it became to blame the obese, but the more popular it had become as a knee-jerk response to all the complications. Not since HIV/AIDS had we so much hate towards the victims when we were pretty sure it wasn't their fault for being caught up in an epidemic no one saw coming.

Humans are social animals with a strong desire to conform and be accepted. But they also sought out the easy explanations for freaky things. If this idea that having more fat tissue made you violent caught on, the obese would be more stigmatized than ever before. Our ability to help them, and fight the epidemic, would become that much harder.

Some obese people had simply convinced themselves that they weren't that overweight. They avoided mirrors and bathroom scales. They bought oversized clothes that made them feel small. It wouldn't surprise me that when some of them saw the Sesame Street murder video clip, they'd probably thought those folks were much more obese than they were.

The cube farm emptied as my coworkers deployed to handle the media onslaught. It was an emergency assignment to inform public perception and understanding of the obese, to dispel any misconception that the obese were monsters. Now, when I wanted in on what the team was doing, I was shut out.

Screw Lyle and his conspiracy theories. I wouldn't call him back yet. I kept the news streaming on the web browser and did my Monday morning reading. It was my intern-worthy job to skim the latest news from the science journals and magazines, and send around a summary of the newest findings for the rest of the Squad to build into their materials.

I watched the post-arraignment press conference live. The prosecutor announced that all of the defendants were charged with voluntary manslaughter and were being held without bail. All ten had pleaded not guilty and were represented by the same defense attorney. The prosecutor took no questions and left.

The defense attorney stepped up to the bank of microphones. She was a small woman in her fifties with blazing blue eyes. She addressed the press like they were a wayward class on a field trip to the courthouse.

"My clients are innocent. They were suffering from diminished capacity. They are filing suit against the Sesame Place amusement park for serving drug-tainted food."

The reporters gasped audibly and the questions poured forth. What kind of food contamination? Was she saying the park was unsafe? How come no one else was affected? The attorney waved them all off and the news channel cut back to the reporter on the scene, who pronounced these claims "surprising" and "hard to believe." Nevertheless, the first question from the studio anchor to the panel of assembled experts was about food contamination as a murder defense. The slick-haired law school professor corrected the anchor by explaining the difference between manslaughter and murder.

I turned it off and called Lyle.

He whooped when he answered the phone. "You have to come up here, Elaine!"

"My coworkers are headed up there," I said. "But I'm not being sent. I told you there was fallout from the Fiesta chips thing."

"Doesn't matter. This story is coming out, finally. The network reporters are eating out of my hands. Your Truth Squad needs to get ahead of it."

I shook my head. "Lyle, I already poked my head up on this and almost got it cut off."

He sighed in exasperation. "But that's not why you have to come up here. I have an informant inside Flawless who wants to expose the entire conspiracy. He's got documents. He even worked on the drug additive. But he will only turn them over to someone in the government. Just get up here. I have to go."

I looked around the empty cube farm. George had been quietly reducing my workload since the meeting with the Director. I didn't have anything else to do today.

It looked like I was going to Langhorne, Pennsylvania.

Washington to Langhorne, which is north of Philadelphia, was roughly three hours. I got on the road after the morning rush hour ended, going against the traffic flow.

I checked my messages at a stop north of Baltimore. George had called looking for me. Great, now I had to lie to him. I called him back from my car, dredging up the first plausible thing that came to mind. He had cut me out; he didn't deserve the truth.

"George, I got your message. I had to run out to handle a custody thing."

"Oh, I'm sorry to hear that. Charlie is eight now, isn't he? Ten? God, time flies. Take as much time as you need. If you need to unload some speaking engagements, let me know."

There was no way I was giving up the little work I had. "I should be fine. It's probably just for part of the day. And there will be a deposition and the hearing down the road. I brought my laptop with me so I can keep going while I wait in the lawyer's office."

George replied, "I wanted to explain why I wasn't putting you on this Sesame Street thing. It's nothing personal. We thought it best to keep you out of any awkward situations. Now that this drug angle has come up, everyone but you can claim ignorance of it, or at least not say anything to fuel that controversy."

"I understand. The FDA will probably take over the investigation now, and see if that defense attorney's claims hold any water. Have you heard anything on that front?"

"No. Look, just to be clear, I want to be sure you're avoiding this whole circus. Route any media requests to me."

I passed a sign for Philadelphia. "Sure thing, boss."

"Good. I'm afraid we'll have a lot of work to do now that the media is reporting the 'controversy' about whether the obese are dangerous."

"Are people really saying that?" I asked, playing ignorant.

"The media has. We're digging for statistics on crime rates by obesity status because we have a dozen inquiries pending. CNN is working on a segment. Fox is running a montage of clips of angry obese people from a variety of town halls and political rallies. The BBC is contrasting American obesity with American crime rates."

"That's ridiculous."

"I know. Take care, Elaine."

Lyle texted me to meet him at the KFC on Lincoln Highway near the amusement park. I arrived about an hour later, bought a bottle of water and sat down.

Ten minutes later, Lyle arrived with the informant, whom he introduced as Barry Prazlewski. Barry reminded me of the late comedic actor John Candy. He was larger than life in every way. He was a good head taller than me and he was carrying a lot of extra weight. He had pasty white skin, large, liquid-brown eyes and a teddy bear demeanor. In his suit and dress shirt, he looked like a business type who was off the clock.

He and Lyle slid into the booth and Barry put a folder on the table. "I'm a project management consultant at Flawless. They brought me in to evaluate the project when it hit a snag ten years ago. It was called Z3bmoz. All I knew at first was that it was an experiment to see if they could make people relax and eat more. I'm not a scientist but, you know, I *have* been evaluating food production processes for twenty years. And I have never seen anything as weird as this."

I shook my head. "Wait, what was it called?"

"Z3bmoz. Probably a production number." Barry held his hands up and brought them down on the cheap white Formica table for dramatic effect. "It makes people forget what they're doing and it makes them very angry. And that was the effect they *wanted* to create. So," he said, looking down at his hands, "I asked them why they were doing this.

"Weird bunch of scientists, these guys. They got kind of quiet, looked at one another, and said it was a counter-experiment. They were trying to replicate a finding where a test subject had gone temporarily nuts because they wanted to understand why that happened. They were real insistent, and upper management backed them, and told me they had to track down what was causing this reaction. For safety reasons, to make sure it wasn't contaminating the product. So I helped them out."

"So far that doesn't sound illicit," I noted.

Barry nodded. "They were messing with combinations of sleeping pills and hormones, trying to find the right mix. Really mucking around with brain chemistry and it made me nervous, but they were really into it. They worked in a strange way—almost by instinct, it seemed, as if they knew the results before they were developed and were deep into the next stage when the results confirmed their suspicions. Mind you, this is brain chemistry, flicking the pineal gland and the hippocampus, but this crew was as comfortable doing that as Joe Blow would be setting up a desk lamp. But they seemed to be getting nowhere, which is why management asked me to check on them."

"So, what did you do for them?" I asked.

"In the end, nothing. By the time I got up to speed on the project and what they were doing, I was put on a higher priority project. I think management had me at loose ends and put me on this until they had something better. I don't ask why; that's an occupational hazard for a consultant."

"Lyle says you know about, Z3bmoz, I mean the additive, right?" he asked me. "Mild hallucinogen that suppresses short term memory mixed with something that causes rage in obese people like me."

"Are you saying they made 3Boz on purpose?" I asked.

"Z3bmoz," Lyle corrected me.

"The additive."

Lyle nodded vigorously and Barry replied, "Oh, yeah. They had the memory suppressant chemical isolated, but when I left the project, they were stuck on what caused the anger. They were trying to create a reverse SNRI, essentially an anti-anti-depressant to replicate the effects. I completely forgot about it until two years ago, when the attacks started."

"Two years ago?" I looked from Barry to Lyle.

"The attacks, yeah, tell her about those," Lyle said.

Barry looked at the table. "There have been twenty that I know of. Some in the lab, some in market tests in select cities, some in focus groups. The company has kept them quiet. Until now, if that's what this is."

Lyle added, "Grand Forks wasn't the first, not even the tenth, Elaine."

Stitcher must have been busy working on his Flawless account. "Do you have any idea why they would want to add this to their products?"

"It's obvious," Lyle said. "They want us to forget how much we've already eaten so we'll keep on eating more of their products."

I replied, "We all do that already. Which is why snacking between meals can be so problematic because, at the end of the day, it's hard to remember the extra cracker or cookie."

Lyle threw his hands up. "Then why do it? And why make obese people angry on top of it?"

Barry opened the folder. "I have copies of some internal documents.

They mention the project by name and the tests to replicate the anger response. They tried everything: serotonin levels, oxytocin inhibitors, vasopressin blockers, and so on. It's not the complete story, but it's better than nothing."

I took the folder. Serotonin was a major brain chemical that helped regulate aggression. Vasopressin and oxytocin both reduced anger and aggression. Oxytocin was the chemical that new mothers experienced that made them warm and maternal toward their offspring.

Lyle watched me as I flipped through the folder. "Give that to your people on the inside when you get back, but you have to meet with some reporters before you go. Deep background."

I shook my head slowly. "No, no. I have to get these documents back to DC. I'll give you names of Truth Squad staff who are already up here. You'll be able to help each other out. The 'obese are violent' narrative will only die if there is strong suspicion that they were drugged. But I have to stay out of the picture. Seriously. I'm in enough trouble already."

Lyle was chagrined, but nodded.

I tore my gaze away from the documents. "Barry, can we count on you? There may be a lot of people who want to talk to you. I don't know how these things are handled, but it could become a big deal. And it would be great if you could retrieve more documents."

The consultant shrugged. "I'm ready to talk. These sons of bitches want to turn us into monsters, like we didn't have enough problems with our social image. You should see the looks I get now. It's just a matter of time before somebody says or does something to a large person. This has to be stopped, even if it costs me my job."

Out of the corner of my eye, I noticed the black nipple of a security camera hanging out of the drop ceiling. I shivered. Lyle's paranoia was contagious. "Let's get out of here."

CHAPTER 13

I**T WAS A LONG DRIVE** home. My mind raced faster than the car. Jim Knox had dropped off the Earth as far as I knew, so I would have to take the documents directly to the FDA. The FDA's testing of additives must have been further along than Jeannie had admitted, but these documents could provide the missing link.

It was nine o'clock when I locked the door to my townhouse behind me. Despite my throbbing bladder, the first thing I did was scan Barry's documents so I would have a digital copy. I hid the originals in my china cabinet and, exhausted, went to bed.

I brought the folder with me to work the next day, feeling like an unwilling secret agent. The morning news was dominated by outrageous accusations about the moral code of the obese. I knew the Truth Squad would be crushed with work. Indeed, the cube farm was deserted again except for a couple of interns who were busy researching follow-up questions.

An urgent email came in from George: He wanted to see me in his office. For once I was eager and happy to help. I felt like I had been frozen out, but with all of the work rolling in, he had no choice but throw me in, too. I didn't care what it was, even helping the interns. I didn't like leaving my coworkers hanging and I didn't want to miss out on the Squad's moment to shine. If there was any silver lining to the Sesame Street tragedy, it would be a national dialogue about obesity that could save thousands of lives.

I brought the folder of Flawless documents with me to George's office. I wasn't planning on giving it to him; I just didn't want to lose sight of it.

George beamed. "I have good news. Your request to return to Human Nutrition was approved. This afternoon, if you can make the move. Your work on this additive thing must have really taken off. Jeannie practically begged me to have you return early. And you've wanted to get back to research. Congratulations."

He shook my hand and wished me the best. I walked out feeling elated. A second chance in Human Nutrition. Without Jeannie sabotaging me. I knew, this time around, how not to repel my coworkers. I could do this.

Jeannie emailed me a cube assignment and said she would stop by to talk this afternoon. After I spent lunch packing, I drove over to the 300 building near Beaver Dam Road. My cube was down in the dusty crash space in the basement. I didn't think much of it. Every organization has temporary office space to house people during renovations or moves, or for visitors who would otherwise have to kill hours between meetings. It was an area that no one felt ownership of. Crash space is fine for teleworking, but it was a dehumanizing prospect for forty hours a week. But I was sure it was temporary. After all, this move had happened all of a sudden. I would make the best of it.

I was busy getting set up, with the Flawless folder out in plain sight, when Jeannie popped her head in. "Welcome back." Awkward pause. "You will do proposal reviews. Your 'broad-based science' degree is a perfect fit." Broad-based was Jeannie-speak for not being an expert in anything. It was her way of belittling PhDs she didn't like.

So it was going to be like that. Reviewing grant proposals was a stab in my heart, and this bitch knew it. I hated that work with a passion. It had already cost me a job and dented my career at my previous agency. Jeannie couldn't fire me, but this was the closest thing.

"The proposals will be sent to you electronically. Scoring meetings are every week—you'll get an invite. I want a weekly report, written, about what has happened. Don't bother the other staff and you can skip the staff meetings. Oh, and the printer has resume-quality paper inside."

I folded my arms. "George said you practically begged him to send me back."

She stared back at me and produced a fake smile that lasted exactly two seconds. "Remember, George is in PR."

I read through every document in Barry's folder again, maybe just as a way to stitch together the shreds of my dignity. I searched the literature for work similar to what these Flawless researchers had done. Deconstructing an unknown physiological reaction is much harder work than simply retesting the suspect item again. It didn't take Lyle's paranoia to see that these guys weren't testing the additive for intellectual curiosity or safety concerns; they wanted to produce it on a commercial scale.

It was critical that I get these documents to someone who could do something with them. Barry could have taken them to the FDA himself, but I think he and Lyle wanted a buffer until he became more comfortable with ratting out his employer. Lyle and I were that buffer for the moment. Since I was the fed, that meant it was on me.

There was only one person I could think of contacting and I didn't want to. I had wrecked almost all of my remaining relationships at BARC already and really didn't want to make it a clean sweep. But I had no choice. I went looking for Jim Knox.

He was walking down the hall outside his lab, listening patiently on a cell phone. He brightened when he saw me, a good sign. After a few "yeahs" and "okays," he hung up.

"How are you, Elaine?" He gave me a hug and looked sheepish. "I'm sorry I haven't returned your phone calls. Gag order from Jeannie."

"I hope I didn't get you in too much trouble," I replied.

He shrugged it off, looked around and said, "Let's talk in my office."

On the way there, I filled him in on my misbegotten return. He groaned and closed the door behind him.

"So how bad was she to you?" I asked.

He waved it off, but I could see the hurt. "Don't you worry about me. I'm a big boy and I can put up with The Harpy. So you got turfed back here by George and Jeannie has it in for you. Just like old times."

"Not entirely." I held up the folder. "This is from a whistleblower inside Flawless." I filled him in on meeting Barry as he thumbed through the documents. His eyes grew wider. "Can you get copies of those to Dr. Straub?"

Jim looked at me over his reading glasses, as if thinking about how to respond. He looked back at the documents again. "No. Jeannie is running this real tight. Everything goes to her, and she liaises with her counterpart in FDA's CFSAN. No staff-to-staff. The reason, she says, is so that everything is properly documented and handled, *unlike last time*." He rolled his eyes.

"Maybe you should just give it to Jeannie yourself, score some brownie points with her?"

I swallowed hard. "If I give it to her, will she really turn it over to FDA?"

Jim shrugged. "It could help out the investigation, and that's a big point for her. Maybe she'll even let you out of the grant review dungeon. Then she'll make us all review some of them again. Hmm... maybe it would be better if she didn't see that." He made a halfhearted grab for the folder.

I hit him on the arm and laughed. I was relieved it was like old times and he didn't hate me. I reclaimed the folder and marched down to Jeannie's office. I knew if I tried to schedule a meeting she would never see me. So I popped my head in her door.

"Jeannie, a contact of mine found an informant at Flawless who passed along these insider documents. They could break open the Sesame Street investigation."

She was skeptical but took the folder. After perusing the contents, her head snapped up when she realized I was still standing there. "Thank you. Is there anything else?"

I fidgeted a second. "Will you send that to FDA?"

She smiled at me in a way that felt like cold steel against my neck. "Absolutely. This will make us players in this investigation. Keep me updated." She looked at the folder and then back at me. "But don't let it interrupt your grant reviews."

Jim had nothing to worry about on that front, apparently.

Until my phone's alarm dinged that night at home, I had totally forgotten about my premiere on national TV. That entire trip was dominated in my memory by the Flawless incident. I had received reassuring emails from Melanie that my clip would air. When they'd publicized the release dates for each episode, I had filed it away for safekeeping and promptly forgotten about the whole thing.

The interview segment included RJ's voiceover, which essentially repeated my long-winded explanations or summarized existing research. The editors made me look good, even my bug eyes and curly hair.

Before the commercial break, RJ's voiceover teaser for the town hall segment mentioned that "things got heated." They edited it to look like a mob scene, one of those angry town halls that erupt over immigration or taxes. I remembered a couple of angry questions from the audience but nothing like what they had hyped. They edited the questions and answers so that there was intense emotion on display every moment, except for the ten-second clips of me giving my speech. They showed the sobbing woman while the audio played off the more angry audience members yelling at me. It appeared ten times more exciting, especially with RJ's melodramatic narration. And my responses sounded flat and ridiculous. But the show included half of the speech's main points. And the other half were covered in the interview.

The texts, emails and calls flooded in to me after the show ended. Charlie congratulated me and joked that he wanted to know how I could be so calm with an angry crowd, but yell at him about doing homework and chores. Friends who I hadn't heard from in ages got in touch. I assured everyone that the show was a one-time thing and nothing to get too excited about.

Ma called too. We were both suckers for reality TV shows, so this wasn't unusual. "Elaine, you're famous! You've been on national TV. Everyone was watching you: all the relatives and everyone from my office. When are you going to be on again?"

I sighed. "That's it. Nothing else."

"Now, come on, dear, I may be your mother, but you did really well up there. After all that exposure, you may even get a television deal! Maybe you'll be like those doctors who have their own talk shows!"

"Ma, I was sent back to Human Nutrition, reviewing grant proposals from a storage closet. I may be getting back to research, but it's going to be a long slog."

There was a long pause. "But why? You did such a good job on that show. Why would they do that before it even aired?"

She wouldn't understand. I suddenly wasn't in a mood to explain. I took a deep breath. "It was best for them and me."

"Oh. Oh, dear. I'm sorry. You're having the worst run of luck, aren't you? Are you having trouble getting along with others again?"

I smiled. "Even when I'm trying to be nice, things seem to backfire. This time my burned bridges bit me in the butt."

"I was afraid this would happen someday, dear. You always have stood your ground so... strongly. It gets you in trouble. If you could just be a bit more accommodating, you'd have a much easier time, I'm sure. You and Bob may have been able to work things out—"

"For the hundredth time, that was just sex, not a relationship. It was never going to work," I retorted. She had been pressing this point since I'd told her I was pregnant eleven years ago.

"Forget I mentioned it. The world is full of other people trying to do their best. They won't all measure up to your standards. If you can't be somewhat accepting of their limitations, then you'll be facing this again and again."

We both sighed. If only my father were alive. "What would Dad say?"

Ma laughed. "He'd probably say something I don't agree with and would lead you into even more trouble. He was so protective of you that he would probably have gotten all agitated and said some hot-headed nonsense that wouldn't help."

"Like, don't compromise, stand your ground, don't let them get me down?"

"Something like that. Plus, he'd threaten to drive over to Route 1 and tell those people to treat you better." She paused. "So what will you do now?"

Once again, my mother had asked the awkward question I wasn't ready to answer. It wouldn't take long for me to go mad from reviewing grant proposals. It would pay the bills, and plenty of scientists do it, but I'm not that type. Other scientists hover around one protein for their entire career, or one analytical technique, but I couldn't be chained that way, either. I could hunker down and hope that Jeannie left sometime in the next twenty years or eventually changed her mind about me. Otherwise, I would have to leave BARC and start over again, but with twice the baggage. A two-time loser. Maybe Ma was right and one of the reporters covering the Sesame Place story would interview me now that my *We Will* segment had aired. "I don't know yet. Too many variables in flux right now."

"You're speaking in equations again. I went over the line. I'm sorry."

"It's all right, Ma," I said. She was so touchy about how to talk to me.

"Different subject. How's the custody hearing going?"

I groaned loudly.

But everything depended on the custody hearing. If I lost Charlie again, or perhaps lost all rights, what would I do? Reviewing proposals seemed small fry compared to that particular hell, which I had been avoiding thinking about.

"Different subject. I bet you'll get a few dates now that you're a TV star."

"Do you think this is cheering me up?"

"Have you gotten any messages from interesting men from your past, hoping to reconnect?" She meant Bob, naturally.

I checked the social media sites I belonged to. All the old friends were female. It was Support-Your-Girlfriend Night, apparently. Which was great, because my not dating was an old sore subject between us. "None," I replied.

"Right. Well. I'm going to hang up now, dear, because the more I talk, the more I'm tasting my own toenails."

She could be so predictably weird sometimes. But that night as I wallowed in insomnia, her questions kept banging around my brainpan like hiking boots tumbling in a dryer.

CHAPTER 14

THE NEXT DAY I WAS hip-deep in grant applications, progress reports, and statements of work for upcoming RFAs. RFA means "request for application," if you didn't know. Reviewing a grant application is not simply a matter of reading it and then spewing comments and opinion. Each required a careful read, scrutinizing who the PI (primary investigator) would be and the likelihood that the project would provide worthy results.

In addition, most of the proposals touched on areas outside of my current expertise, so I had to do additional studying just to properly understand them. Nutrition research covered so many different niches that I had to farm some out to the actual expert in that niche and harangue them for comments.

Appearing on national TV seemed to have happened to someone else. No one mentioned anything to me about it and no one visited my cube in the dusty temporary space in the basement. So, when John Stitcher called me, I was actually eager to talk to anyone. But the sound of Stitcher's urgent, gruff voice blasted away any relief. "Elaine, you did great, a helluva job. Are you on any other segments? Too bad, too bad. Listen, I need your help on this fucking Sesame Street debacle."

The hairs on the back of my neck jumped to attention. Did he know about my trip up to Langhorne?

"Flawless is freezing me out," he said. "My own client, who wants me to deal with these crazy-shit claims at this amusement park, is now fucking with me. The execs are running around with thumbs up their asses about the contamination allegations. So, I make the usual rounds of junior-level execs and I get fucking stonewalled. The media is sniffing around Heinz, Sysco, Pepsico, Flawless, other big food vendors for the park."

"What can I do?" I replied.

"Fucking food makes fat fucks lose their minds and murder skinny fucks? That's tabloid bullshit, but now these cocksucking journalists have it in their teeth and won't fucking let it go. Tell me your Truth Squad is all over this shit. Please."

"I'm off the Truth Squad and back at Human Nutrition." I gave him George's number.

"You're not out of this, Elaine, not by a long shot. If I find out someone at this company is playing me, and they are actually responsible for this, I will fucking freak. I want you to keep your ear to the ground and let me know if anything pops on your end."

I wouldn't tell him about Barry. The temptation was there, because Stitcher could run with that info maybe better than anyone else. But Stitcher couldn't be trusted—I was sure of that. "Are you saying you want me to tell you if the government confirms that your client is drugging overweight consumers to kill skinny ones?"

Stitcher didn't hesitate. "Absolutely. This shit stinks and I will find out sooner or later. You never know when I could return the favor. So, anything you can do would go a long way over here. Honest. I gotta fly now. Later."

After Stitcher's call, I ate lunch quickly in my cube, stressed and alone. Before I could get back into my work, my attorney Sandy called to ruin my day even more.

"Elaine, Bob has filed a counter petition for full custody, with no visitation rights or any other involvement from you. The petition claims that you are an unfit parent because you are unstable, have uncertain career prospects, and have a history of erratic behavior."

My eyes flooded and I almost whimpered in response. I stopped, cleared my throat, and said, "Okay." My voice broke like a violin string snapping in the middle of a note. "Sorry, you caught me off guard."

"I think it's a negotiating ploy," Sandy said. "We bet full custody and so, they called us and raised the unfitness charge. They want us to negotiate and they're trying to provoke you into overreacting. I think they want to settle."

"Oh really? Settle? Are you kidding? If I'm unstable, it's because of him."

"Exactly my point. This is just stupid lawyer dirty tricks. Unless he knows something that you should share with me."

Bob was going all in, to keep this stupid gambling metaphor moving forward. Maybe I had underestimated how threatened he felt by the whole thing. Maybe he saw my petition filing as an attack on his parenting fitness. It was, of course, but I never said he was unstable. That self-absorbed bastard.

He hadn't been this upset before about the custody case. In fact, he was almost smug. I figured the same degree of embarrassment and humiliation would be in store for me. But this was vicious. Something had changed. I tapped my finger. Well, my work situation had gone downhill, but I was still employed. Returning to Human Nutrition was hardly a bad thing.

"I may know what he really wants," I said. "He thinks that my involvement in this Sesame Street food scandal has undermined his lobbyist job. He thinks that I'm some kind of anti-industry crusader out to hurt him by hurting his clients. But all I do is review grant proposals for USDA."

"I see. Can you talk him down?" Sandy asked. "Because otherwise we'll have to retaliate in kind and this will get really ugly, and really expensive, really fast. And it won't do any favors for Charlie."

"But don't you make more money if it takes forever?"

The question lingered out there for a second, its boldness acting like a depth charge in the conversation. Finally, Sandy chortled. "Hon, I don't milk each client to the last dollar; I like return business because of client recommendations and word of mouth."

"I'm sorry. I shouldn't have put it that way. I'm short on tact these days."

"It's okay. Just make sure you fix that before you talk to Bob again. I'm going to end this here to keep your bill low."

"Thanks." Time for another chat with the father of my child. How did you talk to someone when they had accused you of being unstable? Well, the first thing was to get a hold of yourself. I needed a solid ten-minute weep, easy to get away with in this deserted cube farm, followed by several hours with these lifeless grant proposals. I'd only cried in front of Bob once, and I would never, ever, do that again. Unstable, my ass.

By the time I got home that night, I was calling myself the Grim Reaper. An email, call, or visit from me now struck dread in the heart of Human

Nutrition scientists. *Here she comes, taking us away from real work with impossible deadlines on stupid grant proposals. Hurry and hide, make up an excuse.* Jeannie was making me the office pariah to those few people who still hadn't learned to fear or loathe me, yet.

I ate half a can of vegetarian chili, cold, while I read through two more proposals about enzyme inhibitors. Yes, I had brought proposals home. These were in the stack that I needed to study up on first before scoring them. I may have been overdoing it, but when I told truth to power, I needed it to be factually correct and well-researched. Yes, I lived in the library at college and grad school: Dorm rooms were a waste of money for me.

Having been sufficiently numbed, with my mind calm and rational, I called Bob a little after eight. He knew my number, had to know I was calling about the new legal action, so whether he took the call or not would say something. I figured that by this time, he would be home with Charlie, helping him with his homework.

He took the call and we stumbled through some monotone pleasantries. He didn't offer to put Charlie on the phone and I didn't ask. We both knew there was unpleasantness to discuss.

"Why are you making these accusations?" I blurted.

"You did the same to me," he replied defensively. He sounded just like Charlie when he was caught in a lie and trying to save face. I pushed that thought away.

"I said that Charlie would be better off in my custody. I would never, ever say that you are an unfit parent, and possibly a threat to him. You're a good dad and you love him. Do you think I'm a threat to him?"

"I've got better things to do than answer your questions," he said. "Okay? I don't consider you a threat to him. You're a threat to me. Is that why you called?"

I cradled my face in my palm, trying to keep cool. "Do you want something out of me, related to work, Bob?"

"I'll cancel the petition if you stop your crusade. I'm two steps from getting fired. The boss is worried about appearances. I have to keep explaining the connection between me and the woman trying to kill our client. You wouldn't believe the spot I'm in right now. I'm being punished by having to work a fundraiser tonight for some damn freshman congresswoman who has no shot at reelection."

I realized the background noise I heard wasn't the TV. It was other people in the room. "Where is Charlie, then?" What was Bob doing still at work? I hoped Charlie wasn't tagging along, stuck in a corner playing video games or doing homework.

"He's at a baseball game with a friend. Relax."

"But it's almost dark outside. What about his homework?"

"Don't start. He's fine. I was hoping he would join the team, but he wants no part of sports," Bob said with disappointment. He'd actually sounded like a real parent there for a second. Sports were huge in his family.

The reason was Charlie's size, the unspoken subject between us. Bob had always waved it off as baby fat. He said I was "hypersensitive" whenever I brought it up. But as Charlie grew bigger and older, Bob just stopped talking about it altogether.

I shook my head. Charlie's waistline was not the issue right now. "I've been reassigned back to research. I read grant proposals and oversee contract paperwork all day. I'm not even looped in on the Flawless investigation. I'm no longer involved, okay? Your wish is granted, master."

"I didn't know that. Not a stable job situation, huh?"

I groaned. "Bob, are you going to stick with this petition of lies?"

"Are you going to get the government off the industry's back?"

"I already told you that I can't do anything about that."

"Well, Elaine, then I'll see what I can do about this petition."

"I'm not stupid. That means no."

He chuckled as he hung up, the bastard.

I'd bought a video game console a few years ago for Charlie when he visited. I ended up playing the exercise game included with it when I was angry, which had been a lot the last couple of years. And right now, I was white-hot homicidal.

Each user had a lifelike avatar to represent them in the game, with the face being based on a photograph of your own face. I selected mine and went straight into boxing. My opponent, as usual, was a Bob avatar.

I just punched and punched until I converted all that anger into sweaty, throbbing arms. As I ended the session for my character, the game's cutesy icon asked if I had seen Charlie recently, as the last time he had played was

543 days ago. His avatar appeared on screen, rotating with a photograph of him making a goofy grin mapped to his avatar's head. The webcam had captured his chubby physique and I found myself staring at an almost lifelike representation of my overweight son from last year.

Even the game machine thought he was fat. All of the ramifications of childhood obesity punched me in the gut. Type II diabetes, premature development, blood pressure and cardiovascular stress, wearing down knee joints, depression and so on. And I couldn't stop it.

Hot, angry tears burst from my eyes and a string of decidedly non-maternal words burst from my lips. I sank back on the couch, sweaty and crying.

I needed to get my son back.

CHAPTER 15

I T WAS WEDNESDAY NIGHT A week later and the doorbell rang just as I'd pulled the last batch of oatmeal raisin cookies, made with chickpea flour, out of the oven. It was almost eight o'clock. I had no idea who it could be.

The only thing that had changed in ten days, sadly, was that I became more efficient at grant reviews. I resorted to bribing subject matter experts to provide timely feedback with baked goods. My reputation in the office was on an upswing thanks to high-carb, sugary treats. I had realized that I just needed to tempt their lizard brains to win them over.

Eventually, Jeannie retaliated by making me the project officer on several grants. As project officer, I had to read and sign off on progress reports from existing grantees. I also had to answer the endless requests for summaries, justifications, and updates that a whole gallery of management types wanted on every externally-funded project. Anyone with a technical background could do this role, but with all the grants floating around, it added another crushing mountain of reports to read and write.

I told Jeannie I was happy to do it. I don't think twisting that bitch's knobs by feigning sweetness amounted to lying. And the look on her face was priceless. But I needed others to help me, so my oven was getting a workout.

When I looked through the peephole, I saw Lyle looking around nervously. I opened the door.

"Good, you're home!" he clapped his hands.

My fingers tightened on the doorknob. "How did you know where I live?"

"The Web. Come on. We have to go. Barry wants to meet us at a Chinese restaurant in Bethesda. He has more information."

I looked at him, stunned. "What makes you think I'm going to do that? What if I were busy? What if my son were here?"

Lyle looked dazed, like he had been hit in the face with a soccer ball. "You have a kid? I didn't even think you were married."

I bit my lip and gave him an impatient look.

"Oh. Sorry, I was raised Catholic and I just, you know, assume... Do I smell cookies?"

"They're for work, not for you."

Lyle looked over his shoulder. "Look, can we talk about this on the way?"

I shook my head. "No. I'm finished with this business."

He pleaded with outstretched arms. "Come on. Don't be that way. I think you want to hear about what Barry's found."

Well, like the cookies, more insider information from Flawless might help improve my standing back at the office. And Bob already thought I was some vigilante taking on the food industry so I couldn't lose anything more on that front. "Okay, let me get my sweater."

We walked out to his vehicle, an old smart car that had serious wear and tear on the interior. I sat with the dashboard in my lap, or at least that's the way it felt. Lyle started the whimpering engine. We wove around back roads on our way towards Bethesda because, Lyle explained, only the truly crazy would take the Beltway, especially at night. As usual, there was a couple of ounces of truth to what he said.

"Where's your son?" Lyle asked, making small talk.

"He lives with his father," I looked out the window.

"Oh. Does he visit?"

"Not enough," I said in a tone that ended that subject.

Lyle zipped us through traffic silently for a few moments. "This is so much fun. Are you serious about wanting out of this?"

"It's complicating my life. Causes problems for me at work, even for Charlie's dad—"

"His dad?"

"A food industry lobbyist. Apparently, he's getting grief about me poking around this Flawless stuff."

Lyle grinned maliciously. "He's in for a rough month then."

"Great, he'll fight me that much more about custody."

"Oh. I'm sorry. My sister had to fight her ex over my nephews. He wanted to take them with him to Houston. Houston. Can you imagine? Kids breathing in that bad air, playing in some former oil patch? How long were you guys married?"

"Never were. Just shut up and drive, okay?"

Lyle seemed a bit hurt by that, but kept his mouth shut the rest of the way to Bethesda.

We met Barry at the kind of Chinese restaurant that has pink linen tablecloths, shiny black chairs, and a thriving takeout business. Several couples were enjoying their tea and some college-age kids were at a large round table attacking a number of heaping dishes. Barry was in the back with a pot of tea and a bowl of crunchy noodles.

He handed a folder to each of us. Inside were reports on testing of the additive's hypnotic and aggression effects, and its toxicity. Next was a marketing plan for the chips, a salsa, and eighty-calorie snack packs of cookies loaded with the additive. After that were progress reports on the additive's development with milestones and budget information. Finally, there were printouts of email-chain discussions about whether to disclose the additive or not.

It was a treasure trove. This would nail Flawless to the wall. I wanted to run straight to the FDA.

When Lyle uttered an astonished profanity, Barry smiled proudly. "This wasn't all me. Turns out several people in the company are pissed off about the additive."

"Do you trust these other folks?" Lyle asked, not taking his eyes off the printouts.

Barry shrugged. "Ironically, I had to convince them that *I* could be trusted. They had been sharing these documents between themselves already. But none of them could bring themselves to blow the whistle. But when I showed them that email chain, they opened up."

"This is terrific," Lyle said. "This could blow the whole thing wide open. Elaine, do you understand these testing reports?"

I flipped back to them. "I'm not an expert in neurology or brain chemistry, but it looks to me like they've been trying to play with the pineal gland and hippocampus, tweaking the serotonin production, inhibiting vasopressin production. They created a protein that converts adipose to fuel these rage juices, which is why the larger someone is, the worse they get."

Lyle looked at Barry. "I want to make sure that this isn't much ado about nothing. A lot of food conspiracy theorists out there dance around about simple sugar production or vegetable extracts and vitamins that have scary names. I don't want my paranoia to be discredited by basic science."

I was unsure what to say. No one had ever mentioned a way to use adipose to block oxytocin receptors or depress serotonin levels. USDA, FDA, and others spent a lot of time trying to balance safety concerns with trade secrets. Often, the only way to evaluate the health and nutrition effects of a compound was to get it out in the open and have an eager pack of scientists test the hell out of it over a period of years. But you couldn't do that with the secret Coca-Cola formula.

"This is a dietary weapon of mass aggression," Barry said. "Manipulating serotonin levels and blocking aggression reducers are serious business. Probably a national security problem, given how things go these days. But why would they want an additive that did this, other than to make heavy-set folks the scourge of the country?"

"Discrimination against the obese is undeniable," I said, "but why would a food company want to increase it?"

"Like an oil company insulting SUV drivers." Lyle added. His conspiracy nut gears were working. "You can't ostracize a third of the population. If it doesn't make sense, maybe it's something else. Maybe they're trying to push obesity discrimination to a ridiculous degree so there's a backlash. Or intimidate skinny people into becoming obese. You know, increase obesity acceptance, damp down anti-obesity efforts, make it more socially acceptable."

Barry and I stared at Lyle. "That's crazy," I said.

"They spent a lot of time and money on this," Barry countered. He pointed at the folder in Lyle's hands. "They could have produced better value for the money by backing a nutrition campaign or just shaming overweight people with mean billboards funded through some astroturf group."

"Maybe they were trying to create an army of angry zoned-out obese people to march on Washington and demand that the government stop enforcing food labeling," Lyle joked.

We both looked at him again.

"The marketing plan covers national distribution," Barry said. "Renting shelf space, cost estimates for end displays, a TV ad campaign, sponsorships, the whole nine yards. This was going to be a flagship entry product for Flawless. Why would they taint their breakout products like this? Something doesn't add up here." He looked at us and then around for eavesdroppers, but the restaurant was empty now. "I wonder if there's some kind of internal sabotage going on. Someone trying to ruin the company just as it tries to break out big."

"How could a saboteur do that with all of these company resources? And why?" Lyle said.

Barry rubbed his chin. "Flawless has been around a while in the processing business. Now they're trying to become a food manufacturer, competing with the big boys. Chances are the company will get bought by Pepsico, Kellogg, or Proctor & Gamble. There may be some executives who want to see this venture fail. And a food recall out of the starting gate would do that. The company would drop the whole thing and crawl back to its familiar business lines."

"I'm having trouble buying that, and I buy into a lot of conspiracy theories," Lyle said.

Barry shrugged sheepishly. "I've seen worse: A new CEO shakes things up and the old guard fights back, regains control through dirty tricks, and shuts down the new ventures. But I've never heard of anything this elaborate, or dangerous."

That echoed the concerns Stitcher had. Factions within Flawless working at cross-purposes. One of them was cutting out the company execs and possibly Stitcher. This was an eye-opener to me, because I think of corporations as monoliths, moving in one direction with a single purpose. But they're just clumps of people like any other organization, infighting, scheming, striving, and failing. Like government agencies. "How many people gave you these documents?" I asked.

"Half a dozen, at least," Barry shrugged. "My contacts said many of these documents came from people in other departments."

"Are you sure you're safe doing this, Barry?" Lyle asked.

"Sure, why not? Safety in numbers. I'm not a lone whistleblower anymore."

We reviewed the documents one more time so that all three of us were clear on what they contained and what they didn't.

I told them about how I'd turned over the other documents to Jeannie. Since she acted like her star would rise because of that first batch of inside info, this should make her ecstatic.

Barry pushed the folder across the table to me and reached for a fortune cookie. "Then take these in. Maybe your luck will change."

Not if Bob or Stitcher find out about this, I thought.

Barry left the restaurant before us. The owners were giving us dirty looks while they stacked up chairs, so Lyle and I left only a few minutes later. Lyle was tight-lipped until we were back in his car. "My mind is spinning. Do I tell my press contacts? I mean, this is huge."

I shook my head. "It's premature. These documents could pressure the FDA to move too quickly. If there's external pressure to do something from the press, or Congress, things could go wrong fast."

"But I want to keep the food contamination story going in the press. And this is the smoking gun." He navigated the empty, dark streets of suburban Maryland. "I can't believe they would screw with food like this. Kids will eat this. Mentally unbalanced people will eat this. Someone already died because of this!"

"Why don't you give a copy to the Sesame defense lawyers? Tell them to talk to the Grand Forks DA. By the time either one goes public, hopefully FDA, or the FBI, will be ready to act." *And it would get me off the hot seat*, I didn't say.

"Unless the defense lawyers think this is too farfetched, even with proof like this," Lyle said. "You'd be amazed at how people can disregard the plain facts at the end of their nose if it runs counter to what they believe. Or if it runs counter to what they are paid to believe."

I grunted. "If that happens, go to your press contacts."

"They're tired of only having me on deep background. They want to put me on camera, or at least quote me. I can't do that."

I looked at my co-conspirator and shivered despite the late-spring humidity blowing in through the open window. The press would treat him as a crank. "Not a good idea."

"No. For now, at least. But this is becoming my life," he said.

"That's not healthy, Lyle. This will blow over eventually, you know. Life will return to normal."

His shoulders sagged a bit. "Probably. Too bad, you know. I love busting the balls of these corporations."

We were passing through downtown Silver Spring and stopped at a deserted red light. I turned to him. "Why are you so committed?"

He glanced sideways at me. "These bastards piss me off. The country has gotten fat—poisoned really—on this crap food and they don't care. I had Type II diabetes. When I was diagnosed, I lost it for a while. But then I went hardcore on my diet and exercise. Now, I can't look at a Hostess Cupcake without feeling sick."

I tried to imagine Lyle overweight. I couldn't.

"But these bastards!" Lyle pounded on the steering wheel and the whole car shook. "They're still trying to get me to eat their crap! They make diabetic-friendly junk food. They're like profit machines feeding on human misery. The food may as well be a bag of broken glass, like that old Saturday Night Live sketch, where the immoral toymaker defends selling kids bags of broken glass. Just infuriates me." He shook his head. "Modern life is bad enough to give you a nervous breakdown every day. They don't have to add to it."

I nodded. I knew plenty of people across the food industry, but they weren't evil. Considering that Bob's job put food on Charlie's plate, I considered him in the non-evil category. Except for the custody fight.

"What about you?" he asked. "Why do you study obesity?"

I sighed. "An unhealthy commitment to the truth. I believe the science behind why obesity happens can drive the policy, which can end the epidemic." *And my son will need that help, if I don't win this court battle*, I thought. Then I silently prayed to God for help on that one.

Lyle shook his head as he headed south toward Bowie. "And you think these food titans will let that happen? And I thought I was crazy."

CHAPTER 16

WITH ALL THE EXCITEMENT ABOUT Barry's latest revelations, I had completely forgotten about tomorrow. Lyle's enthusiasm was enough to distract me on the ride home. But when I stepped in the townhouse and thought about the next day, I remembered why I had front-loaded so much of this week's grant review work. The reason I wanted to avoid staying up late tonight. The reason that an industrial conspiracy had felt like a pleasant escape.

The deposition in my custody case was tomorrow morning.

Standing in my living room at well past ten, with the Flawless folder hanging limp in my hand, I panicked. Adrenaline shot through my fingers and toes and I felt a bicep muscle twitch spastically. Maybe Lyle was rubbing off on me. It felt like the night before a final exam in a class I'd forgotten to register for, much less attend.

The source of my angst, in addition to the sky-high importance of the custody fight to my life, was the memory of my deposition five years ago. Charlie was in kindergarten back then and all I knew was that Bob wanted to revisit the custody arrangement. What happened was that I found myself facing a roomful of antagonistic strangers, with my waste-of-space lawyer cringing and wincing.

Bob's lawyer had sent in the most lecherous old white guy they could find to run the deposition. His name was Andre. He had a white comb over and a long thin nose. I remembered him like the deposition had happened yesterday. He was probably a partner who hung around just for depositions involving young women.

My massively inept, but cheap, lawyer was named Brent. He started off nervous and withered to silent. What could I do? I was a single mom who had paid for four-and-a-half years of day care and graduate school loans on a GS-12 salary. I couldn't afford better.

Old Andre had started by asking me about Charlie's home life, his progress in pre-K, and where he went to preschool. He spent a long time on my day care arrangements; how many hours Charlie was there, how often his caretakers changed, whether it was licensed. We covered immunization records, whether he had made all of his infant appointments, and his history of illnesses and diseases.

Andre's mellow voice was hypnotic honey that made me sick to my stomach. He clearly liked to hear himself talk and his questions typically included preambles, prefaces, examples, and digressions. So, when he asked me how Bob and I met, I was lulled into giving a straight-up answer.

Andre didn't want to know only how we met; he wanted to know the entire shape of our relationship. When I implied that it was a single-date kind of thing, he actually sneered, right before letting loose. He spent ten minutes dissecting a one-night stand that lasted barely twice as long. I had to explain what conference it was at, how much I'd had to drink, had I met Bob before, and so on.

It was at that point that Brent went silent.

So, Andre asked, had I had any other one-night stands before? Ever been pregnant before? When did I lose my virginity? How many sexual partners had I had? Brent finally objected, but Andre made some noise about relevance to the fitness of the mother, especially as Charlie aged and became aware of such things. Brent relented unhappily, the putz.

The aftermath of the one-night stand: Did we date again? What happened when I learned I was pregnant? Did I consider abortion, despite being Catholic, since fornication wasn't a deal-breaking sin for me?

He pressed on about whether either I or Bob tried to build a relationship in advance of co-parenting our baby. Again, me being Catholic and all, did I consider just marrying him? Why not? I wasn't expecting to answer any of these questions and stuttered my way through half-assed responses.

Andre continued. Did I see other men before or after my "assignation with Bob," as he called it? What was my social life like since Charlie was born? Any single mother, hell, most of my married friends with kids can tell you that any mother's social life hits the skids after birth. But Andre didn't buy that. He asked if I went clubbing, picked up guys, brought anyone home, used an internet dating site, etc. I said no to all of that. Again: Mom with young child and full-time job equals no time or interest.

By the time he asked whether I masturbated or not, Brent was thoroughly defeated and I was shell-shocked. I realized that the law firm must have poked around in my life somehow, learned which romance novels I checked out of the library or bought online.

Andre insisted on an answer. The stenographer looked sick to her stomach, but waited for my response.

"Yes. Like almost every other adult," I said.

When Andre asked how many sex toys I owned, I stood up to leave.

Andre apologized profusely, despite the sneer spread across his face. "Leaving the deposition would not be a wise choice, Dr. Cassano, and I'm sure your counsel will agree with me. He would also remind you that lying in this deposition, under oath, is perjury and subject to criminal prosecution."

When I sat back down, he demanded that I list the sex toys I owned and how they worked, just so it was clear for the record, he said. And this was how, at a deposition about child custody of my five-year-old, I had to discuss the feeding and caring of my clitoris.

Even worse, having just relived that traumatic episode, I was now scared shitless I would have to repeat it again tomorrow morning.

When I hired Sandy to represent me, she was aghast at how that deposition had gone five years earlier. Society still got mileage out of portraying mothers as whores, she reminded me, and when they want to discredit you as a mother, they paint you as a whore. She assured me that no such nonsense would be permitted this time around. As I knelt by my bed to pray, I prayed she was right.

With all that horrible history weighing on me, I managed only four hours of half-asleep dozing. I dared not take anything to help me sleep; I couldn't risk oversleeping or appearing out of it the next day. When the alarm went off, I sprang into the shower on a bolt of anxious energy and hit the road with an empty, churning stomach.

The deposition was at Charlie's lawyers' firm, in some office park out near Tyson's in Northern Virginia. I would have to wrestle the morning rush hour, which was getting worse all the time, to get there.

After a couple of wrong turns, near-accidents, and construction delays, I parked my beat-up car and dashed into the morning heat. Sweat glued my camisole to my back. Two hours in a car had creased my business suit and the lack of sleep left the darker than usual circles under my big eyes. I must have looked like a strung-out drug addict stuffed into respectable clothing.

Sandy was waiting for me at outside the law firm's door. She gave me a reassuring squeeze on the arm as we walked in together. The receptionist escorted us to a conference room with a grand view of NVA sprawl. I was relieved to see that the stenographer was not the same one as five years ago. In fact, I didn't recognize anyone in the room.

Before I knew it, the deposition was underway and I was answering the usual self-identification questions. Bob's lawyer was a tall, thin man named Gary with old-fashioned eyeglasses who came off as a cold, abstract law professor more than a practicing attorney.

The discovery process was for asking about anything and everything related to the custody case, and whatever was said in the deposition could be used against me in the hearing. It made my dissertation defense sound like old friends shooting the breeze.

"Is it correct that you have not had custody of Charlie for five years now?" Gary asked.

"Yes," I said.

"Have you seen much of him since then?"

I described the weekend visits that had become more infrequent and how I took him to the doctor on the last one. I even added that we play Pokémon together. Gary actually cracked a smile when I mentioned that. Generally, you weren't supposed to add anything to your answers beyond the basic truth, lest it get you in trouble during the hearing, but Sandy said a deposition is also a live performance in some ways.

First of all, this was being videotaped, and it would help if I was warm and human. Second, Sandy coached me to work the other side a bit; if I could get Gary to smile or react positively, it would be that much harder for him to treat me badly or a viewer to believe I was cold and impersonal.

"Tell me, Dr. Cassano: How do you plan on approaching Charlie's teenage years? What is your opinion on underage drinking? Dating? Teen sex? Playing sports? Academics? Staying out late?"

Charlie was ten now. I wasn't sure what the rules of the house would be when he was sixteen, but I probably sounded stricter than I wanted to be. Of course he wouldn't be allowed to drink or date.

"Would there be an adult male figure in Charlie's life if he lives with you?"

Sandy sat a little straighter in her seat, ready to object. If I said no, then Bob could say that Charlie would be losing a father figure if I gained custody. If I said yes, I sounded like a slut who would be bringing home strange men. As usual, I stuck with the truth. "I am not seeing anyone and don't expect to in the future. I want to keep Bob involved in Charlie's upbringing and not replace him."

"Then why do you want to take custody of Charlie away from his father?"

I chose my words carefully. "I don't think that Bob can care for Charlie as well as I can. Charlie's health is poor and he is gaining weight. Bob dumps him on the parents of Charlie's friends a lot because he works late. I also have concerns about how Bob will handle his teenage years. I want him to have a moral center that I don't think Bob is too keen on."

"Do you think that my client is a good father?"

The central question. I pursed my lips. "He clearly loves Charlie a lot. But all of Charlie's illnesses, his weight, his diet, the late nights, it just adds up to Bob being unavailable to providing a sufficient level of care day in and day out."

"Do you have records of these doctor visits?" Gary asked. Sandy distributed copies.

"What do you see as your flaws as a parent?" Gary asked.

I thought about it for a moment and smiled. "I am the no-fun parent. Eat your vegetables, do the homework, get a good night's sleep, put the video games away. But I'm too forgiving when he misbehaves because I'd rather teach him than discipline him. And I'm too blunt and can hurt his feelings accidentally." When Charlie was four, he asked me if God and Santa Claus were the same person. I blurted that God was real and Santa Claus didn't exist. Given how long he cried, that may have been too much truth at once.

Gary switched to another tack: my job. What a relief. After verifying the basics about where I worked, my income, education, and background, he asked, "You were recently on a reality TV show, weren't you?"

"I was interviewed as a professional expert on a show about the obesity epidemic. As part of my job at the USDA. I also gave a speech and took questions at a town hall."

"Things went out of control at the town hall, right?"

Was he really asking about this? "Some people in the audience didn't like what I said about the causes and remedies for obesity. Some people asked for help."

"The kind of spectacle that reality TV is known for," he said.

"Objection," Sandy said. "Counsel's opinion about reality TV is not relevant. Dr. Cassano provided her expertise as part of USDA's public education campaign."

Gary moved on. "Could you explain why the police wanted to question you after the town hall?"

"The sheriff and the district attorney asked me to advise them on the physiology of obesity in a criminal case. I was not in any trouble."

"We have had reports that say otherwise. We have a report that one local business contacted the authorities about your activities there. While no charges were filed, you left town immediately afterward, right?"

My mouth fell open a little bit. He was talking about Stitcher. Had Stitcher talked to them? Did they know what really happened in Grand Forks? That Stitcher thought I was on his side?

"Why don't you call John Stitcher as a witness and have him explain what happened in Grand Forks?" I said. "The two of us got along just fine when we met there."

Gary looked like I had just thrown a spear through his chest.

"Objection: hearsay," Sandy added, looking perplexed. "Unless counsel has affidavits or other proof of these reports that they can share."

"Withdrawn. Strike that from the record." Gary said quickly. "That was an overnight trip. Does that happen a lot?"

"No. Recently, I transferred back to the Human Nutrition unit. I review funding proposals and the hours are pretty steady. Very little travel."

Gary shuffled papers. "Reviewing grant proposals, serving as project officer. Yes, I see. That involves site visits, though. Who will care for Charlie when you are on these trips? His father can't get him to school in Maryland from where he lives in Virginia."

I hadn't thought about that. I didn't know if Jeannie had thought that far ahead. She had designated me the project officer on any new grants awarded. I was sure she meant for me to take that over eventually. It was the kind of assignment that took a PhD, but left no time for research. The perfect punishment. "My mother lives in Silver Spring."

"And does she work? And how can she get him to school and get to work?"

"She has flexible hours," I said curtly.

"Why did this transfer to Human Nutrition happen?"

"I want to conduct research, not public relations," I said.

"This isn't the first time, or even the second that you have had to change jobs. Can you explain why this continues to happen to you, even at different agencies and with different supervisors? Remember that you are under oath."

I cocked my head to the side and glared. "When I see something wrong, I speak up, and I don't play office politics very well."

Gary said. "Are you an outcast at work, with a career at a dead end?"

"Absolutely. Proud of it."

Gary gave me a look but flipped the page to his next question. "Do you think that obese people are more violent than other people?"

"No, there's no research to support that claim."

"Do you subscribe to the view that something or someone is turning them violent?"

I said cautiously, "There are ongoing investigations on this question. It's too early to say. My opinion will be based on the research when it's completed. Which could be years from now."

Gary folded his hands. "Do you interact with conspiracy theorists? Those who believe there is a secret plot to use food to harm the country?"

"I have talked to some of them, yes. They regularly approach people like me who work at the USDA, FDA, and CDC with claims and accusations."

"Are you working with one right now?"

How the hell did they know about Lyle? I looked at Sandy. She objected based on relevance, but she looked as bewildered as I felt.

"The relevance," Gary said, "is that my client claims that Dr. Cassano is not psychologically stable. She takes outsized risks, has ruined her career and has become a conspiracy theorist. This instability prevents her from providing a stable life for Charlie." The judge overruled the objection and Gary waited for my answer.

How could Bob know this? I didn't doubt that he saw any threat to the food industry as baseless. Like many a lobbyist, he drank the Kool-Aid long before taking the job. But a difference of opinion didn't amount to the person you disagree with being mentally unstable, did it?

Either Bob's lawyer knew Stitcher or had hired a private investigator to dig up dirt on me. Or both. Bob might already know about Lyle and Barry, and the Flawless documents which I had yet to turn over. Was this the industry's ham-handed way of making me back off, or was this Bob scrambling on his own to keep custody? Maybe these were the paranoid ramblings of an unstable single mother.

I cleared my throat and my mind. "The pursuit of truth using empirical methods, which is what science is about, must examine all claims. We try to discard a claim and only grudgingly accept it if no one can discard it. Scientists make poor conspiracy theorists."

Gary didn't blink. "And yet you associate with extremists who think food is deliberately contaminated and who demonize the obese. People who have their own mental stability problems."

"Objection. Counsel needs to ask a question and stop maligning my client's job and associates," Sandy said in an irritated-but-bored-tone, as if this nonsense were all that was keeping her from playing tennis.

"Dr. Cassano, what will you do when you end up in jail and Charlie gets off the school bus and no one is home?"

His lobbyist father is more likely to end up in jail than his scientist mother, I wanted to shoot back, but didn't. Instead, I said, "What would I be in jail for?"

"That's not relevant. Please answer the question."

"I would call my mother and have her get Charlie. She's closer than Bob and more reliable. Bob would be next on my list."

"Do you harbor an animosity toward the food processing industry?"

I shook my head no. "I'm no socialist. No one can work at BARC and believe that every food company is bad. A lot of researchers cycle in and out of the industry, or go to academia and work on industry-supported projects."

"Why, then, are you persecuting the industry? Is it to hurt my client? To ruin his ability to do his job?"

I dipped my chin to glare at Gary. "I'm not persecuting the industry. And my work has nothing to do with Bob. The recent media circus over whether the obese are inherently more violent is clearly prejudicial and ugly. If we can find the real reason for these incidents, they will not be vilified like this."

"Have you become obsessed with this cause?" Gary asked.

"No." I wanted to say *I am obsessed with getting my son back*. But I knew that lawyers liked to twist statements like that.

The questioning continued about my behavior and underlying psychological state. I answered mechanically when Sandy's objections didn't shoot down a question. Bob's lawyer was grasping for any hint that I was unbalanced, but there were no medical records or other substantive indications for him to work with. And Sandy's objections made it clear she wouldn't let Gary even get near my underwear drawer.

For the rest of the deposition, my mind was elsewhere, trying to figure out how Bob had found all of this out. Bob had indicated that Stitcher was the food lawyer none of the others wanted to hear from, and was perhaps feared by them. And Stitcher seemed to like me, so it probably wasn't him. I was stumped.

Sandy and I decompressed over an early lunch at an empty chain restaurant at Tyson's. She had a salmon salad and I opted to assassinate a club sandwich with extreme prejudice and hunger. She took a huge forkful of salad when the food arrived. "So, what did you think?"

I pulled the toothpicks from the sandwich. "I wonder if Bob hired a private investigator," I mused. "They knew too much about too many things."

"Don't worry," she assured me, "If they had something concrete, they would have gone further. They were just trying to rattle your cage. You did great."

I chewed the turkey, hitting the tangy smoothness of Swiss cheese and the bacony crunch of bacon. I really shouldn't have skipped breakfast. "Do custody cases go this far into work-related issues?"

She nodded. "In DC, I've seen criminal investigations, election campaigns, and office politics all get tossed into custody and divorce proceedings. For many people, work is their life and when both people work in the same area—oh brother—*everything* is on the table." She took a swallow of iced tea. "I once had a couple bring in their current bosses *and their previous bosses* to be character witnesses and discuss their performance appraisals."

That made me feel a little better.

"Just keep your nose clean from now until the hearing. If they have a private investigator after you, they may try to dig deeper now."

With the sandwich done, I moved in on the pickle. I couldn't stand greasy chips or fries. "It freaks me out to have a professional stalker going through my garbage."

"Don't think about that," Sandy said. "Focus on how, at Bob's deposition, I'll get answers about how they found out all of that information. If he really paid for someone to snoop on you, we'll let the judge chew on who is the most unstable."

I drove home with the AC blasting. I needed a nap, but I still had work on my schedule. I couldn't shake the feeling that I was being watched, even in Beltway traffic. Enduring another deposition had left me rattled and nervous enough, but now I was on edge, even when I got home. I showered, changed into another work outfit and carried my baked peace offerings to the office to take my mind off the deposition.

Charlie called me when he got home from school. Hearing his voice on such a lousy day was like a ray of sun bursting through a dark purple storm cloud. "How was the deposition, Mom?"

I smiled, proud of his sympathy. "It was fine, honey. Why are you worried about it?"

There was a pause. "I heard Dad talking about it with his lawyer. He used to think it was funny how things went last time, when he won. But this time he wasn't laughing. He was worried that they were too rough on you."

"What did he say?" I asked in a guarded tone. I had no doubt that Bob was stupid and childish enough to relive the details and embarrassment. But with Charlie in earshot? It was inconsiderate to air any of the custody stuff around him, but sharing the personal aspects of the fight between us was that much worse.

"Nothing, really," Charlie mumbled.

"Mmm-hmmm. We're trying to keep you out of this as much as possible. Did you hear something that upset you?"

"Dad thinks you're trying to get him fired. And he's afraid that it was because of the earlier deposition. He wasn't happy to hear about how they treated you."

Which meant Bob really believed I was trying to fire him. He must be under pressure at work because of the Flawless scandal. The expression on his lawyer's face to my name-dropping of Stitcher made more sense now. Stitcher was not helping Bob with the custody case. He must have been leaning on him about something related to me. "Let me state clearly for the record that I don't want your dad to be fired. There's nothing that I have done that should affect his job. And if I did, it was an accident. You can tell him I said that."

"Okay. He kind of overreacts when he feels threatened," Charlie replied, with a tone that implied there was more he didn't know how to say.

"Are you looking out for me, honey?" I said. When did the child become the parent? Was it at age ten these days? The answer, of course, was no. And that was why I felt a lump in my throat. It was just because my little guy cared so much.

"I worry about you, Mom."

"Thank you, kid, that's really sweet of you. It was just a lawyer asking a bunch of questions and me passing around paperwork. Really, it went fine."

"I don't want either one of you to be hurt. I wish this custody thing didn't have to be either/or. But I know you two could never live in the same house. I probably know that better than either one of you does."

He probably did. I laughed.

"I'm serious. You two live in totally different worlds. And I like parts about each one. You know, neither of you have never asked me who I want to live with."

Because that was a big no-no in custody cases. It puts way too much pressure on the child and places the adults, the parents and the judge, in an awkward position. "That's because we're probably both afraid you'll pick the other parent," I joked. Even Bob wasn't dumb enough to put Charlie in such a spot. I was sure his lawyer had given him the same lecture Sandy gave me about keeping Charlie out of this as much as possible. He was too young to weigh in on the custody decision, and exposing him to details of what was happening was not good for him.

Charlie laughed hard. "You make it sound like picking teams for kickball."

"Yep. And no one plans on asking you, okay?"

"I wish I could give you a hug right now, but I have homework," he said. We said goodbye. He went back to his world and I went back to mine. And in mine I called a conspiracy theorist to see if he could spy on Stitcher and find out if the foul-mouthed lawyer was pulling the strings on my custody case.

CHAPTER 17

THERE'S A LEGEND AMONG THE nutrition science crowd that an industry astroturf lobbying group once spied on a nutritionist to catch her drinking Slurpees while eating a bag of M&Ms. The nutritionist had to move to Montana and change her name. While it's a ridiculous urban legend, it spoke to the nervousness we nutrition researchers feel when approaching our own food choices. What if someone saw us buying a tub of ice cream and accused us of being hypocrites?

But I am a hopeless lover of Italian food. There's something about garlic, oregano and tomato that makes me salivate. Perhaps it was because I could tell how much my parents enjoyed it and how much my mother despaired that she couldn't make it nearly as well as my father's mother. My fear was that a cousin or aunt would see me buying sauce in a jar. But hey, single woman, working full time, I don't have time to make my own.

So, I grocery shop late on weeknights, in the worst weather, when Trader Joe's is mostly empty. The Washington area has a contentious relationship with spring. Most years, we leap out of winter in a flash of cherry blossoms and then the summer heat and humidity are draped around us until autumn. Other years, spring creeps in as a slight warming hidden by clouds of pollen, and bone-chilling showers and grayness. This spring seemed intent to exit with warm temperatures and rain. It had been gray and miserable since I left work and now a steady downpour was turning the streets into canals of yellow-green pollen soup.

My phone rang as the rain pounded on the roof of Trader Joe's. It was either Lyle or Ma. I hoped, as I pulled the phone out of my purse, that it was Ma. But it was Lyle.

It was not that Lyle annoyed me. No, I feared what he was calling to say. I was surprised he had volunteered to spy on Stitcher after I told him about my odd deposition, but Lyle was incensed that the food industry plumber might be mucking around in my family affairs.

"What are you doing right now?" Lyle asked.

Right on cue, the Trader Joe's manager announced over the store public address that a child had found the store's hidden teddy bear and had won a prize. Everyone clapped raucously. Charlie never believed there actually was a bear, no matter how much the Hawaiian shirt-wearing employees tried to convince him. I'd have to tell him I'd finally witnessed an actual bear rescue.

"You're not home," Lyle observed.

"Uh, out grocery shopping in Silver Spring."

"You have got to come down here to DC," he said. His voice was low and excited. It sounded like he was driving.

"I have ice cream to get home before it melts," I said, heading toward the checkout.

"Ice cream? Ha, okay, okay, I'll meet you at your house."

"Can't we talk on the phone? Or do you think it's bugged?" I said it half-jokingly, hoping he would laugh.

He didn't. "No, I doubt it. You have to *see* this. It even matters to your custody case. Sometimes, Elaine, I'm a genius. Sometimes, doing something seems like a big waste of money and time, but then when it pays off—whoa boy—does it pay off! I'm driving to your house right now. See you in a few."

I was out of the store a few minutes later, sprinting with my canvas bags of Trader Giuseppe products through the flooding parking lot. The rain sheeted until I slammed the car door on it. I just wanted to go home and crawl under something thick and warm. It was a weeknight. I was tired. But I was too curious about what the hell Lyle had found that had any bearing on my custody case. A meeting between Bob and Stitcher and the judge? Stitcher passing around compromising photos of me?

Lyle was waiting for me at my townhouse. That might have freaked me out once, but now I just gave him a grocery bag to carry. He happily shuttled the bags in while I chucked cold stuff in the fridge.

"Wear something warm. We could be stuck in the car for a while," he said. "And solid shoes that you don't mind getting muddy. I don't think this rain is going to let up."

I grabbed a hoodie and we left my house a minute later. Lyle started talking in short bursts, like a human Uzi, as he drove towards DC. "I tailed Stitcher for two days. Home, work. Followed his car. That guy is always on his phone. Always. That'll give you brain cancer, you know. Europeans are all over that. As usual. Radiation in those doses, God. But why should he worry about that? Hah!"

"Lyle. Lyle?"

"What? Yes?"

I put a hand on his shoulder. "Relax. Can we have a few minutes of silence? I'm afraid you'll hyperventilate. Just drive."

"Good call. Yeah. But this is good stress. It's not bad stress. Okay? No really, it's not. This is so frickin' huuuuuge."

I wasn't going to ask what it was until we passed RFK stadium. The streets were mostly empty and the rain had slacked off to a steady drizzle. As we made it to the more rundown side of Capitol Hill, I spoke slowly. "Let's start with the basics. Is this related to my custody hearing?"

"What? No. Why would you think that?" Lyle looked at me like he thought I was crazy. "No, it has to do with the food industry. God, keep up, woman!"

"I don't know what the hell you're talking about then."

"Here, tell me if these coordinates change, okay?" he handed over a smartphone that showed a DC map with a blinking dot. I zoomed in and the dot was in a Capitol Hill neighborhood south of Independence Avenue.

"That's Stitcher's car," Lyle explained. "An old Studebaker Speedster. Can't believe he parks it in DC. I put a tracer under the bumper. Tells me if he's on the move. It'd be better to track his cell phone, but I my contacts in the telecom industry don't take my calls anymore."

We drove down Stitcher's street. It was packed with brick and clapboard townhouses that seemed obscenely smaller and quainter than mine in Bowie. These were built a century and a half ago, it looked like. Some of them probably were originally slave quarters or very small shops.

There were no lights on in any of the windows in Stitcher's house and no one was on the sidewalk. The tiny yard was devoid of grass, replaced with simple-but-elegant landscaping, much like his office. The windows were all barred.

"He could have left the house on foot," I said. People did that in cities.

Even lawyers. Maybe I was cranky because it felt creepy to be window peeking on a rainy night.

"In the rain? Well, it's stopped now, I guess," Lyle said. He turned at the end of the street and we drove off.

"Where are we going?" I asked. It seemed like a big waste to come all the way into DC just to drive by a dark house.

"We'll come back; we're just early. And there's something I want to show you at Lincoln Park. Hey, did you turn over the Flawless documents yet?"

"Yes. My boss now looks at me in a different light. Like she can't decide if I'm a spy with loose morals or a total wack job. She nearly jumped out of her chair when she read them." I had wanted to celebrate what looked a bit like a new opportunity to revive my career, but reminded myself that this was Jeannie and she would find some way to screw me over.

"Do you think she shared them with FDA?"

"Definitely. My boss thinks our snooping turns into prestige for her. Evidence that Flawless intentionally did what it did is priceless."

"Good, good. We'll need that," Lyle said offhandedly and turned on to East Capitol Street.

Lincoln Park was a green square located between the Capitol and RFK stadium. It hosted a smattering of people walking their dogs or letting them run around on the wet grass. There was some kind of sculpture in the center under lights that I couldn't make out from the road through all of the soaked trees.

"Stitcher goes for a walk every night at the same time. Weather doesn't matter." He handed me what looked like an older-model camcorder as he slowed down for a speed table. "Look at that woman walking her dog in the park over there. Now look at her through this infrared scope, it will show you her body heat signature."

I looked through it, completely bewildered at what Lyle was up to. The middle-aged woman's exposed skin gave off a yellow-orange hue while her body under the sweatshirt was a darker orange-light purple. She stood out clearly against the ambient dark purple of the night air. A pretty nifty device to spy on people at night that you couldn't see clearly.

"How expensive is this thing?" I asked. It dawned on me that Lyle had taken this snooping thing way, way too far.

"What do you think her BMI is?" Lyle asked, waiting to turn left to continue around the park.

I looked at him a long second. "What the hell are we doing here?"

"Stakeout. Do you think she's overweight but not obese?"

I shrugged. "Yes. So, what?"

"The infrared signature is affected by body fat. A really obese person still shows heat coming through despite the extra insulation. But a skinny guy like me will show up bright. Look at me through the scope."

I pointed it at him. He radiated yellow heat from head to toe. The brightest colors came from his warmer mouth as he talked. His clothes were a mix of fuchsia and orange.

"Okay, I'm going to drive around the park a few times. Test the scope out on any other people here, and see if you can spot other heat sources." He rolled the windows down. "But the infrared doesn't work through glass."

We circled the park slowly for the next few minutes. A young woman jogged past us in a sports bra, radiating like a small sun. She jogged right past an older guy shuffling across the park who turned to watch her pass.

The older guy showed lighter colors around his face and a vibrant dark-blue from his cheeks and neck. The trees he passed by were almost as black as the empty air, nearly the ambient temperature.

I understood Lyle's point: Different layers of fat obscured the body's heat signature enough that this scope would take notice. Was he trying to sell me a diagnostic tool for the USDA to estimate body fat?

"Time to head back to Stitcher's," Lyle said.

"Are we going to spy on him inside his house?" I asked.

"No, that scope doesn't see through walls or windows. Police helicopters have high-end infrared detectors to detect indoor marijuana farms—"

"Wait, I don't understand," I said. "What does this have to do with Stitcher?"

Lyle smiled ferociously but said nothing as he turned back on to Stitcher's street. His silence was not comforting in the least.

We continued down the street and turned onto another. All of them looked the same to me by this point. We reached a commercial drag along Independence Avenue. Lyle parked beyond a cluster of corner bars so we could watch their entrances. He swung into a parallel parking maneuver that I was convinced would plow into vehicles on either side, but the smart car slid right in.

"Should be any minute now. Turn the scope on and be ready."

I felt uncomfortable sitting in a parked car at night, with a guy, pointing an expensive thermographic imaging device out the window. Not that I was worried a second about Lyle. And anyone who has seen a smart car up close would agree that it's too small to do anything more salacious than making out. It was probably my imagination, but it seemed like we radiated suspicion: man and a woman sitting in a parked smart car with tinted windows, which were cracked just enough to stick scopes and cameras through.

I distracted myself playing with the scope, holding it out the window and scanning around. I could tell which cars had been parked recently, because their hoods burned yellow with orange edges.

I felt drops on my hand and considered the plastic case of the infrared scanner. "Is it okay for this thing to get wet?"

Lyle shrugged. "It's meant for firefighters to rescue people in burning buildings with smoke and water everywhere. It's fine. Unless it starts to pour. Someone's coming." He raised his camera to his eye and began snapping pictures.

"Did you buy all of this equipment just to spy on Stitcher, or did you already own it?" I asked, then thought better of it and said, "Don't answer that. Either way, I'm creeped out."

Two men and a woman came off Independence Avenue and went into the sports bar on the far side of the street. They scurried through the drizzle under an umbrella that was too small for all three. They were young and wearing trendy t-shirts no doubt, three yellow-and-blue figures darting through the infrared dark.

"Wrong bar," Lyle said. "Wait, here comes Stitcher."

I eyeballed him without the scope first. I could see from a distance that it was him: cell phone to ear, skinny guy, walking swiftly. He had a derby on, like you'd expect from a duffer his age, but no umbrella.

I raised the scope to my eye, and then put it down. "Something's wrong with this thing," I said. I must have knocked it out of adjustment. "I'm not getting a signature on him. Is the rain affecting it?"

"Nothing wrong with that scope," Lyle insisted behind a grin as he snapped Stitcher's picture.

I scowled at Lyle and looked again, paying attention to every detail. Stitcher's entire face and body registered absolutely nothing more than the deep purple of the trees, sidewalk and buildings he passed. Only his orange-looking cell phone registered any heat. "He has no heat signature. What does that mean?"

"You tell me, Dr. Cassano."

Perhaps there was interference in obtaining a reading. The scope wasn't defective, but the weather could be affecting it. Maybe Stitcher had some kind of fiberglass coat that hid his heat signature.

Well, I knew what it couldn't be. Because that was impossible. I tried to remember other reasons, besides the obvious, that a human body would give off a very low level of heat. Human body temperature couldn't drop much below ninety degrees Fahrenheit without hypothermia setting in. Below eighty degrees, it meant death. If the reading on Stitcher was accurate, his body temperature was roughly fifty-five degrees, which was the air temperature outside. In other words, he was either dead, or the most lifelike, well-cooled android I had ever seen.

Were there any medications that could mimic deadly hypothermia? None that would allow a person to walk around normally like this.

Stitcher was on our side of the street, passing closed sidewalk cafes and laundromats. Lyle's expensive camera snapped away as I tried out one explanation after another, discounting it immediately and hunting for another one. Android, ablative makeup, skin prosthetics? This was just one of those scientific puzzles, a brain twister, that I had to figure out. But I ran out of logical explanations and sighed.

"You want me to say it?" Lyle said. "Dead man walking right there."

Stitcher snapped his cell phone shut and went into a bar in a converted row house.

I shook my head. "That's crazy. This makes no sense. He must have some kind of covering that hides his heat signature."

Lyle grunted dismissively. "And on his ears, his neck, his chest, below his clothes and inside his mouth?" He showed me the pictures he had just snapped. Although the picture was green and grainy, Stitcher was not wearing a ski mask or heavy makeup. "He's just dead."

"Impossible."

Lyle shook his head. "I found this out last night. I had a friend look at Stitcher's finances. No credit card transactions or checks written to any grocery store in the last five years. Plenty of spending in restaurants and bars, but not three meals a day. More like once a day, usually at a bar."

"Maybe he uses cash?" I said. "He *is* older."

"He credit cards everything else. Socks, dry cleaning, housecleaning, you name it. He doesn't buy food, because he doesn't need to eat."

"Shit, Lyle. I mean… shit."

"Hang on Doc. Here comes some more people." We raised camera and scope to watch four people walking in pairs down Independence. They crossed the street to our side. One couple registered heat signatures, the other couple didn't. "Any heat?"

"The two in front are registering, but not the two behind them," I reported tonelessly. So much for equipment malfunction. And the unlikely explanation that Stitcher had gone to a lot of trouble to use some unknown makeup to block his heat signature became untenable with two more guys just like him walking down the street. Logically, once you've ruled out the impossible and the unlikely, it may be time to revisit your assumptions about what was impossible. Another part of my mind whimpered in a corner, under a blanket, like a traumatized puppy.

"What the hell does any of this have to do with my custody case?" I whined.

"Damn," Lyle said. "I recognize those guys! They're industry execs. The one in the three-piece suit is Gil, he's on the board of half a dozen firms in the meat processing industry. Ken, he's been all over the industry going back half a century. Now they both sit on corporate boards, run industry trade groups, consult for the industry's lobbyists. Power behind the throne types, you know, with half a dozen business cards, all of them conflicts of interest up the ass. Jesus."

The couple with normal heat signatures walked past us, but the food execs entered the same door Stitcher had gone in. No one else was on the street. The rain started up again, pounding the car roof in big angry splats. I pulled in the infrared scope.

Lyle showed me the pictures. Both men were elderly, with deep set eyes, scrawny and gaunt, like Stitcher. One was bald and had a skull that seemed only nominally wrapped in skin. The other was wearing a toupee. If they were seen separately, no one would bat an eye, but taking the three of them together, with the lack of a heat signature, they all looked similar to one another.

"Ghouls," I said. "Zombies."

"This is huge," Lyle said. "Stitcher was an anomaly, but these other two. God. Dead people, ghouls, running the food industry. People who don't even eat food. But why? I'd love to know what those three are chatting about in there. Maybe I should go have a peek."

My stomach began to hurt. There had to be a logical explanation. I closed my eyes and tried to focus on the normal things right around me: the seat, the rain, Lyle's incredibly lousy ideas. But the lizard part of brain was running around my skull like a gibbering, sobbing toddler with snot running out of her nose.

I put my hand on Lyle's arm. "No. They may know who you are. And there may be no one else in there. We should just leave."

"Are you okay?"

I looked at him like he was an idiot. "No, I am not okay. I just found out that the already scary man who may be screwing with my custody case, and my career, is apparently a walking corpse."

Lyle dropped me off at my townhouse during a steady downpour. He promised to dig further into Stitcher's lack of life signs. By the time I stepped inside my front door, I was wet, chilled, confused, and upset. Once inside, I sat down on the welcome mat and cried for a while.

What I had seen tonight seemed to have tossed me down a rabbit hole into a world I didn't understand. I was either going to look crazy or go crazy in the normal world that already had doubts about me on that score.

Eventually, I stopped crying, wet and spent, and stood up. In quick succession, I changed into comfy clothes, grabbed a beer from the fridge, and watched two recorded episodes of *We Will*. The town had split into two factions: those who despised the show and everything it was trying to do, and the mayor and her allies. I guess reality TV had to follow the sharpest drama, even if it was just people yelling at each other during town council meetings.

Almost instinctively, I called my mother after turning off the TV, to gossip about the show. It was our girly thing to do. But until she answered, I forgot that it was later than I thought and she would not have been watching the same thing. When she picked up, I said, "Oh, sorry, Ma. I forgot it was so late."

She chuckled. "I couldn't sleep anyway. I don't like the sound of rain on the roof. I wish my bed were on a lower floor so I didn't have to hear it right above me."

"This storm has to let up at some point."

"Not until after midnight. The news says Alexandria is already flooding," she replied. Ah, global warming: a disaster that science could explain but not prevent. How not-at-all comforting. "What's wrong, Laney? I can hear trouble in your voice."

I closed my eyes. "My belief system took a blow to the head. Well, not religious beliefs. Belief in science. I saw some things today that I don't know what to make of."

"Can our faith help?"

Not unless it meant that I had just witnessed three resurrected souls. Catholicism definitely allows for the dead to rise from the grave and for miracles to heal the sick. But there was nothing remotely religious about John Stitcher. He was too real, too crude, too modern to be a product of that. Saviors swearing into cell phones? It made no sense.

My brain made another mad dash to find a rational, scientific explanation for his corpse-like appearance and failed. Again. Now I understood what it meant to go catatonic: All other activity ceases while the person continually fails to mentally process the un-processable. "I don't know. Maybe if God gave me some guidance or strength. But I don't think religion or science can explain some of the things I've seen."

Ma was silent for a moment. "I'm sorry. How did the deposition go?"

I groaned. If my mother were a dentist, she would avoid one aching tooth by pounding on another until it hurt worse. But she meant well. I sighed and tried to figure out a way to sum it up. "There seem to be powerful people who don't want me to have custody of Charlie. And they have no damn business getting involved, but have anyway."

"That's awful. As usual, I don't know understand. Why?"

"I wish I knew. It feels like everything is crashing down in some way. Work, custody, reality. Of course, Bob's lawyer is using everything against me."

"You're not just talking about one bad day, dear, are you?"

I took a swig of beer. "It's been a bad five years."

"Are you drinking? Ugh, you get so damn maudlin when you do. Like a broken-down country singer."

Did country songs reference the undead and vasopressin inhibitors? I doubted it, but I didn't know much about music. I liked light jazz and on special occasions the blues, because it made me horny. Why that was the case is a long story about something that happened in college, but I wasn't in the mood to think about it.

"Cheer me up, Ma. Tell me it will be all right."

There was a pause. "Oh, honey, I don't know. Now you've got me worried about losing Charlie."

"Jesus Christ, Ma, could you have done that any worse?" I got off the couch, stomped into the kitchen and poured the rest of the beer down the drain. Like a lot of people, I'm susceptible to my vices, but sometimes they disgust me before I can indulge them fully.

"I'm sorry, Laney, I am. I can't give you false hopes. What I do know is that you're better than these problems and you will handle them."

I trudged upstairs, plunging the townhouse into darkness. "That sounds better. More of that please."

"You are a PhD scientist, for crying out loud, and smart, too. You're a good mother and you stand up for yourself more than anyone I know."

I put her on speakerphone as I changed into my pajamas. She stumbled through some more compliments and encouragement. When she didn't overthink it, Ma was a natural. And then, "The deposition must have gone better than last time, right?"

Ma sounded laid back when she asked questions that were burning a hole in her head. I had never explained how that first deposition had gone so badly and I was sure that made her curiosity even greater now. She probably assumed that was why I was feeling down. And after she had pumped me back up, she probably expected that I would reciprocate and tell her what happened. The deposition almost seemed like a comical distraction compared to Stitcher the walking corpse and his ability to make food industry lobbyists pee their pants.

"It went much better than five years ago," I replied.

"It must have, because that last one really upset you."

A pause lingered for several seconds. I don't know if it was the beer, my exhaustion, shell shock, or just having to speak truth no matter the consequences, but it all tumbled out of my mouth. "Yes. This time they didn't force me to talk about how often I masturbate or what sex toys I use or how much of a slut I am."

Ma inhaled noisily, just as I'd expected, but maintaining decorum had bottomed on my priority list tonight.

"This time, they just questioned my mental stability and competence as a scientist. But that's because my lawyer is much better this time around."

Ma gasped. "I can't believe Bob would do that."

I lay on my bed and took her off speakerphone. "Charlie called me after the deposition to make sure I was okay. He said that even Bob was worried his lawyers had gone too far again. I hope we crucify that bastard during his deposition."

Ma couldn't stomach revenge but she held her tongue this time. "So, how does this affect your chances of getting Charlie back?"

The million dollar question. Based on the deposition, my chances were probably fair. But if Bob's attorneys were linking up with Stitcher, who knew? He could have a gypsy put a hex on the judge and make me lose the case or something. Reality was broken around anything having to do with Stitcher, and I didn't know what that meant for the sane world where custody hearings happened. The worst part was that I couldn't breathe a word of this to anyone lest there be some psych evaluation or other inquisition of my mental state. Sandy wanted me to keep my nose clean for the time being, and that meant following Lyle around tonight was a huge mistake.

"Until tonight, I would have said it was even odds. Now, I don't know. I don't know if powerful interests are against me, or against Bob, or don't care about Charlie's custody. But they seem to be involved."

"Is there anything I can do?" Ma asked anxiously.

Now I was scaring an old woman about losing her grandson late on a stormy night. I snuggled under the covers. "Ma, if Bob's private investigators come asking you if I seem mentally stable, digging for dirt, tell them the truth: All us 'I-talians' are nuts."

She laughed. "Elaine, that's not funny."

The constant patter of rain, Ma's indignant voice sounding small out of the phone, the beer, it all made me drowsy. "Goodnight Ma. Thanks for talking to me. I love you."

CHAPTER 18

W HEN I WOKE UP FEELING great the next day, I decided that the previous night was a bad dream. On the way to work, I popped open the sunroof, let the wind blow my hair and smiled under my sunglasses as I zipped past blossoming apple trees. This time of year always seemed ripe with the promise of summer ahead.

My good mood didn't falter when Jeannie stopped by my cube. She spoke in a low, confidential tone. "Flawless told FDA that it is pulling its Fiesta Chips off the market and any other products with that additive. They made this decision right after FDA and our labs both confirmed that there were concerning levels of this mood-altering substance in them. I've got to hand it to you, Dr. Cassano. This is some great work you did."

"Oh my God, that is such a relief," I said. This would make Barry ecstatic and it meant Lyle finally won a fight. And there was a sheriff out there who was a lot smarter than he looked and who deserved a congratulatory phone call. Plus, wait, was Jeannie making nice noises at me?

"But," she added, "the recall won't be publicly announced. The official story is that their extended market testing is over and they've decided not to move forward with their own products. In return, the government will not pursue them on this. And we can't study the contaminant. That's the deal and apparently it is extremely fragile, an eleventh hour agreement."

My mouth fell open. "But they poisoned people. Someone died; others were seriously hurt. And now those people will go to jail because of it."

"I don't like it, either. And we should have received some credit for this, but it doesn't look like that will happen, either."

I swallowed. "That's a cover-up."

Jeannie glared at me for a second. "I've been told to think of it as settling out of court. Apparently, the Flawless executives didn't know that this contaminant was added and are very upset. They are taking measures to improve their quality control. Since they are cooperating fully, the government won't investigate or prosecute."

I blinked a few times in disbelief. "But what about the *Sesame Street* murder? That won't go away. There are people on trial who are probably innocent."

Jeannie closed her eyes and leaned against my cube wall. "There is nothing that you or I can do about that. It was made very clear to me that we have to abide by the agreement. I was told that we should focus on how many lives we saved by stopping this contaminant from going nationwide. If you or I or anyone here at USDA interferes, we will only make things worse."

I folded my arms. "They patted you on the head and told you not to be a bad girl."

She nodded. "You don't want to know how often that happens at my level."

No, I didn't. "So, what do I tell my sources?"

"Tell them that Flawless has withdrawn the products and ended their market testing. That's it. Nothing about contamination, or infighting in the company, or the deal with the government. That's sensitive information you have received in your role as a federal employee, not meant for public consumption. It's killing me, too. This would have been a nice feather in our cap, here. I just hope this earns us a chit for the future."

I nodded my head while my stomach grew nauseated. Wearing the big girl pants meant having some discipline and not spewing your version of the truth all over others. I seethed, though. But I was keeping my nose clean, remember?

"Are we good?" she asked. "Great. You did a phenomenal job on this, Elaine. Thank you. Next month, we'll discuss your role in the division. See if we can't find you some time to get back into research." She gave me a little smile and walked away.

That should have made me really happy. The road back to my old career. But it felt like a bribe. Part of the cover-up.

Later that day, I read the same paragraph three times. I realized I had been on the same page for ten minutes. I gave up and called Lyle on my cell phone. The cube phone suddenly seemed poisoned and dirty to me.

He whooped after I told him about the voluntary recall. "This is fantastic! Do you think it's good news?"

"Yes, but I can't say much more," I replied.

"Is there a gag order? Are you telling me that I can't talk to my media contacts?"

"Exactly."

Lyle gasped. "What the hell? How could you agree to that?"

"I had no choice. My boss says that any clumsy-footed moves by us will just mess up whatever the government is up to."

"And the innocent *Sesame Street* defendants?" he asked.

I sighed. My office phone began ringing while Lyle was winding up for an epic rant about the injustice of it all. It was Stitcher's number. I shivered, thinking about his body temperature.

"Call you back," I said to Lyle. He was really sapping my celebratory mood, anyway. "It's Stitcher calling me."

"Wha-?" Lyle said as I hung up.

"Dr. Cassano," Stitcher said, "are you happy now?"

That infrared image of him, all purples and dark-orange, with no life-indicating yellow heat, was all I could think about. And then there was the gag order.

"Yes, that additive was monstrous." I winced at the Freudian slip.

"Wish I knew about that shit back in Grand-fucking-Forks," he said. "Why the hell didn't you tell me about this? I could have stopped this before *Sesame Street*, before the government stomped in like a drunken bear with a goddamn sledgehammer."

"How?"

Stitcher sighed. "The last two days, I've been busting my ass trying to cut a deal between the FDA and my fucking client, who didn't even know about the additive. If you had just told me what you knew, I could have shut down this motherfucking bullshit myself. They pay me a lot of money to keep them out of smaller trouble than this."

I wished I could laugh. "Flawless execs didn't know what their own company was adding to their product? Were they shocked, shocked, to find out that someone added a chemical targeting obese people?"

"Elaine, you don't understand. This was probably sabotage. Someone in the company, maybe aiming for the c-suite, didn't want Flawless selling its own products. 'That's not what we do' and all that crap. They undermined the entire thing by contaminating the products and embarrassing the company. The execs had no idea what the lab monkeys were told to do. Heads will fucking roll, I can assure you of that."

That matched what Barry had said, except that those opposed to the snack products were the ones outing the contaminators, because the additive was so, uh, monstrous. It was possible that Stitcher either didn't know this or was warping the whole story. I didn't trust him at all when I thought he was alive; I trusted him even less now that I knew he was dead.

"Tell me this, John: what was the point of producing this additive? Why not just throw rat droppings into the assembly line? Occam's Razor says there's another reason. What were they doing? Demonizing their customers?"

"It's stranger than you'll probably believe," Stitcher replied. "The lab dorks were trying to do the exact opposite. They thought that they could stigmatize skinny shits by making fat fucks rude to them, thereby de-stigmatizing obesity. They made the additive—don't ask me how—so that fat fucks wouldn't turn on one another. But they went overboard."

"But this is neurochemistry at a level our experts have never seen before," I replied, keeping my voice down. "No one knows how to manipulate brain chemistry like your lab monkeys did. No. One."

Stitcher clucked his tongue. "These idiots are off limits, per the agreement between Flawless and the government. The company will crush the shit out of these lab rats, believe me. I nearly wrung out their fucking necks myself when I found out. I called to see if you and your pals will stick to the agreement."

"They didn't tell me what the agreement is. I was told to shut up," I replied.

"Okay. Well, could you tell your conspiracy pals to lay off, as well? Because we really need the media to take a breather on this. The more that conspiracy shit crops up, the more defensive my client gets and the worse things become."

I snorted derisively.

"Come on, Elaine. This isn't Agatha-fucking-Christie as your loony-bin friends make it out to be. It's typical internal corporate politics and standard-issue miscommunication."

And beyond-cutting-edge neuroscience, but he obviously wanted to pretend that wasn't the case. I said, "I've already told them to lay off."

"Thank you. I owe you, but remember I would have owed you a lot more if you'd just leveled with me earlier. I gotta jump, but we should have lunch sometime."

"Do you even lunch?" I blurted. And then quickly, "Or does that mean you just make phone calls sitting down?"

Stitcher laughed and laughed. "Christ, Elaine, I needed that. I'll be in touch."

And the dead man hung up on me.

CHAPTER 19

Until Lyle called me two weeks later, in my mind the Flawless incident was over and done with. The FDA had done its thing. Flawless was probably firing the knuckle-headed chemists who had tainted their Fiesta Chips. Stitcher thankfully had not followed up about meeting again. I had only two things to concentrate on: the custody fight and salvaging my career. On both fronts, I felt I had made progress.

Bob was grilled by Sandy in a deposition. She asked him about how late he worked, Charlie's weight and frequent illnesses, and how he managed to take care of Charlie on a day-to-day basis. The answers, while initially evasive and defensive, were illuminating. Bob bristled at having to go through Charlie's medical records, all of the colds, strep, bronchitis, and so on, plus the damning height/weight chart. My son had become a latchkey kid who was growing up on a steady stream of junk food and babysitting by his friends' parents.

Bob truly believed that his late hours were critical to supporting Charlie. He thought he made up for that with Sixers box seats, boating and other activities I could never afford. He went on about how his extended family enriched Charlie's life. He spun a heart-warming story, but Sandy would come back to questions like: Who helps Charlie get his homework done? Who makes sure he eats properly? She was relentless.

Lyle called me right after dinner on a weeknight in late June. It had been unseasonably cool and rainy earlier, and I had my kitchen window open to let the cool damp breeze into the townhouse. Tonight my big plan was to catch up on all the reality TV shows I had missed.

"Barry's dead," Lyle said breathlessly. There was a loud background hum. He was driving somewhere in that ridiculously small car of his.

"What happened?" I asked. Barry was such a lovable guy that it broke my heart, even though I barely knew him.

"He choked on a burger, his neighbor said, or had a heart attack while he was eating it. This doesn't look good; it doesn't look good at all. I'm disappearing." Lyle pounded on his car horn. "Slower traffic moves to the right!"

"Lyle, calm down. His death could just have been an accident."

"Come on! The fat guy who outed a junk food scandal chokes on a burger? Not very subtle."

I reached over and closed the kitchen window, suddenly feeling chilled. "You're being extra paranoid. The Flawless additive has been pulled. Who would want Barry dead now?" And why?

"Retaliation? Who knows? Hey, asshole, pick a lane and stick with it! I'm sorry, sorry. What was I saying?"

"Lyle Nunez, you need to calm down before you die in a car crash," I said. "How many energy drinks have you had?"

"I only remember the last three. I'm hitting the mattresses, Elaine, before they get to me too. I suggest you do the same." His horn punctuated the sentence.

I shook my head. First things first. "Lyle, pull over or I *will* hang up."

I waited until the background crunch of tires on the shoulder died down. Lyle was muttering under his breath about me being a pain in the ass, but that only made me smile.

"What?" he said in exasperation.

"Driving like a madman will only draw attention to you. Do you have any other sign that they're after you?"

"I don't need one, Elaine. This is your friend Stitcher fixing the leaks at Flawless."

"He is not as powerful as we thought. We knew more about what was happening than he did. And he's no friend. Do you have any proof that he killed Barry?"

"No way, Elaine, no way. The burden of proof isn't on me. He's the puppet master, don't you see? Meeting with the movers and shakers, showing up in Grand Forks, this guy has his dead little fingers in every pie."

"Don't say that," I said, wincing.

"What? Are you kidding me? Okay, you don't want to dwell on it? To me, this is just horseradish on the shitburger. Fine. Point is, until proven otherwise, he knows all and sees all. He's probably playing stupid with you, for sympathy, or because he hopes you're a necro."

"A what?"

"Necrophiliac. You know, into screwing dead people."

"Lyle, stop." I rolled my eyes. "If he's omniscient why didn't he stop us from delivering those documents to the government? Why did he let *Sesame Street* happen? He is really pissed that the additive escaped. He's been in damage control mode ever since."

"Bah. Circles within circles, I don't know. The CEO didn't know, Stitcher didn't know, no one knew that a bunch of lab geeks tampered with their flagship product? That's ridiculous. Open your eyes!"

"You need proof to convince me that things are other than they appear," I said evenly, trying to drain some of Lyle's frantic energy out of the conversation. He must have been really spooked, because he had gone full tinfoil beanie on me. "I'm serious. Show me what you got. In the meantime, I'm going to get on with my life. And that includes going to Barry's funeral rather than hide."

"You just love poking these people in the eye, don't you? Damn it, I'm trying to warn you so you'll protect yourself. But it's your choice. I don't want to attend any funerals, his or yours. Can't stand those things. Anyway, I'm getting back on the road, um, or highway or dirt path, or whatever I'm on. Don't try calling me on this number because I'm chucking this phone in thirty seconds."

"Say hi to Tony Soprano for me."

"Ha ha. Mafia joke from the half-Italian because I'm hitting the mattresses. Ha ha. Take care, Dr. Cassano."

I waited a minute and then called his phone number, expecting him to pick up. Lyle was at least half-full of bluster and exaggeration, and I expected him to answer sheepishly. But the phone rang and rang, probably sitting in a ditch by the road.

I shrugged and continued to clean up my kitchen. Then I watched the two-hour season finale of *We Will*. They dragged it out, of course, by recapping the season, including a clip of me sternly laying down the law about how to fight obesity. I listened closely for any factual errors they might have made, but surprisingly they did pretty well.

All of the show's contests wrapped up. The town made its weight-loss goal and unlocked millions of dollars in donations for more obesity-fighting efforts. The new farmer's market was thriving. A lighting technician won the crew's own weight-loss contest. RJ and the mayor led a celebratory 5k.

Seeing RJ sweating in tight, scanty exercise clothes took me back to my interview with him. I did like to poke the know-it-alls when I could. That was why I'd taken the Fiesta samples home. That was why I was so vicious with reviews of supposedly top-notch researchers. I felt the urge to call Stitcher and see if he even knew about Barry. I bet he didn't. If there were more layers to the Flawless story, I had a feeling that Lyle would know before I did and that I would know before Stitcher did.

Besides, Sandy had told me to keep my nose clean. The custody case was all that mattered. I had to keep reminding myself of that.

The overhyped series finale, Barry's death, and Lyle's freakout drained my batteries, so I went to bed early and played a guessing game where I tried to pinpoint where Lyle would go to hole up. The last spot I remembered thinking of, before I fell asleep, was some lousy cabin in the Shenandoah.

Someone grabbed my shoulder. Which was odd, I thought as I woke up, because I was alone in bed in my locked house. Was Charlie staying over and having a bad dream? Was I having a bad dream right now?

I looked around, slightly bewildered, my eyelids sticking together. Maybe the sensation was from an instantly forgotten dream? That had to be it. When you jerk awake so hard you think someone shoved you.

Another shove. There was someone leaning over my bed. Not Charlie.

I slid sideways, away from the intruder. For years Ma had told me to buy Mace. But I had always dismissed her concerns about a single woman living alone as old-fashioned. Should have bought the Mace.

The intruder pinned my shoulders with strong, chilly hands. I keep my room very dark, without even the light from a clock, so I couldn't see much of the bastard's face.

I couldn't escape. Terrible thoughts raced through my mind like a rapid-fire ticker tape: rape, torture, death, Charlie motherless. Terror ripped through my sleepy fogginess as various reflexes kicked in. Adrenaline, heart rate, flight or fight.

"Elaine," my attacker said in a dull tone. There was no anger or adrenaline behind it. "I won't hurt you. The Flawless scandal is over. Prazlewski is dead. Stick to your research papers. No more crusading. Or horrible accidents will happen to you."

His breath was a gust of lukewarm wind brushing against my face, smelling like spearmint. I didn't want to think about how this asshole would look on an infrared camera. I knew he wasn't Stitcher, though: too tall, bearded, the wrong voice. But just as dead.

"What do you want from me?" I demanded.

He looked around. "Where is Lyle Nunez?"

"I don't know. Out on the road somewhere, hiding, he wouldn't tell me."

The dead thing groaned like he had walked into an express DMV hoping there wouldn't be a line. I tried to sit up but he shoved me back down. I wanted to tell this thing to get the hell out of my house, but he was angry and my tongue wouldn't move.

He dipped his head lower until his bearded chin was right above my forehead. He inhaled deeply, smelling my hair or something. The creep-out factor tripled, my stomach started to turn, and I kneed him in the stomach.

He grunted in surprise and then chuckled, unhurt. He puckered his lips like he was going to kiss my forehead.

Dizziness and exhaustion fell on me like a heavy tarp. My eyelids fluttered and my stomach felt like it was being pulled up through my throat.

"Hmmm…" he said in a husky, intimate tone, "Your soul is tasty. I could do horrible things to you."

I grew weaker. I had no idea how he was doing this, other than that he was drugging me with some aerosol anesthetic, even though his hands were still holding me down. Maybe his breath was that bad.

Consciousness became an iffy proposition. I could feel my heartbeat slowing down and my nerve endings seemed to recede into the distance, like I was detached from my own body. And this was no dainty damsel-in-distress fainting spell; I was scared out of my mind, wide awake, with my adrenaline pumping and my heartbeat hammering. But I was slipping away despite all of that.

If you had told me that there was such a thing as soul-eating ghouls ten months ago, I would have snorted in derision. Groped for an explanation about fainting. But there was a dead man sucking my consciousness right out of my head and even now, I can't explain how he did it with empirical science. Call me half-convinced.

I kept wiggling my toes to keep contact with reality and my own body. *As long as I can wiggle them*, I thought, *I'll be okay.* I had a feeling that if I lost control of my toes, someone would eventually find my body in a dumpster or a shallow grave.

The assailant sat back, as if shocked, and leapt out of the bed. Consciousness returned in a rush. Maybe he had squeezed the right pressure points, I thought, despite still being in mortal danger.

He pulled the sheet up and wrapped it around my head several times. This was it, I thought, he'll strangle me, and a sudden surge of fear made me pee.

I thrashed against the linen. But the smothering pillow never came down and the sheets didn't tighten around my neck. But in the middle of the night, crazed with fear, groggy from deep sleep, damp from pee, it's amazing how lost you can get in a twisted sheet.

I finally freed my head and looked around. I could hear him moving around downstairs. It took a couple of more seconds to free myself of the sheet.

I dashed downstairs to the front door. It was still locked. I ran to the back door out of the basement, but it was locked, too. The first doubts about what happened began to creep in. Maybe I had dreamt the whole thing. But the crotch of my shorts was wet and I could still smell the spearmint from his breath. I went back upstairs and opened the front door, hoping to find him lurking in the bushes. Urine-soaked pajama shorts or not, I was going to kill this guy if he was hiding in my shrubbery.

The townhouse development was a still life. No one about, the streetlights casting their bronze glow on parked cars, and splashes of green trees and lawns. I heard a car, down where my street connects to the main road, and saw a pair of taillights. It could be the intruder, but there was no way I would catch him now. I didn't even know what kind of car it was.

I went back inside, locked the door, and turned on lights to see if he had stolen anything. Everything was just as I had left it. Undead midnight visitors apparently weren't into rape, murder, or robbery. Just sampling your soul and looking for conspiracy theorists they thought could be in your bed. Ugh.

I have never been afraid of the dark. Things that go bump in the night always have logical explanations and those explanations always dispelled any fear my wimpy brain could conjure. I yawned my way through every teenage vampire romance, no matter how enthusiastic my friends were when they shoved them into my hands.

But as I sat there at my dining room table in the middle of the night, shaking, I tried to ignore the dark corners and unlit rooms. I felt violated, my home's implicit protection having failed. It was a hollow feeling, like I was living in a bus station anyone could easily stroll right through at any time. When you think about it, a house only has thin drywall and some siding separating you from all the evil in the world.

Calling the police seemed the obvious thing to do until I tried to think of what I would say and how they would respond. Crazy single lady has a bad dream and pees herself? Cops were the ultimate wielders of Occam's Razor and for good reason. And a police report with my name on it would not help in the custody fight. Keep my nose clean and so on.

I could go stay at Ma's. I really wanted to, but I couldn't worry her. And if they were watching me, I didn't want to lead them to her.

I felt parched and drank a bottle of water. I couldn't call Lyle if I wanted to. I was tempted to call Stitcher and see how he reacted. Was he as ignorant as he claimed and acted, or was he toying with me? It didn't matter because I couldn't find his number.

I wondered if he was still up in the wee hours. If he slept at all. There were now five people I had run across who happened to be walking around with no discernible vital signs. No, no, no, I didn't want to think about that. Not tonight. Not until the sun came back up.

I climbed upstairs, changed the sheets, and took a shower. I was shaken, but didn't feel all that scared. There was something about an assailant breaking into my house solely for the purpose of lobbying me to leave his company alone that was pathetic.

The undead K Street crowd now made house calls 24/7. I stood under the showerhead, giggling uncontrollably. It turned into a short cry of fear, confusion, and frustration. Barry dead, Lyle gone, and me attacked. What did they want from us? Why now, after the additive had been recalled?

I didn't sleep until dawn, then gave up and went to work as my own kind of zombie.

CHAPTER 20

BARRY PRAZLEWSKI DID INDEED DIE at a fast food restaurant. He was forty-eight years old. The cause of death in the obituary was listed as a brief illness. The obituary also said he left behind an ex-wife, a mother, and two sisters. I said a little prayer in my cube when I read that. He was a good soul, who did right, and I wished I had gotten to know him better.

I decided to attend his memorial service. I was pissed at whoever attacked me and this felt like a relatively safe act of defiance. Unlike Lyle, I wasn't hiding or running. I always felt better operating in the open, all cards on the table. And it would keep my nose clean. God, I had come to hate that phrase.

I called Stitcher to see if he knew anything about Barry or the attack on me, or at least see if he could pretend he didn't know anything.

"Who the hell is Barry Prazlewski?" he asked when I informed him of Barry's death. "I mean, it's terrible. But why should I give a shit?"

I explained that Barry was the Flawless mole. A loose end that the FBI might have been interested in talking to.

"This is the first I've heard of it," he said defensively, although I hadn't accused him of anything. "Once again, everyone, including you, keeps me out of the loop until the fan is thoroughly shit-caked. Jesus Christ on a fucking corn dog. Is it possible this guy just died of natural causes? The food industry doesn't kill people. At least, not violently or quickly."

"The same night, I was attacked in my own house by someone warning me to stop crusading against the food industry, specifically Flawless."

"Get the fuck out of here." Stitcher paused for two full seconds. "Wait, are you serious, Elaine? Are you okay?"

"I wasn't hurt, but I think I scared him off. He seemed intent on scaring me, but then he attacked me. I peed myself a little, although I don't know why I'm telling you that."

"Attacked you? Did you go to the hospital, call the police?"

"No, he didn't punch me, nothing like that. It was like he was a vampire or something. Trying to eat my soul or my brains."

A long pause. "Well, let me look into that shit and get back to you. The execs are not behind this, I can goddamn guarantee you. And they sure as shit would never kill one of their own employees."

"Then who?"

"There's two possibilities. There may be some real slick-haired, ladder-climbing cocksuckers in Flawless who may be trying to scare you. Complete frat-boy cowboy arseholes. The ones who okayed the Fiesta additive to undermine management's new business line. Aren't office politics fun?"

Talking to him wasn't making me feel any better. "Flawless has pissed me off royally. So, I'm going to be completely up front with you, Mr. Stitcher. You have connections, and power, and a way with people. I need you to do something about this. Barry Prazlewski was trying to protect the health and lives of his customers and may have given his life for that cause. And I cannot have people breaking into my house and threatening me or my family. Can I stress this enough?"

"No, yeah, I got it, Elaine. I got it fucking cold. I will find out what happened. And then I will administer the appropriate pain to someone's asshole until it's raw. I can promise you that."

"Why should I believe you?"

"Because if it *is* the dumbasses I'm thinking of, they need their balls fed to a rabid bear. They've been calling the shots, undermining corporate, and frankly exposing the whole industry to a galactic standard fuck-ton of scrutiny. MBAs like to play cloak-and-cell phone even though I've warned them about the consequences. Now I may have to shove a post hole digger up their asses. Which I will enjoy immensely."

"Wait, you mentioned two possible groups behind this. Who's the other?"

Stitcher cleared his throat. "Ah, they are a totally different class of assholes. I don't think they have their dick in this orgy, but I will check. Discretely. I'm not exactly on the best terms with them. It may take a little time."

An image of a quilting bee of a dozen undead old ladies came to mind. Old ladies who didn't like uncouth lawyers with profane mouths and nonexistent morals.

"Any one else you know of who may be trying to kill me?"

He laughed. "Fuck no. It's a small number of people in the world who would go all Goth burglar on someone. Gotta jump. Yell if you need anything, except I don't do fucking hugs and shoulders to cry on."

"It would never occur to me to ask." I hung up.

Later that night, Stitcher texted to suggest I attend Barry's memorial service. I was half a bottle of wine into crashing on my couch. His message and the vino helped me sleep through the night without interruptions or visitors. I still hadn't heard from Lyle.

Barry's memorial service was at a funeral home in Fairfax on a morning with a bright blue sky and streets still wet from overnight rain. His older sister greeted mourners at the entrance to the viewing room. She was gregarious and warm, and reminded me of Barry, with the same straight brown hair, friendly eyes, and heavyset figure. She had two boys in their early teens next to her who looked surly and awkward in formal clothes.

I took her hand. "I worked with Barry. I talked to him just the other day. Such a good man. I can't believe he's gone. It's such a shock."

"Thank you. Our father died at the same age from a massive heart attack. Barry always said that he figured he wouldn't make it to fifty, either. He had his first heart attack two years ago and I don't think he took care of himself." She shook her head. "You said you worked with him?"

"Yes, and what impressed me the most about him," I said, "is how he was always so concerned that contaminated food could make people become sick and possibly die."

"I know," Tricia said. "His company really loved him. The vice president told me they would take care of the funeral. They brought in a funeral planner, the funeral home, an estate lawyer, and the company paid for everything. They've made this as easy on us as they possibly could. The company must have really loved him."

"I'm sure they did," I said, trying to hold back the truth. But it blew right past my lips. "He was dedicated to making sure that the company's food was safe. I'm sure his work has saved thousands of lives. He really left his mark on the company."

Barry's sister cooed and thanked me for saying such sweet things. I excused myself before I said something too truthful and went to the casket to pay my respects.

The dead never look like they did in life, I reminded myself. An image bubbled up of my father looking diminutive and foreign in his casket. It was a memory I didn't want to revisit. He had looked like a wax statue of himself, not quite right, but close. It had plunged the reality of his passing straight through the optic nerve and right into my grieving brain, making it real to me for the first time.

Lying horizontal meant that Barry's substantial double chin and jowls framed his face in fat ripples. It made him look older. He wore a dark blue suit that would have been slimming except he seemed to barely fit in the casket. The couple of times I had talked with him, I was focused on his face, or the documents he had. I must not have realized how large he was.

I knelt and prayed to God to guide such a gentle soul to his final reward, to help his family in their time of grieving. The image of Barry's girth came to mind and I asked God to give strength to all of those battling with their weight. Our country was creating tons of fat that we were now carrying to our graves in super-sized caskets.

It was madness, I said to God. *We don't know how this madness started and we don't know how to stop it. Is it just an unintended consequence of maximizing profits in a highly competitive food industry? Or is there something more nefarious behind it, as Lyle believed? And where does resurrecting the dead fit in? Either way, it all ends up with good people who barely fit into a casket, humanity burying millions of pounds of fat tissue with our loved ones. Regardless of what caused this epidemic, God, please help us figure out how to stop it from ruining millions more lives like Barry's. Amen.*

I stood and drifted back against the wall to watch the other mourners pray, cry, and grieve. I wanted to scream the truth about Barry and the world to everyone in the room.

"Is there anything you need, ma'am?" someone on my right asked me. I turned to face one of the somber attendants. He wore an expensive-but-forgettable dark suit. I'd noticed these guys when I came in; they scanned the crowd like feral waiters paid on commission.

"I have a question about how the body was prepared," I said. "I know this probably isn't the right time."

"It's okay," the attendant said, touching my elbow gently.

I nodded. "Why didn't the mortician make Barry look thinner? Lying down like that just makes his size more…obvious."

The attendant stepped close enough for me to smell his aftershave and said in a low tone, "People prefer that we present their loved ones in the most lifelike manner. That means with the fewest possible alterations."

I knew that. That wasn't what I wanted to know though. "Does a family ever request that you make the deceased look better? Or thinner, in this case?" I asked.

He shook his head. "That is not standard practice and the typical funeral home would not be able to accommodate that, outside of reconstruction services. If the deceased doesn't fit in our standard casket, we have other, larger options that can make the deceased look smaller. Maybe we should have used a larger casket in this case. Are you feeling okay, Miss?"

"Uh, I'm fine, thank you." I walked away and he watched me for a second, but then turned to steady a chair a child was tipping over.

The reality was that not only was I fine, but I had an epiphany. Barry had given me one final revelation, just from seeing him in his casket.

At the door, the other attendant gave me a small gift bag as I left. Inside was a fancy remembrance card with Barry's birth date, death date, and a short inscription. There was also a small plastic figurine of a dove in flight. My bold entrance, meant to show the Flawless creeps that I would not run from their ghoulish bullying, had resulted in scoring one of their gift bags and an entirely new way to think about the obesity epidemic.

I fought my way back around the Beltway through lunch hour traffic to work. Rather than eating, which didn't appeal to me, I spent my twenty-nine minute lunch trying to track down Lyle and learning where all the fat went.

At Barry's memorial service, it occurred to me not to view the obesity epidemic as the result of an industrialized food system, a wealthier society, a more sedentary lifestyle, or other factors of modern life. Those were all insufficient on their own to explain the problem.

I had been caught up in the conventional lens the epidemic was viewed through. My time on the Truth Squad had reinforced this view of the epidemic as a confluence of unrelated factors. My worry over Charlie had made me think about it in terms of the custody fight and what one parent could do to protect her child against this scourge. Even Lyle's old-fashioned conspiracy perspective only captured one aspect: corporate greed.

As a systems biologist, I should have been using a different analytical lens. Imagine that each person in the country was a cell in a large, organic being known as the United States of America. As a collection of over three hundred million cells, we all functioned in various emergent systems in the U.S.: the economy, the culture, the political system, transportation, and so on.

The obesity epidemic was an emergent property of that system. It was like an inflammation. Over half the cells were currently swollen, and over a third were obese or dangerously swollen. The system was producing a Niagara Falls of fat, all locked in the bodies of its individual cells. The cells' distress also stressed the organism's other systems in interconnected and interrelated ways.

This was causing various other systems to react: straining the health system, the food industry producing health-conscious products, accommodations for the obese in transportation, and now even the funeral system. That tidal wave of fat tissue washed up in funeral homes like the one I had just left. The funeral industry had to adjust to burying or cremating a lot more adipose tissue than it had since the dawn of human funerals. The adipose wave crested in liposuction clinics and on the traveling free liposuction clinic that was so popular that the *We Will* producers did a whole episode about it.

Was fat an accidental byproduct of the epidemic or was the it the point? Any organism can experience inflammation as a side effect of something else and at some point, the inflammation became more dangerous than the cause. But sometimes, the infection causing the symptoms relied on the symptoms to spread itself, like cold viruses irritating nasal passages to induce sneezing. And sometimes, one organ in a body could benefit from a danger to another.

Systems analysis could provide a disturbing take when applied to the obesity epidemic. What if a subsystem of the American meta-organism was benefiting from the epidemic and had found a way to cause it, or prolong it? Who gained when the country gained weight?

The health care sector profited from more sick people. The exercise and well-being industries benefited from people trying to lose the weight. That didn't mean that Gold's Gym, York Barbell, or Catholic hospitals had caused the epidemic or kept it going. Most of these businesses were profiting from obesity either reluctantly or indirectly. Others that profited directly could not influence the epidemic much, despite their intentions, good or bad.

The food industry was an obvious potential culprit, simply because they profited from every unnecessary calorie consumed and had a lot more power than Gold's Gym. But from my work at USDA, I knew food producers faced tiny profit margins as cost-cutting pressure had grown more extreme over time. They were by no means innocents, but they were so wrapped up with hitting market share and earnings targets that they could barely keep their heads above water. They had people like Stitcher running interference for them in perpetual crisis mode.

Furthermore, I could think of no reason why food companies would want obese customers. Sure, they would prefer that people consumed four thousand calories a day, but only if there was a magic pill that burned half those calories just as fast. Obesity, if anything, was a problem for them as it drove customers away from their products and forced them to devote resources to a series of ever-changing health-conscious products.

And how did ghouls fit into the U.S. organism? Necrotic cells or cancerous cells? My mind groped for a metaphor but the unreality of the undead running the country, much less involved with the food industry, made me ignore it. Well, the one thing all the ghouls had in common was that they seemed inordinately skinny. Fat-free dead people.

Intuition is a funny thing. It bubbles up through the subconscious, from some well-hidden, Spock-like brain that we don't realize is constantly ticking. *Follow the fat,* my intuition said, as if this were a Watergate of obesity. Fatty tissue, or adipose, was the one thing that everyone turned away from when it came to the epidemic. The Truth Squad focused on obesity's health impairments like diabetes, joint failure, suppressed immune systems, everything but what people were carrying around. The media shunned obese people other than the occasional lovable comedian. The obese themselves tended not to own mirrors or scales to avoid visual reminders of how much fat tissue they had. Even scientists had little interest in adipose tissue. But we were producing tons of it.

What was the upside of the American organism producing all of this fat and inflaming two-thirds of its own cells? It was a question no one was asking from a systemic standpoint. Obviously, it was because everyone assumed that there was no upside. I needed Lyle's help to at least think of the craziest reasons so I could rule them out.

I found articles about the funeral industry adjusting to larger decedents. Deeper and wider caskets, body-lifting machinery, even different makeup techniques were required. Embalming differed only in increasing the solution injected into the body to compensate for the additional mass. The bottom line was that the deceased's body mass, the obesity itself, was worked around, rather than altered, just as the attendant had told me. Fat had become a cost-driver for the funeral industry, an inconvenience. It was unlikely they appreciated the epidemic.

It was surprising to me how minimal the embalming process was. Barring autopsy or a severely damaged body that needed reconstruction, morticians treated the dead with efficiency and economy. And if the deceased's body didn't fit into a standard casket, they could upsell a wider and deeper one.

Stitcher called me just as lunch ended. I hesitated. Something about talking to the dead the same day as a funeral creeped me out. But I answered, anyway; I was afraid that he had fingers in my custody case and I had to keep on his good side.

"How was the funeral service?" His tone was smug.

"Um, wonderful. The family is relieved the company handled absolutely everything. Did you make that happen?"

"The Flawless CEO felt horrible about the whole thing. The food industry is not full of heartless monsters, you know."

I winced. "Yeah, okay, if you say so."

"Whoops, I have a client calling. Gotta jump. We still need to grab lunch. Call me." He hung up in a way that reminded me of a cheating husband hanging up on his mistress when his wife walks in.

I needed Lyle. There were pieces about the epidemic, faint suspicions and half-formed thoughts. But I didn't know how to put them together into a proper conspiracy theory. I wasn't deranged enough, yet, and they seemed so silly to me. But how to find Lyle? He could be anywhere by now, drinking beer by a stream with no cell phone or GPS. And someone as paranoid as him wouldn't just scoot to a motel in town. He would go off the grid.

His business card listed him as an independent consultant to health care companies. The card had a phone number and an email address. I left a vague and mysterious message.

By evening, I still hadn't heard from him. Was it possible that he had quit his consulting job when he went into hiding? He could take a sudden vacation without worrying about answering to a boss, but it would cost him his clients. I didn't think for a second that Lyle would do something extreme like that. He was too nervous to just walk away.

I looked at his card again. He offered several types of services, mostly having to do with data management of health records and producing health statistics. He advertised that he was a certified SAS programmer. SAS was a statistical software package that the health industry used extensively.

Lyle had worked for various medical research firms, health data analysis shops and so on, according to an old resume of his that I found online. Over the years, he had written papers for SAS user conferences on various techniques to calculate and display medical statistics.

There were no associations or meetings or conferences he would likely attend in the DC area or from Philadelphia down to Richmond. He must be working for a client and he probably stayed local.

I eventually found him in the SAS Institute's course guide. A person listed as L. Nunez was scheduled to teach a class this week in Rockville, about an hour's drive from BARC. I left work in time to make it to Rockville when the class ended.

Since it was the end of the day, no one gave me a second look when I strolled into the SAS Institute's training center in a mid-rise office building. Some classes were leaving for the day and people were milling around the snack area.

Lyle was poking at the snacks, oddly enough. He nearly jumped in surprise when he saw me. A scowl clouded his face. "How the hell did you know I was here? You weren't," he lowered his voice, "you weren't followed, were you?"

I shrugged. "I came here directly from work, and left earlier than I usually do. I already got a stern talking-to from a ghoul, in my bedroom, the night that you disappeared."

He raised an eyebrow. I sighed. I hadn't come out here to drive him further into hiding. I needed his help. Damn my tongue.

"Not Stitcher, someone else," I explained. That didn't help calm Lyle one bit. "Look, we were caught up in some nasty infighting at Flawless. Stitcher assures me that Flawless is punishing the people who made the Fiesta additive and came after us and Barry. The company paid for Barry's funeral, helped the family out, and so on."

He rolled his eyes. "Great. Case closed. A murdering company goes free again in America. So why are you here?"

"I wanted to run something by you about why the epidemic is happening."

That had him hooked and we rode silently down to the ground floor in a crowded elevator. We walked into an overcast afternoon on Rockville Pike and I explained my systems analysis of the epidemic and how we could follow the fat. I could tell it had piqued his interest.

"Weird," he admitted, as we walked to his car. Naturally, it was parked in an open lot further down Rockville Pike. Lyle didn't do parking garages. "It's probably profit, pure and simple," he said as he opened the door of his smart car. "More food sold, more pharmaceuticals, and finally, a bigger coffin at the funeral home. Every business profits off the epidemic. The fat they can just throw away. Isn't corporate revenge the simplest explanation here?"

I shook my head. Trust Stitcher or not, I didn't believe he would act like that if we were a loose end to be swept away. "Unless they sacrificed the additive to conceal something else, something bigger. And they needed to scare us off to make sure we didn't keep looking. A systems biologist, a conspiracy theorist, and an industry whistleblower somehow upset the applecart quite a bit."

Lyle looked me over. "You should have laid low when I warned you. Look what happened to Barry."

"You should have been at his funeral," I shot back. He looked hurt and I shook my head. "He had a history of heart trouble. Look, am I way off base here? Tell me, and I'll go back to my regular life, which could use the attention."

Lyle shook his head. "Of course there's more. You have to ask yourself if drugging obese customers was really a mistake. Even if they bungled it, the fact remains that they tried to manipulate their customers at a level far beyond anything done to addict them to salt, sugar, and fat. And short-term profit was probably not the goal here."

He got in his car, started it, and rolled the window down. "Don't call me. I'll call you. Please don't ever track me down again. I won't sleep tonight, thanks to you. Jesus. I'll call you if I find something."

He backed out quickly and scooted away.

CHAPTER 21

I CALLED CAROL, MY CUBE MATE from the Truth Squad, for advice on finding a plastic surgeon. As a result, I learned the intimate details of each elective surgery done by anyone she knew. She gave me the names of five body-contouring centers and anti-aging facilities in the area. I told her I had to go when she started suggesting what kind of 'work' I should have done. Thanks a lot, Carol.

I looked into all of the anti-aging centers. When insurance doesn't cover a procedure, they really go all out on the marketing. I bet they showed up on time for appointments too. I made an appointment for a free consult at the one that did the most liposuction.

The body contour center was in a medical office building in College Park. The soft lighting and futuristic, neutral decor made me think I had walked into a spa. The staff were perky and perfectly gorgeous. They whisked me into an exam room that was plastered with before-and-after photos of eyebrows, necks, bellies and boobs. A stocky white doctor in her fifties with short gray hair bounded into the exam room with a big smile on her face and a cross swaying from a necklace.

"Nice to meet you. I'm Dr. Paula Garrison. Call me Paula. Are you here for the after-photo?" she asked, mock-serious. "Because there's no way you need anything else done, dear."

I laughed despite myself.

She settled on the stool. "What could I possibly do for someone as pretty as you?"

"Thank you. I just have some questions about liposuction. I saw that traveling liposuction clinic on TV and until then I hadn't considered it."

"That's fine to just have questions. We're getting more and more people asking about it. Either from watching TV or seeing our work on friends and family." Paula laughed. "That clinic is like a traveling commercial for us: We're getting booked up faster these days. So, tell me: what bothers you about your physique?"

"My butt and stomach," I said. What did you think I would say? Every woman has some issues with her appearance. Especially if she's north of thirty and has had a child. And is afraid of turning into her Italian grandmother, whose arms flapped like wet sheets on a clothesline.

Paula rolled into a well-oiled sales pitch. She told me about ultrasound-assisted liposuction, a technique that uses lasers, and what the unlikely side effects and complications could be. She showed me before and after pictures of people who had similar work done. She described studies that found vast earnings and mortality differentials between the obese and normal weight, for those worrying about getting their money's worth. I bit my tongue when she breezily cited these studies. I bit down hard.

"Lets have a look at you. So, were you thinking stomach, thighs, breasts, posterior, or arms?"

What's wrong with my arms? I thought as I stripped down to my underwear. I was in my early forties. Was that when it started happening to my grandmother?

Paula looked me over and had me turn around. "Like I said, you're in good shape. We could tighten some things up: the tummy, the underarms, the backs of the thighs, give you the look of a twenty-year-old beach babe. Any concerns about your face?"

I looked in the mirror. Who doesn't have concerns about their face? But that wasn't why I was here and I shook my head.

"Okay, what about your breasts? Let me see, if you don't mind."

As I undid my bra, I figured this was the best time to ask my real questions. "Uh, what do you do with all the fat you remove?"

Paula stared at my chest and had me turn around. "That gunk? It's medical waste, like blood and any other tissue removed from the body. Goes in a biohazard bag and you never have to see it."

"Huh," I said, with my tits hanging out in the chilly exam room. "Where does medical waste go? The landfill? I've never thought about that before."

"I think it's incinerated, using a special procedure, like when bodies are cremated. Anyway, Elaine, it's absolutely nothing to worry about. Our equipment is professionally cleaned after each procedure and we follow the strictest protocols. We want return business. We don't grab the cash and do poor work, like some places."

She tapped her pen against her lip. "You're a b-cup and at your age, some women want either less or more, or to fight gravity. What do you think?"

I looked at my chest in the mirror. Sure, my tits weren't what they were before nursing Charlie or when I was in my twenties. But, honestly, I didn't care all that much. It wasn't like I was dating or flouncing around in a bikini on a beach.

"You must dispose of a lot of fat here. And with people getting obese so much these days, that's got to be a lot of fat getting burned."

Paula nodded. "Every year it's more. You'll find that doesn't affect our pricing though. I think we charge a small fee for the waste handling but not by the pound." She laughed.

She ran through some projected pictures on her tablet of what my stomach, breasts, hips, butt, and thighs would look like with some reduction. But it was the reduction in my net worth that erased any thought of actually pursuing this.

I shook my head. "Well, here's the thing. I recently went to the funeral of a friend who was obese. I don't want to look like that when I go, I guess."

Paula nodded. "I'll print these pictures. Take them home and think about it. I think you're a good candidate for having some small procedures done, if you want. Do you have any other questions?"

This was hard, because I'm wired to tell the truth and this was a pile of lies about to pour out. I looked at the floor as I got dressed. "I have some religious beliefs about not letting go of parts of my body. I have all of my baby teeth. When my son was born, I kept the placenta. I really need to know more about where my tissue would end up and if I could maybe hang on to it."

Paula looked at me like I was crazy for a second. I could imagine I would become the anecdote *du jour* at the water cooler this week. "What kind of religion are you?"

"It's an old, European, Earth-worshipping thing. A family tradition from the Balkans. Part-Druid, Wiccan."

Paula nodded, not understanding, and smiled. "This tissue we would remove is not bone, or an organ. It is just fat. That won't last. Think of it as a foreign body, a splinter, that you don't want any more."

I smiled as sweetly as I could. "But this was something that my body made, that it doesn't want to get rid of."

"I'll have Nora, the office manager talk to you, okay? We want you to be comfortable with the procedure." An array of pamphlets appeared in her palm, like a sleight-of-hand trick. "It was so nice to meet you, Elaine."

Nora was a tired, middle-aged blond who looked annoyed to have to talk to a patient. "You want to know where the medical waste goes? I'm sorry. We can't waive the fee for that."

"I'm not concerned about the fee. I wanted to keep whatever was removed."

Nora squinted at me. "What the hell would you want to do that for?"

"Religious beliefs. Kind of a psychological hangup, too."

She shook her head. "Regulations say the waste has to be properly handled and disposed of. We transfer it to our medical waste servicer."

I smiled. "Who is that? Maybe I can talk to them. It's kind of important to me not to lose whatever is removed. I have baby teeth at home. And kidney stones." The lying was becoming easier the more I did it but the taste it left in my mouth grew worse. Like spoiled lunch meat.

"Huh," Nora replied. She led me back to her tiny office. She told me to have a seat while she rifled through her filing cabinet.

"Excuse the mess," she said as she dug. "I'm the billing expert again since we had someone quit. Okay, here we go. We contract with this place," she said. "Lowest cost and local. They pick up three times a week." She photocopied an invoice for a company called Medshine. The invoice had marketing copy in a corner that claimed it was a total medical waste solution company that provided sharps containers, waste pickup and disposal, and compliance solutions for local, state and federal OSHA and EPA rules and regulations.

I thanked her and left.

I called a number of other liposuction and body-contouring businesses. I asked about their medical waste removal vendors and the amount they thought they produced each month. By the time I began calling funeral homes about how they handled medical waste, I had a smooth spiel rolling off my tongue, much like I did back on the Truth Squad about exercise and diet.

The funeral homes all claimed that they did not do liposuction on their clients, even to improve the appearance of the deceased. Turning a three-hundred-pound heart attack victim into a one-hundred-eighty-pound corpse would really upset the family, one mortician told me.

The only time a funeral home produced large amounts of medical waste was in the aftermath of messy autopsy cases, or when substantial reconstruction was needed. Embalming was designed to be minimal and not change the appearance of the deceased.

I looked into Medshine, too. It had been gaining a larger share of the medical waste market nationwide by beating out bigger competitors, like Stericycle, on price. It was becoming the Walmart of medical waste. I found some articles from a few years back about its competitors lobbying for OSHA and EPA to investigate the company's disposal practices. Nothing came of it that was public.

Medshine was a privately held corporation and shared little information about itself, unfortunately. I would have to rely on Lyle for more. Did it have corporate ghouls on its board of directors? That seemed far-fetched. But then again so did ghouls with law degrees and lock-picking skills.

The memory of Barry in his casket stuck with me, though. It could be that this was unconnected to the Fiesta additive, or to Stitcher. Maybe I was imagining a connection because Flawless was trying to generate fat and the funeral home was paying to dispose of it.

But there was a torrent of fat flowing through American society like a river full of ice floes. It must matter where it all ended up. Some place in the American business world must have a vested interest in keeping that fat flowing.

It wasn't landfills. Medical waste couldn't be dumped in regular landfills. There were state regulations about proper disposal. There were concerns about toxic substances, like lead and mercury, health concerns about HIV-positive blood and hepatitis B, and simply the ick factor about bones, eyeballs and amputated feet showing up in unexpected places. Most medical waste, such as human fat, had to be incinerated before a waste company could dump it in a landfill. Fat, being flammable, would not survive that treatment.

There were some accounts of people finding unique uses for human fat tissue. Reconstructive surgery techniques used a person's own fat tissue to rebuild other areas of the body. On the creepier side, a plastic surgeon in California used adipose to fuel his car. Years back Peruvian gangs had killed people to sell their fat on the black market. But for the most part, it was slimy, bloody stuff that everyone wanted to simply go away.

I had wasted a good chunk of the afternoon on this, which was manageable until Jeannie emailed me a bombshell. Someone in Congress had begun asking ARS a bunch of pointed questions about our grants on obesity and nutrition research. It was probably a case of sour grapes, where a loser in the grant process called their congressman.

But for me it meant that there were QFR, or Questions For the Record, that USDA had to answer, so I had to scramble. The QFR demanded to know if any grants had found the magic answer to the epidemic, why the ARS was giving these grants, what process and criteria were used to award them, how much oversight ARS provided of awardees, etc. The section on the awards process and criteria went on for over a page. Hopefully, this didn't mean one of our grantees had been featured on the local news in one of those stories about your tax dollars funding stupid studies. The news media loved to trivialize scientific inquiry, sometimes egged on by politicians like former Senator Tom Coburn. It didn't take much to freak out members of Congress.

Congress had also involved the USDA inspector general and this meant that the bureaucracy involved in my day-to-day work would triple, at least. It also possibly meant an audit. For the next few days I had to drop my morbid side research and focus on pushing paper with bullet points printed on it about grant review procedures.

Two nights later, Lyle wanted to meet at the College Park Ikea to discuss new developments. He didn't say why. After work and having a small dinner at the nearby Potbelly's I found him in the Ikea lobby, holding one of those stubby pencils and an order form.

"Why are we meeting here?"

He held up the order form. "I need a new office chair and I want a woman's opinion."

"I thought you used to be married. Isn't your ex available?"

He shook his head. "She doesn't return my phone calls unless the alimony is late."

"I don't even know what your house looks like," I said. When he held up pictures on his phone, I groaned. "I thought we would talk about the thing."

"We are," he said as we rode the escalator up to the showroom. "That free, traveling liposuction clinic tour nearly fell apart over the issue of how to dispose of fat from the road. A company named Medshine stepped in and offered to haul it away for free." Lyle grinned. "It's privately held by a shell corporation that is owned by three separate hedge funds that are ultimately owned by two associations with ties to the food industry."

"Stitcher and his pals? Really?" I asked, looking at the price tag on a couch.

He nodded and we moved on to the home office area. The store was mostly empty tonight. Lyle sat on a couple of desk chairs, and made careful notes about each on his blue-and-white order form.

"Stericycle and its other competitors complained about Medshine's business practices and regulatory compliance. They didn't like that Medshine undercut them on price. Medshine shrank their market share by using medical waste service as a loss leader. They figured out how to profit off it another way."

"How? You can't recycle it, much less resell it."

Lyle flashed a smile. "Not legally that I can see. But it offers other waste 'solutions' and consulting that may really be the moneymaker. Safety protocols are all the rage post-Ebola." We took a shortcut to the modernistic work desks and office chairs of every shape and color. Lyle sat in an expensive black mesh chair. "Medshine has three waste collection and processing centers in the DC region. Most trucks drop off or pickup and go directly to third party incineration facilities. Easy to follow. But other trucks go from Medshine to an industrial plant in Anacostia. It was fenced in and I couldn't see anything."

"Who owns the industrial plant?"

He shook his head. "No name, other than a faded sign that says 'food manufacturing and processing.' I checked the DC tax records and a corporation has owned the land for forty years. The corporation doesn't seem to exist, which doesn't mean much, with all the companies that are privately held today."

He sat in what looked like Captain Picard's chair from the bridge of the *Enterprise-D*. Yes, I know what that chair looks like. Dr. Kate Pulaski, the second-season replacement of Dr. Crusher, was a hero of mine, and Beverly Crusher and Data were not that far behind. I get a thrill when scientists are portrayed on TV. Sue me.

"Anyway, I tagged the trucks with transponders to follow them on GPS. They all headed for one particular loading dock."

"Were they dropping off or picking up?"

"Dropping off. After the run to the plant, they returned to Medshine and parked for the night. That suggests they were making a delivery and came back empty. I videotaped them coming and going from the plant and they rode lower on the way in."

We were both silent as that point sank in. Finally, Lyle said, "Any reason I can think of for a delivery from a medical waste company to a food processing plant makes my skin crawl," he added.

My mind rifled through the various possibilities and permutations. The most likely explanation was that Lyle had it wrong and the trucks were returning to Medshine with biowaste or some food byproduct, like pig's eyeballs, or something toxic.

"You said to follow the fat," he said, as he popped out of the plastic chair. He tried a navy-blue, fabric-covered chair with no arms. He spun around a little and adjusted the height. "The question is," he said, "do you have the stomach to find where this all may end up?"

I furrowed my brow. "Why? What is it? You're holding back."

"Because we can't track the waste behind closed doors. It either stops at the incinerator or a landfill, or it goes somewhere else." He lowered his voice a notch and leaned forward. "I couldn't see what was unloaded."

What would a medical waste facility send to a food processing plant in truckloads every night? Sterilized containers for biohazardous material? Latex gloves and breath masks that worked just as well to protect from chicken blood as human blood? There had to be an explanation that made sense.

I recoiled at the idea of leg bones and chunks of human fat floating in a vat of tomato soup. I shook my head. "You're not saying that Medshine is shipping medical waste to be included in food we eat, are you?"

"I wouldn't rule anything out, given that there are ghouls speed-walking the streets of DC. But it could be animal feed, or fertilizer, or latex gloves. I'm not sure what this facility produces."

"Well, we don't know *what* is happening. We don't have enough information to make any conclusions," I said.

"The trail leads to that plant," Lyle said nonchalantly, as we passed through the children's section. There were a number of cute things I could have gotten Charlie, except that he was probably too old for them now. A white-hot fear that I was already losing him gripped my heart and squeezed until adrenaline shot out to every nerve ending.

We went downstairs to the warehouse section to find the armless chair upholstered in black fabric that Lyle wanted. The cavernous warehouse section was nearly empty. As it happened, they were out of the black-fabric model. They had green, blue, and beige. Lyle ultimately chose the navy-blue version after complaining a solid five minutes. He unpacked the boxes and shoved the pieces into his smart car, with its tiny trunk.

Lyle wiped his hands and looked at me. "So, are we going to sneak into the plant?" When I laughed at him, he shot back, "What? Do you have any other ideas?"

My wheels spun. "Can't we just look at their corporate records?"

Lyle raised an eyebrow. "The corporate records are private, or at the IRS, and they don't hand over that info to people like us."

"But you're talking about breaking and entering." And anything that could jeopardize the custody case was a non-starter. "Maybe I can get the FDA to investigate. Otherwise, we walk away from this."

Lyle gave me a look that said he wasn't walking away from anything.

"No, Lyle. You like being outside of jail, and you like your life not getting destroyed. Right?" When he nodded half-heartedly, I rubbed my face in frustration. I was tired. "Let's get out of here. We'll think of some other way."

CHAPTER 22

WHEN I TOLD LYLE I would look into investigating this food facility through work, I had just said whatever would make him drop the idea. My hope was that he would forget about it, or I would also hit a dead end and that would be the end of it.

So, I made some informal inquiries at work. I asked people casually, at lunch or in the hall, if there were any reasons why a medical waste company would make deliveries to a food processing plant. Instead of hearing plausible answers I hadn't thought of, I received puzzled looks and people at lunch asked that I stop talking about medical waste. Jim Knox suggested that I call the FDA; there was probably a report on this factory sitting on a shelf somewhere.

I was mulling doing just that when Sandy called. "I met with Bob's lawyer after digesting both depositions."

One part of me revved up for good news, but the cynical part took a big, nervous breath.

She continued, "It's clear we have a better position now. He no longer has a fiancée to provide supervision and stability, plus his long hours, the missed school events, and the illnesses damage his credibility."

I did a fist pump. "You're worth every dime," I said. Probably not something you should tell your lawyer, but I was excited.

"Well," Sandy continued, "it's not all good news. His lawyer ambushed me with a dozen industry lawyers when we met. They wanted to go over every word in the previous custody decree and argue about each sentence in both depositions. They accused you of using your government position to hurt Bob's case, threatening his means of living, and catching the agricultural and food processing industries in the crossfire. They brought up this tortilla chip recall and the whistle-blowing episode earlier in your career that you told me about. They tried to make the reality TV show appearance sound unethical and scandalous. They said they have grounds to ask the USDA IG to investigate your conduct."

I smacked my forehead. "Bob doesn't have the clout to pull this off. He's on thin ice with his bosses. It can't be him behind this." Stitcher and his pals had to know about this, though, if they weren't pulling the strings. Which meant that at the least they weren't stopping it, or at worst, they were doing it. Maybe this was Stitcher's subtle way to make me give up pursuing the truth.

Sandy sighed. "Nevertheless, you've upset someone with real juice. Bottom line: You don't want these industry lawyers involved; they'll bankrupt you, possibly get you fired, and Charlie will be out of college before the custody hearing actually happens. As your attorney, I'm advising you to stop doing whatever has bothered them. I realize that may not be feasible for you from a work standpoint."

I rubbed my forehead, feeling a tension headache starting. "But even if I could do that, it wouldn't guarantee that Bob gives up custody, right?"

"No."

"Well then, what else can I do?"

"You could gain enough leverage to make them back off, but that's hardball," Sandy said carefully. "I know you're a fighter, and you've taken hits for your beliefs, but this is major league, Elaine. And I don't think you can win that fight."

"And I can't prove a negative either. I can't prove that I'm not doing anything to hurt these companies. I review grant proposals all day. That's all."

"True. But I suggest you reach out to them and make them believe that."

Great. Lose Charlie to Bob or lose the truth to Stitcher, or gain some mysterious advantage over them both and still maybe lose Charlie in the end. If there was another alternative, I had better figure out what it was.

I didn't have a choice about what to do, really. I couldn't use my job to appease these industry jackals and secure Charlie's custody, even if I wanted to. I could sit still, do nothing, and let Bob and Stitcher both get what they wanted while I got nothing. Or I could do something. Try to get that leverage that Sandy had mentioned. But I didn't have to be stupid about doing so. I needed to find out if these industry lawyers were getting their information from inside BARC.

USDA had been accused on a regular basis of collusion with the industries it oversaw, as most regulatory agencies are. I had never witnessed anything like that, because of course if I had, I would have blown the whistle. But if these industry lawyers were watching me through my own organization, I had to know before I followed the fat any further.

I started by taking Jim Knox out to lunch at a Mexican place on Route 1. He was plugged in with the who's who in all of the health, food and nutrition agencies and the biggest names at universities.

If this were some Dan Brown thriller, Jim would be the sage, gentle friend who turns out to be the evil mastermind who betrays me in the end. But this was real life and Jim Knox was a granola-crusted hippie who never ate more than half his food at any restaurant. He always took a doggie bag back to the lab to see how much more fat, sugar, and salt they had crammed inside his entree. He was deeply committed to improving food safety and the public's health. During the time that I had known him he had declined half a dozen lucrative offers from the food industry.

I waited until after we ordered chimichangas to update him on the custody case and the appearance of the industry lawyers. Jim turned three shades of gray.

"I'm a little worried that someone in BARC is helping them. Like Jeannie," I said.

Jim laughed. "She dislikes you, definitely, but her primary concern is climbing the ladder. She won't bring down the IG on her unit, and threaten our research programs, just to spite you. No one here would."

I breathed a sigh of relief. "Okay. Different subject. Can you think of a reason why a medical waste company would make shipments to a food processing plant every single weeknight?"

"Um, maybe delivering latex gloves and other protective gear," he answered.

"Every single night?"

He wrinkled his brow. "Oh."

"Let's say that would be equivalent of a three month supply delivered each night," I said. I had rummaged around in our labs' supply room for the boxes of face shields, gloves, breath masks and surgical scrubs and had done some volume estimates given the size of the trucks that Lyle saw.

Jim peered at me through his bifocal glasses. Then he rearranged his silverware on the tablecloth and shrugged. "What are you after, Elaine?"

I cleared my throat. "You've been around, seen a lot here. Would you have any reason to think the government has been involved or even is aware of a secretive effort to make people obese?"

He looked at me funny. "People at CDC, FDA, and NIH dropped everything they could to jump on the Fiesta additive. People canceled vacations because of this whole obesity killer thing. It's why we went to school, and why we're here. Nobody has ever tried to help spread the epidemic."

He looked at the tortilla chip he held in his hand. "Is it the extra lime juice or the extra salt that makes these so tasty? Anyway, once in a while, we get political hacks who do what they think is the industry's bidding, to swing their next post-government job. And it almost always backfires. The IG, Congress, senior management, someone finds out and undoes the damage. You've seen this with research grants, right?"

I rolled my eyes. "We're going through another round of Questions For the Record from Congress on the anti-obesity research grants."

"See? Anything the government has done that indirectly aids the epidemic, like declaring ketchup a vegetable, is widely ridiculed by the media right out in the open. A government conspiracy would never get the oxygen it needs to survive."

"So, how about those Nationals?" he said as the waitress brought the food. Jim gave her a big smile. "I'll tell you right now I'm going to need a box. This is just too much!"

He winked at me and we talked about baseball, his obsession, and then how his grandchildren were perfect while his grown children were a mess. No shoptalk: No one discusses *E. coli* over refried beans, cheese, and ranchero sauce.

It wasn't until we were riding back to work in his pickup truck that he cleared his throat. "Elaine, you've been asking some odd questions lately. Medical waste, fat tissue. People are starting to ask questions about you."

"Eh, just chalk it up to me being a systems biologist," I joked.

Jim grinned. "It would be better for you if you dropped the subject. You're going to need help if there's more heat coming down on the extramural research. Or you really piss off the industry."

"I will," I replied. At least at work I would.

I spent the rest of the day on the Congressional assignment and then tried to squeeze in some grant reviews. If Congress had any sense of how much time and money was spent responding to their inquiries, they would probably be outraged at the waste and demand another round of answers to explain it.

When I got home from work that night, there was an email from Sandy wanting to know how to proceed. She said it was my last chance to pull back. I had to call Ma first for advice.

I told her the latest about the custody case and then asked. "Am I doing the right thing?"

Ma took a big breath. "Charlie's future is at stake, his home environment is not good and he needs you. You can't give up; you can't compromise. Maybe others could, but you just can't."

"But even if it means losing him?" I said. "I feel as if I've doubled down on this and am risking everything."

"Every mother has to give up her children when they're grown. Even if you win, you'll only have, what, seven more years before he goes to college?"

"I know, but those are the critical years. The ones that really count, you know?"

Ma paused a second. "Are you okay, Elaine? Something is wrong. You don't ever doubt yourself like this. At least, not to me." When I was growing up she'd always said that strong-willed and stubborn does not attract boys. And now she was dinging me for not being stubborn enough. "I have doubts all the time, I just don't let you know about them most of the time."

"You're not going to kidnap Charlie and move to Europe, are you?"

"Ma, no! Of course not. You know I wouldn't." God if she thought I was capable of that! I could hear Bob's lawyer telling the judge: Her own mother wonders if she is unstable, and thinks she's capable of kidnapping her child.

"I'm sorry. Some people do that kind of thing when they're losing custody. Especially mothers. Anyway, you're thinking about something, but you're not sure what you should do about it."

I was thinking about that food factory in DC, with the Medshine trucks rumbling in tonight, like every night.

"Dear, you have to do what's right, no matter what the cost. Your father did too. But that's the way you are and there's nothing you could do about that even if you wanted to. It's the only way you can live with yourself."

"Thanks, Ma. Love you."

I emailed Sandy that I was not giving up. I didn't mention whether I was going after leverage or surrender. I couldn't walk away from following the fat. Even if Stitcher was exerting pressure on me through the QFR and through the custody case. If there was a far-ranging conspiracy, my stubbornness on the custody case would backfire unless I had some leverage. I had to know what was being delivered to that factory in DC.

Lyle came by Saturday night. I felt like I should do something to welcome him, but offering him sweets or baked goods seemed wrong. He wasn't my son, or a date. He was a co-conspirator. What was the protocol for that kind of visitor?

It turned out that Lyle wouldn't have noticed if I offered him a double cheeseburger while dressed in lingerie. He was a babbling, sweaty mass of nervous excitement and distrust. He came in, his gaze darting about, and then mumbled about going to his car to get something.

He returned with some handheld electronic equipment, which he said detected listening devices. He swept every single room and the backyard. He used his infrared scope to look for people watching my house from the back and the parking lot out front.

I waited at my dining room table while he bustled about, my chin in my hand.

"We should really meet somewhere else," he said as he came in from the back deck. "I might have missed something."

"Wouldn't they follow us then and still listen in?"

He bit his tongue, impressed with my paranoia, and asked to check the crawlspaces. Satisfied, he returned to his car and came back wheeling a large suitcase. The suitcase contained two laptops, a tablet, and a roll of hand-drawn blueprints, all of which he put on my kitchen table.

On the tablet, he had video of the trucks rolling in and out of the waste facility on the weeknight we would make our attempt. He paused it for each Medshine truck, estimating the cargo capacity and how much weight it was hauling by how the shocks bounced when each truck turned into the facility's driveway entrance.

I put my hand on the map to get his attention. "Okay, do you understand how much I'm risking by doing this? I am in the middle of a custody hearing where I am petrified to get a parking ticket. We can't get caught."

He nodded, turning serious again. "Relax. You don't even have to go in. This place uses low-skilled, low-educated Hispanic labor. I chatted up some of the *amigos* after their shift. They said the job is terrible. There's high turnover so they get a recruiting bonus. So, I pretended I have bad English and got a job there—started two nights ago."

That was ingenious. It wouldn't be breaking and entering then. "Lyle, that's great!"

He grinned proudly. "They make cheese sticks and single-serve milkshakes. I feed plastic into a wrapping machine and set up the milkshake boxes. They showed me the operation really quickly; that's what the blueprints are based on."

Dairy, which has a high fat content. "Did you see what the Medshine trucks bring in?"

"No, but they take it to the warehouse loading dock. The warehouse guys hang out on the dock smoking on break, so the warehouse is empty. The shift supervisor hides in his office, especially on breaks. I could slip in there, take some pictures."

I shook my head. Just reading a package label was not worth it. The only way to know anything was to test the material. To hold the samples over Stitcher's head and demand a legal ceasefire. "We need samples of what Medshine brings in and the products they're making there. Do you know how to collect samples so they don't become contaminated?"

His eyebrows arched and he shook his head.

I sighed. "Then I have to go in and get them."

"Uh, forget samples. It's too dangerous. What? You're the one concerned about getting caught. What if it's sealed up, or locked?"

"I'll take a Swiss Army Knife and cut them open."

"A knife?" He rolled his eyes. "You may need a key or a crowbar or half an hour. This is a really, really bad idea."

"If I hadn't brought back the Fiesta samples, Flawless would be selling those chips now," I pointed out. "Samples or the deal is off."

"You're killing me, Elaine. Oh my God. Fine. But you have to be quick about it. And technically, taking samples is theft," he added.

I groaned and looked at him, fighting the urge to rethink this entire thing. "Maybe I can get a job there?"

Lyle winced. "Everyone there is short, poor, and Hispanic. The boss would be highly suspicious. No, that's not going to work. I have to sneak you in."

"How?" I asked.

"Hm. There are no patrols along the six foot fence, and it's not well-lit." Lyle pointed at a location on the blueprints. "Here's a dark spot along the right side here for you to climb over."

"Uh, climb over? Don't they have cameras watching the fence or something?"

Lyle displayed pictures of the place during the day. There were no cameras, inside or out. In this day and age, I found that a bit strange. Were they cheap, or did they not want to record whatever happened inside?

"What about checking ID badges? Internal alarms?"

He unrolled the plant's blueprints. The west side of the building had a warehouse and a loading dock, and the east side was a wall with a few emergency exits. The northern end connected to a single-story office building. The production floor occupied most of the rest of the building, with small rooms at the back for the locker room, break room, bathrooms, manager's office, and supply closet.

"I can let you in before the midnight break. You hide here, in the supply closet, until break starts. Everyone hits the bathroom and then the break room. You hide before break is over and then leave while we're back on the floor and it's clear."

"What's the production floor look like?"

Lyle shrugged. "They didn't show me much more than my station. There are pipes, conveyors vats, ovens, and presses. You'd get lost pretty easily. Just go to the warehouse and back to the supply closet."

We kept rehearsing the plan for another hour. We also developed two backup plans that involved pulling fire alarms and running. He left me the blueprints and maps to study. I prepped homemade sample kits that fit inside a fanny pack when I wasn't studying the plan. After practicing the plan for several hours, we were ready to go.

CHAPTER 23

I PLOWED THROUGH WORK AND PREP for the custody hearing with grim determination. Planning to commit a felony at the end of the week tends to overshadow everything else. I began following every law and rule to the letter, as if matching the speed limit exactly now would make up for a criminal act later on. I even flossed my teeth twice a day. It was awful.

Finally, it was Friday night, the night Lyle thought trespassing and theft would go easiest. He had learned that many of the workers would have a few drinks in them before their shift began.

I took Route 50 west into the District. The food processing facility was in an industrial area with warehouses, garages, railroads, printing operations, and the like. It was deserted that late on a Friday and I felt conspicuous being in one of the few cars on the road. Luckily my weathered, fifteen-year-old Corolla wasn't out of place in front of the cinder block auto body shop that I parked by.

I hiked in a half-mile to the plant past the dark and shuttered businesses. When I found a really dark spot along the fence, I climbed over. Or tried to. The fence rattled and vibrated so much I jumped off. I tried again, attempting to be quieter, but my foot slipped on the dewy, wet chain link. I had to start over again despite having caused a racket. With my heart thundering in my chest, I stayed low and quiet to see if the guard at the front noticed. Ten minutes passed and all I heard was crickets.

I tried again, this time using my arms to pull me up more than my legs pushed. I hadn't climbed anything in years, but I did take a weight-lifting class and hoped my just over forty body could manage this. I made it. Once on the ground, I quieted those goddamn rattling chain links.

I waited by the fence in the dark to see if anyone came around to see what the racket was about. The nighttime chill went right through me. There were no signs of life outside the facility, other than the smell of something burning that shouldn't have been.

The plain steel wall of the factory building was dotted with cheap orange lights and a couple of doors unevenly spaced along the wall. The loading dock was on the opposite side. I could hear trucks rumbling out by the street as tonight's Medshine deliveries arrived. I couldn't see them, but the rumbling grew closer as the trucks made their way to the loading dock. There was a brief spasm of beeping as each backed up to the dock.

Lyle's shift went from ten until six in the morning, with lunch at two and breaks at midnight and four. Lyle would slip me in before the first break in the fire door on this side. Which meant either waiting in the glare of those lights and hoping no one snuck a cigarette early, or running in from the dark when he opened the door. I stayed in the dark.

Twenty-five minutes to midnight, the doorway to my right opened. A person in a blue coverall and puffy white hair net looked out. I hesitated a second to make sure it was Lyle. He made the hurry-up sign and I ran into the light and inside the building.

We were standing in the short back hallway. The supply closet was right by the door. It was noisy even back here. It smelled like burned barbecue and ammonia.

"Here, put this on," Lyle said, handing me blue coveralls. "It will make you look less conspicuous if someone spots you. There are fifteen of us here tonight, including the boss. Four on the loading dock, ten on the floor, and the boss in the office, as usual."

I took the blue coveralls and ducked inside the supply closet. I hid the fanny pack under the coveralls. I didn't know how much time I would have to take a sample, and I needed easy access to the specimen cups and baggies inside, but it would be too out of place to wear it on the outside.

When the break chime sounded throughout the building, I set a fifteen-minute countdown on my watch. I waited till Lyle gave me a soft all-clear knock on the closet door and then hurried out to the production floor.

The production floor was brightly lit and crammed with machinery, a jungle gym of sheet metal and steel vats. Lyle's sketches were relatively accurate, but his appraisal of the stench was understated. It reeked like bad milk left simmering on a stove for hours.

The assembly line was set up so that the ingredients and final product were handled right by the warehouse to make trips between them shorter. Ingredients were loaded into the large, stainless steel vats on one side of the warehouse entrance and the finished product was loaded into crates on the other side. I hoped this meant I could concentrate on this small area, get my samples and pictures, and get the hell out.

The vats were fed from a raised steel-grate platform. An entire pallet of sacks that looked like cement bags were stacked three high. I imagined the worker would slit the sack and pour the contents in. Alongside these pallets were empty green plastic drums. They had no identification or markings and contained too little residue for a sample.

I speed-walked around the perimeter of the production floor, taking care to make sure the guys on the loading dock weren't looking back in my direction when I passed the giant door that led to the warehouse.

I tiptoed up to the platform where they fed ingredients into the vats and peered inside. I filled a sample cup with what was advertised as dry flavor powder. The vat fed by the green drums was empty but caked in what looked like dried pancake batter.

I brought out specimen cups and filled them with each.

"I'm going to get a Coke," I heard one of the warehouse guys say. He was headed to the break room. I hid behind the stacked pallets of powder bags and waited for him to pass by.

When he disappeared down the hallway, I scooted over to the pallets of finished spray cans and what looked like cheese sticks. The cans were labeled McDotty's Cheesy Food Spray, a brand I had never heard of.

I hunkered down behind the pallet of finished cheese sticks and peeked around the corner, waiting. The dockworker walked by twenty seconds later, his wallet chain swinging from his faded jeans.

There were only eight minutes left before break ended, and I wanted to be gone two minutes before then, just in case. I worked my way backwards from final product packaging to where the liquid cheese was poured into the plastic wrapping. The heat pouring off the cooker made me sweat. I couldn't imagine working in this heat for eight hours. I plucked two still-gooey cheese sticks off the conveyor belt, using a sample baggie as a glove.

I still had to get in the warehouse and sample whatever had come from Medshine. I was still holding out hope that it was simply latex gloves and hairnets.

The warehouse guys were all out by the trucks, no doubt taking a breather from the stench. Half the warehouse was an enclosed refrigerated space, which made sense if they were producing dairy products. I took note of each different dry item outside, though, including a small pallet of latex glove and hairnet supplies that had been delivered a month ago from another medical supply company. Not Medshine.

Five minutes left. I slipped through the plastic door strips and entered the refrigerated area. On the left were stacks and stacks of eggs, a single pallet of butter and two pallets of cream. Odd that they weren't using eggs on the production floor that I could see. Maybe they produced several different products here.

On the right were shrink-wrapped pallets of boxes of finished product: McDotty's milkshake drinks and cheese sticks. One of the pallets had a pallet jack underneath it. I stepped around the pallets and walked further into the refrigerator. The earlier chill I'd experienced came back. The thin coverall didn't insulate all that much.

In the far corner were several shrink-wrapped pallets of the green plastic barrels I had seen out on the floor. They were labeled emulsifier and date-stamped with today's date. By volume, they were by far the most prominent ingredient in the place.

I spent a moment searching these green drums for some label, mark or other sign of where they came from. Every other package in the warehouse was festooned with advertisements for their supplier. None mentioned Medshine.

Finally, I found a shipping form taped to the shrink wrap of one pallet of green drums in the corner. Among the order numbers, bar codes, and shipping address was small print that said Medshine. Any doubt I had about a medical waste company supplying ingredients for processed food disappeared. I tore the sheet off and stuffed it in my fanny pack.

Three minutes left. I needed to go now, but I couldn't leave without a sample of whatever the hell was in these medical waste drums. It'd be fine if I was just quick about it, right?

I pried open one of the lids—with my Swiss army knife, thank you—and was dismayed, but not surprised, at what I saw. Inside was a viscous yellow sludge, marbled with streaks of rusty red, brown, and white. It smelled like rancid lard. It was a tub of fat. Human fat, if I had to guess.

I took out my phone to take a picture of it. The camera app kept crashing. It didn't like the light level and wouldn't focus. When I finally got a picture it was blurry because I moved the phone before it was done. Seconds ticked away like a solemn drumbeat in my head. I hate phone cameras and jammed it into my pocket. Samples were more important than pictures.

I dipped a specimen cup in and put it in a sample baggie. Then I did it again. I resealed the drum carefully.

Now I had two minutes to scoot.

I peered through the transparent plastic flaps at the rest of the warehouse. No one was in sight, but I could smell cigarette smoke. I kept the stacked pallets of milkshake flavoring between me and the loading dock as long as I could. Then I bolted across the open space through the warehouse back to the production floor.

I had to at least get back to the supply closet before break ended. Otherwise, the workers would find me. I hustled to the giant doorway to the production floor, feeling more exposed than I had since I climbed the fence.

The break chime buzzed loudly. I jumped and adrenaline rushed through me like a liquid bath of gasoline. Then I looked at my watch, knowing that there was more time left for me to make it to the supply closet. There was: just under two minutes.

Management had shorted the break. What had screwed over the workers a little now left me standing on the production floor, twenty yards from the back hallway. And I could hear people walking down it, headed toward where I was standing, immobile with fear.

Naturally, Lyle had assumed that management really allowed a full fifteen minutes for the fifteen minute break. With my two minute cushion of time, it should not have been a problem. But I had chewed up that cushion to get the last sample of the yick in the green barrels.

Now I was stuck.

I did the only thing that made sense, which was to sneak onto the production floor and head away from the back where workers would be coming in. I just needed to buy some time, find a door on the far side, and slip out quietly.

The machinery on the floor shielded me from the view of anyone coming up the rear hallway. There were stainless steel workstations, a complicated conveyor belt system, stacks of supplies, and large piping that created layers of cover to hide behind.

I crept around the north side of the floor, keeping as much sheet metal between me and the workers as I could. I passed a door that led to the office building. I just had to reach the side door before anyone saw me. The sound of the workers returning, laughing and complaining and mumbling, seemed to follow right behind me.

I stayed low and duck-walked across the south perimeter of the production floor. When I reached the side door, my heart fell into my stomach and sweat broke out across my neck. The door was blocked by a steel bin with an industrial-sized fan on top.

I heard people's voices coming closer but willed myself not to look in that direction. Somehow people instinctively turn towards someone looking at them, even if they didn't know a person was there. Part of me just didn't want to look that way anyway. I knew Lyle would be nervously scanning the whole place to see if I was still here.

I needed another way out. Or I had to hide and wait four hours for the next break without being spotted. I could hide that long if I could find a spot. But the production floor was brightly lit with large fluorescent lights and the machinery was not dense enough to stay hidden from all the workstations. Somebody would wander by at some point and see me. Maybe. But what choice did I have?

I could hear the forklift buzzing around the warehouse now, so going back that way was not an option.

I crouched in the southeast corner, fighting off fear-induced paralysis. Yes, I was scared completely shitless. If I was caught, it was a felony. It would mean losing my job, letting Stitcher off the hook, and losing Charlie.

The only good option seemed to be the office building. I would have to work my way back there without anyone seeing me. Or just run and hope to get away. Oh, God. This was not going well. Didn't Lyle tell me to forget the samples? Why didn't I listen?

"Hey, who are you?" someone said behind me.

I stood up, but kept my back to the voice. A voice that wasn't Lyle's. Of all things to think of at the moment, I realized how out of place I was since the other women in the building tonight were all under five feet tall.

"Hey! *Segurado!*"

"*Que?*" someone else yelled over the steam-driven whine of the cookers.

The guy behind me yelled something that sounded like *intruder* in Spanish. He must have been standing a good bit away from me.

I ran. What else could I do?

I sprinted towards the front of the production floor and turned towards the door to the office building. I was expecting to be grabbed or tackled at any moment. Fear drove me forward.

I tried wrenching open the door to the office building with a fierce desperation. Nothing happened. It was locked. The only other way out was through the warehouse or the back door Lyle had let me in. But both were too far away. I would be cornered before I ever made it. They were going to grab me any second.

I pushed instead of pulled and the office building door swung open easily. What a moron. I ran down a dark hallway, away from raised voices in the factory. The hallway ended at another hallway running the width of the building. All I needed was an emergency exit to the outside.

I looked over my shoulder as the door banged open behind me. Two guys looking silly in white hairnets and worried expressions burst through, walking quickly but apprehensively. Maybe they were afraid I was armed. Or maybe they had never been in the office building before.

Unfortunately, Lyle hadn't been in here either, so I didn't know where I was going. This was Backup Plan Number 3: Run like hell in any direction.

I turned left, hoping there would be an emergency exit on the east side of the building, so I could avoid the truck traffic on the west side. This building didn't have a simple grid floor plan though. It was like a maze. Another turn and I was standing at the edge of a cube farm that was eight cubes deep by a dozen cubes wide.

On the far side of the cube farm, a security guard fiddled with a light switch. I ducked below the nearest cube wall just as he turned the lights on. I was pretty sure he hadn't seen me, but how would I escape now?

With a moment to think and catch my breath, I became concerned about the samples never being tested. It just seemed like a damn shame to be so close. And then I thought of the look on Charlie's face when Bob told him that I had been arrested. Bob would probably be gleeful about it, the bastard.

The cubicles had dull beige carpeted walls four feet high but the bottom had an open space to let air circulate. I could see the security guard's legs moving through the cube farm. I would get caught if I sat still.

While the guard checked the east side, I crept to the west side, matching his movements, hoping to slip around him and down the hallway he had come from.

The guard and my pursuers ran into one another, of course.

"What are you all doing in here?" the guard asked.

"Where is he?" I heard Lyle ask in broken English.

"*Chica. Es chica,*" remarked the voice of the person who had seen me.

I scooted to the front of the cube farm and hoped they kept having their little war council.

But the guard figured out what they were saying. "I'll call this in. Let's split up. Just be careful."

How many people were chasing me now? Was it the entire night shift?

I ran up the hallway towards the front of the building. Lots of doors and ways out, I hoped. The front of the building had a receptionist's desk that doubled as a guard station which, thank God, was currently empty. If this place had two or three guards, I would be caught already. I ran to the door. It was deadbolted. Shit.

I needed to find an emergency exit or a window. I looked for red exit signs, but they all pointed towards the locked front door. Duh.

I chose the hallway to the right. It dead-ended at a locked executive suite. I turned around and ran back to the lobby just as Lyle and two other workers arrived from the other hallways.

Lyle swore in Spanish and grabbed my arm, his eyes full of disappointment. What else could he do?

I was trapped.

From a systems point of view, when a disaster or catastrophe happens, it is the accumulation of several things going wrong. Take the Spanish influenza, for instance. It combined just the right elements that caused various failures throughout the human body. It produced too much mucus in the lungs, it was easily transmitted between people, and the onset was sudden. There was a whole lot of failures or inabilities of the human host to fight the disease that all stacked up. Don't ask me why I thought of the Spanish Flu as I was caught breaking and entering.

Stacked-up failures. That's what popped into my mind when I was cornered. I had made a series of mistakes and bad judgment calls that had led me to this situation. Large mistakes and small mistakes. Not being able to work a camera phone. Grabbing that last sample. Assuming that a fifteen minute break meant fifteen minutes. Deciding to help Lyle in the first place. Getting exiled to USDA. Having a big mouth and a self-destructive commitment to the truth.

I couldn't look at Lyle, who had an iron grip on my arm. I looked at the floor while someone ran to get the guard and the manager.

"*Que es tu problema?*" Lyle asked.

So much for him knocking out the other guy and both of us escaping. But this was no Hollywood movie where we would hit the road and redeem ourselves in the final reel. I would likely be in jail within the hour. I was in too much shock to even tear up.

I realized that when Lyle stressed that I shouldn't risk staying too long, it was because he would let me take the fall myself if caught. He had his own backup plans in case things went wrong.

The guard and the plant manager gathered in the front lobby to gawk at me. The guard asked if he should call the police.

The manager, a short, bald man in a sweater vest, shook his head. "No, I already called management. The boss is coming over. This is a trade secret thing." He turned to his night shift, which had pretty much all gathered in the lobby to stare. "All right, everyone back to the floor. Except you, Rosalita. You stay and be a witness. Si?"

The short woman I had noticed earlier nodded silently. It was clear what she thought of her bilingual boss.

"So, what do you want me to do with her?" the guard asked.

The manager looked me over. "I want to see what's in that fanny pack and you, uh, better frisk her."

I gave the manager a death look. The guard looked even less happy about it, if that was possible.

Rosalita helped me out of the coverall. The guard removed my fanny pack and rummaged through it before stepping up to me. His hands traveled over me for what felt like forever. At least he was chivalrous and used the backs of his hands. When he was done, he bound my hands behind my back with a wire cuff and sat me in the lobby's waiting area.

The manager went through the fanny pack, placing all of the contents on the receptionist's counter.

"It looks like we have a corporate spy here," he said with a smug tone as he held up the sample baggies and specimen cups. He waved the cheese sticks around. Except, of course, they were not cheese, were they?

"Look, dear, why don't you tell us your name and who you work for," the manager said. "Your receipt here says Elaine Cassano."

Ugh. So much for keeping that secret. "I dare you to take a bite of that cheese stick," I retorted.

The manager smirked. "Destroy evidence of stolen inventory? No way."

A car pulled up out front, followed by another. The guard unbolted the front door.

"Rosalita, dear, go back to work, *por favor*," the manager said.

Rosalita looked from him to me and then walked up and shook her finger in my face. "You don't take this job from me. I have kids to feed, *puta*." She spat at my feet and stalked off with her head held high.

"How come you didn't call the police?" I asked.

The guard looked at the manager; he was wondering the same thing.

"We deal with corporate spies in our own way," the manager said.

"What are you going to do, grind her up into the food?" The guard deadpanned.

The manager scowled at him. "Yeah, her and the guard who let it happen."

The guard shrugged defensively. "What? She didn't come in this way."

The manager dropped it. "Can you unlock a conference room for us? Thanks."

While the guard rummaged for a key, the front door opened. A thin, wiry woman hurried in, wearing sweats and a haggard look. Behind her, wearing a sport coat, dress shirt and slacks, was John Stitcher.

"What the hell is going on, Raymond?" the lady said to the manager.

Raymond the manager indicated the specimen cups and baggies and cleared his throat loudly. "Corporate espionage."

Stitcher looked at the evidence on the counter, then at me, and shook his head.

I couldn't resist. "Hi John. I didn't wake you, did I?"

Everyone turned towards Stitcher, surprised. He recovered instantly, but his mouth was a thin, grim dead line. "Elaine, didn't we first meet at a police station?"

I shrugged. "I keep turning up at your crime scenes."

The woman only grew angrier. "What the hell is going on?"

The manager cleared his throat again. "She was snooping around the production line and we chased her here. She was stealing."

Stitcher said in a low tone, "Is there somewhere we can talk to her in private?"

The guard escorted us all to a conference room. Raymond told him that no one was to disturb us and then closed the door.

Stitcher grabbed the edge of the table. "Elaine, what the shit-hell are you doing here?"

I met his angry gaze. "I know what you guys are doing here. Making food products out of medical waste. Human fat tissue. I tracked medical waste being delivered here as ingredients in dairy products."

The lady turned pale and her mouth fell open. I couldn't tell if she was offended that I would accuse her of such a thing or surprised that I knew.

I turned to her. "Who are you, anyway? I know who he is and what he does. Are you the owner?"

"Don't answer that," Stitcher said with a hand chop. "She's with the government, so she doesn't know anything."

"Who are you working with?" The woman asked.

I shook my head. "No one. This is something I had to do. Ever since the Flawless incident. Since Barry died." I sneered at Stitcher. "It's personal."

"Do you know how much trouble you're in, Doctor?" The lady asked.

"Breaking and entering, theft, possession of stolen trade secrets, destruction of property, sabotage," Stitcher ticked off crimes on his cold, dead fingers. "Damn shame about the timing, given all of the legal and professional troubles that are butt-fucking you at the current moment."

I didn't have a response to that.

"What should we do, Stitcher? What's your recommendation?" The lady said.

Stitcher stepped back and thought about it for a moment. I could only guess at the horrors that he contemplated behind those dark, dead eyes. What was the worst that a ghoul could think up?

"Raymond, is it? Number one, tighten up the cocksucking security around here. Dr. Cassano here is a fucking biologist, not a Special Forces ninja. And tell those careless dog-fuckers at Medshine that they need to rethink their invoices."

"But what about her?" The lady insisted.

I looked at Stitcher and raised an eyebrow.

"Leave her with me. I need to talk to her. Alone." He looked at them like they were idiot deer in the road. "And leave the evidence here. Now fuck off before my goddamn head explodes."

CHAPTER 24

STITCHER HANDLED THE EVIDENCE WHILE he waited for the others to leave. I didn't know whether to feel guilty, stubborn, angry, or scared. I felt punchy with hopelessness.

The dead lawyer sniffed the specimen jar but shrugged. "Shit, my sniffer isn't what it once was."

I said nothing.

"What crap were you planning to pull with all of this?" he asked, genuinely curious.

"Let the world know what you're doing here. Explain how the food industry is profiting from the obesity epidemic. And how it turned overweight people into killers. And how it is feeding us our own fat."

Stitcher laughed. "Fuck me, Jesus. Elaine, you don't have a goddamn hint of a goddamn clue. You are *not* Upton Sinclair, here. More like Pee Wee Herman. You know there's a conspiracy, but you don't understand its context."

He set the sample bag on the table and leaned over to me. "I'm going to tell you the whole shitty deal. And if I think you're trouble after that, I call the cops and your fucking life is fucking over. Understand? But after you hear this, these asshat clients of mine won't have to worry about you, I bet." He gave a small smile.

What could I do? I nodded.

He waved his hand dramatically. "Yes, there *is* an obesity conspiracy. The various food and agriculture industries have deliberately created the obesity epidemic in the United States. And only because they are dumb motherfuckers who happened to get lucky, it's spilled into other countries. It's our best hope to save the world but the epidemic is only a means to an end."

I gave him a puzzled look and he waved his hand, signaling that I should hear him out.

"The epidemic really does have dozens of causes. That's the beauty of it. But here's the rub: The industry backed each one of those causes on purpose. Partly to deflect blame from the other causes. My favorite cause was cable TV sponsored with food commercials, the ultimate double whammy. But also because the cumulative effect of all those causes sped up the epidemic. You don't believe me?"

"Of course not," I said. "This is about increasing corporate profits. Why else would the industry go to all of that effort?"

"The food industry could have made a Jack the Ripper-sized killing doing any number of things. Our lobbyists could have won subsidies for vegetables or fruit or seafood, but we went for corn. Why? We fucking muscled corn in on the sweetener market in the 70s. You know how goddamned hard that was? You know how controversial that was inside the industry at the time? Corn is not a sexy food, but we had other reasons."

He relished my confusion. "The idea was to fatten people up enough that they would get liposuction every six months, like going to the fucking dentist, and be done with it. We increased plate size; increased serving size; and pushed higher calorie foods, low fat/high sugar, and diabetes medications to mitigate the negative side effects. Take a 100 calorie muffin from ten years ago and today it's 350 calories, easy, and it tastes like bacon. You name it; we pulled all the fucking strings."

This was something he and his undead conspirators had done to the living. It made him seem even more alien to me. "You're openly admitting that the food industry deliberately fattened the American people?" I asked in exasperation.

"Yes, same shit that we did with livestock. We can squeeze every possible bit of product from a cow or chicken, make every damn cell sing for us. When our farmers maximize white breast meat from chickens, we restrict their movement, alter their physiology. We even play with the lights and their sleep patterns to optimize production. This is the same shit.

"We spread vending machines everywhere, underwrote free antibiotics, backed diet fads doomed to fail, passed the Americans with Disabilities Act to add elevators and remove staircases. We funded the Food Network, lobbied the clothing industry to fatten up sizes, fought for trade policies that outsourced calorie burning manufacturing jobs, killed school recess and gym class, even backed TV shows starring fat actors. We backed every single contributor to the fucking epidemic."

My brain was spinning. Was he screwing with me? Was he killing time until the cops arrived? He had an ulterior motive; that was clear as day. But what? I was at his mercy, so why the need for games? Maybe it was the only mode he knew how to operate in. "What do you mean?"

"Every reason you ticked off on your reality TV show, we either got in on the ground floor or jumped on the bandwagon. It couldn't look like it was just the food doing it, right? Our shareholders would have shit a motherfucking brick. The best conspiracy is one that's out in the open but one nobody can blame you for. Who would be paranoid enough to think that someone would orchestrate all of that?"

He was pretty proud of himself. He probably thought he was telling the truth, but I could tell he was also winding me up, playing me. I just didn't know why.

"You'll never believe the shit we pulled." He waved his arms. "We paid off producers but not only for product placement. We paid them to put skinny people in action films, and to give Kevin James and Roseanne Barr TV shows to socialize obesity. Make you want to aspire to be the skinny, big screen hero, but connect with the fat-ass TV goof in between commercials for KFC. We even funded all those fucking vampire books and shows. Vampires are the perfect characters to help fatten up a population: They are impossibly thin, eat like sharks, and fuck everything that moves."

"I know you're dead," I blurted. I don't know where the hell that came from.

He was horrified. "What?"

"You have no body heat signature. Like a vampire. Several food industry executives, too. You're dead, John."

He didn't know what to do with that. He looked at me, then pushed his chair back and stood up quickly. He started pacing the room.

Until this point, I figured I was headed to jail. Now I was worried about surviving the night. And that fear gave me the courage, or stupidity, to keep talking. "What are you? A zombie? What the hell do you eat? Brains?"

Stitcher was distracted and for a second looked like he forgot that I was there. "No, zombies eat brains, don't be goddamn ridiculous. We're ghouls, we eat souls. Besides there's no such fucking thing as zombies."

"Oh, good. You just eat souls."

He waved his hand in circles. "Uh, psychic energy released from the recently deceased. Or, if we're being assholes, the not-yet-dead. But that's not important right now.

"Okay, okay. Shit," he muttered to himself. He looked at me again and then looked away. "Son of a cocksucker. You're good. Okay, I'm a ghoul. It's actually kind of funny; it's a business arrangement. We have—how shall I say—very long-lasting contracts. And for a very good reason."

"Including the one you sent to attack me in my own bedroom? What was his good reason?" I retorted.

Stitcher looked confused. "A fucking ghoul attacked you in your fucking house? Hey, you're not pulling my prick, are you? No, you're sure, okay, no, you're not. Tell me exactly what happened."

I told him the whole story.

"Mother. Fucker." He paced the length of the conference room. Once. Twice. He was pissed but also looked afraid.

He shook his head clear. "A beard? Sounds like Bradley. He isn't with me, I can guarantee you that. Shit. Shit!" He snapped his fingers and reached for his phone and then stopped. "I'm sorry. That was someone else's ghoul."

"Someone else's ghoul?"

He turned back to me. "The undead aren't always on the same side of any issue, any more than the living are. There are factions and shortsighted assholes everywhere, itching to fuck things up for everyone else. Bradley works for the chemical industry. They're a bunch of fucking strident true believers over there. Not nice guys like me. Some scientist or reporter or God forbid, a whistleblower, starts poking around, they just kill the son of a bitch."

"What does the chemical industry have to do with the food industry? Fertilizers?"

Stitcher spared me a glance before whipping out his phone. "It's a long story that you don't need to know and you goddamn don't want to know."

He paced for another half minute and banged out a text on his phone. He continued pacing until his phone buzzed with a reply. He read it and looked at me. "Shit. You're in danger. Bradley and his merry band of shitheads know you're here. We need to fucking leave right now."

"Other side? Why would we leave?" I wasn't following him anywhere. I'd rather deal with the cops, honestly, because right now, Stitcher looked afraid and that terrified me. I was going to end up as a partially decomposed corpse in a field somewhere.

Stitcher's face was lit with a tight, manic energy. It was the closest I had ever seen to happiness on his lined, gray visage. "I know how to shut up these cocksuckers. This could work out very nicely, if you survive. But I need to buy some time." He held out his hand. "You're coming with me."

Stitcher marched me past the guard and out the front entrance. The guard looked up and gave us a wary scowl. Maybe it had sunk in that his job security had been compromised because of my cheese stick heist.

The executive lady was waiting for us outside, checking her phone. She prepared to leave. "Are you taking her to the police?"

Stitcher stopped and fixed her with a hard stare. "No. This bitch is a bigger problem than I thought. And I'm fixing the problem."

The woman looked at him, and then me, and then back at him. I didn't have to pretend to look like I feared for my life.

"Do you know why this happened?" she asked curtly.

"Yes, I do. Because you didn't heed my fucking counsel. I told you to better disguise shit around here. Better security, put a damn sign on the fence, make it look legitimate."

This brought out an executive frown. "Those things cost too much."

"Then live with stowaways fucking breaking in," he replied as he pushed me towards his car.

"You talk to all of your clients that way?" I said after I got in his car.

He grinned. "Some of these dickheads actually appreciate my honesty."

He climbed in alongside of me and cut the plastic cuffs. He drove off the factory grounds. "We're going on a long ride," he said. "Make yourself comfortable. Where were we?"

I buckled my seat belt. "You were going to answer why you and your ghoul buddies want to fatten up humans like cattle, but only eat our souls."

"Let me set the stage. At the end of the 1960s the Green Revolution's food production gains peaked but global population kept booming. We knew there was no damn way the new fertilizers would keep up. On top of that, everyone, from the Nixon White House to the food industry to universities knew that the US was losing its edge. A Soviet scientist could run circles around an American one on math theory: the Viet Cong had outfought us, the Japanese were ready to pounce on our manufacturing, and the Chinese, although still starving, were about to French-kiss capitalism.

"The worst part is that we realized that as dumb as we were, we were losing to countries that were even fucking stupider. None of those countries had people who could do any better than us on food production. And we all read Rachel Carson's *Silent Spring* and shit our goddamn trousers. We were ruining the planet and killing ourselves and the whole thing was out of control. The industry paid guys to run simulations on big mainframes at land grant universities and they showed that we had crapped in our own nest so thoroughly that we didn't have the fucking brains to set it right in time."

"Sure, Nixon did what he could with the EPA and the war on cancer, but it was pissing in the wind. We needed something else and fast."

"We had this brilliant ace in the hole, but we didn't know how to use it. But by the early 1970s, with a baby bust and stagflation, our scientists cracked the code on the biggest genetics problem you've never heard of." Another deathly grin.

"And that is?"

"You know the Superman origin story? Alien baby falls to Earth, lands in a farm field in the American Midwest? Well, in reality, it was just a meteor carrying some frozen biological matter. Cells, DNA, not much like our own, but something our guys could work with. Instead of landing in fucking Farmer Joe's cornfield, the meteor hit a massive corporate farm in the Midwest in 1962. Our property, no need to tell the government. But it took until the early 1970s for our guys to grow a human-alien hybrid with advanced math and engineering capabilities."

The dead lawyer driving me somewhere in the middle of the night had just told me that aliens from outer space existed, and were agribusiness test tube babies. It was so ridiculous that I didn't care if he was driving me into the wilderness to leave my soul-eaten body in a ditch, I couldn't take it anymore.

Could a ghoul become deranged on narcotics? How would you test for that? "A human-alien hybrid? Are you pulling *my* dick, John?"

Stitcher adjusted his body behind the wheel. "They look completely human, but they're a lot smarter than us and a smidge or two on the autism spectrum. We breed alien hybrid eggheads to solve the world's problems, not find prom dates."

"What does the alien DNA do?"

He sighed. "I'm told it increases synaptic connections and growth, memory retention, and creative problem solving. But I tried to put one of these geniuses to work in my firm and she was a complete fucking blank wall, couldn't hack it. So results vary, apparently. You're not believing a goddamn word I say, are you?"

"Of course not. How many of them are there?" I imagined cloning vats and accelerated growth curves from sci-fi movies. I gamely expected him to say that everyone but me was an alien-hybrid body snatcher.

"Over three hundred thousand now. We farm out a few to infertile parents looking to adopt a smart baby. Another sign of the damn apocalypse is the growing number of infertile couples. But most of the hybrids are raised by people in the industry."

I looked at the trees whipping by in the dark. We were headed toward the Beltway. "Naturally, because they must be so cute."

"Ha-fucking-ha. We realized that the hybrids can't ingest the usual fats that humans need for brain development. We flailed around on what they needed until we realized that human adipose worked. But it is in scarce supply."

"In other words, you created alien cannibal nerds," I said.

"Exactly. If you want to create an army of scientific geniuses to solve the world's problems, how the hell do you feed them a special diet like that? Here's the food industry fucking unable to feed its own young." Stitcher shook his gray head. "In the mid 1970s, only middle-aged people—plus ten percent of the rest—were fat. We needed to ramp up adipose production like a motherfucker."

I said, "So you created the obesity epidemic that would kill people, worsen preventable diseases, cause disability and misery, and endanger children. Just to feed your alien babies with high SAT scores. Got it."

"Everything has a shitty tradeoff. My entire career is focused on mitigating the downside. The alternative was even worse, I shit you not."

I closed my eyes. The road hummed along under the Mercedes' wheels. I wanted to argue that the scientific impossibility of all this was beyond ludicrous, but I considered the health status of whom I would be arguing with.

I just wanted to bail out of the car and die in a ditch. But the scientist in me was spoiling for a fight. "So, are your alien cannibal nerds saving the world from itself yet?"

"Sometimes they're a barrel full of sweaty dicks who create more problems than they solve. Like that damn Fiesta additive. But they're starting to make progress. Problem is, the crisis is worse than we thought. Climate change plus environmental damage means as a race we could be out of business in less than a century."

We drove down the dark highway in silence for a minute. There was no moon or starlight and the darkness enveloped everything but the dashboard and the sweeping by of lane markers. I needed to find a way out. The situation only seemed to get crazier with every additional mile we put between us and DC.

"So, what's it like being dead?" Boy, that didn't sound half as chummy as I'd intended.

Stitcher shrugged. "Undead. Brain is still ticking, but the body is in kind of a stasis. You'd think I wouldn't feel anything, but I goddamn itch and tingle everywhere all the time. But it's better than the alternative."

I tried to imagine how dead muscle fibers and nerve endings could still operate without blood circulation, without cell replacement, and still respond to central nervous system signals. My scientist brain gave up.

"And how long do you ghouls last?"

Stitcher chuckled. "We're dying very slowly. Something about arresting cell decomposition. So, maybe thirty to fifty years? Depends on how much soul food I get."

I laughed, alone, and then realized he was serious.

He continued, "I died in 1985, when my bitch wife smothered me with a pillow while I was passed out drunk. God, we were a couple of self-absorbed yuppie assholes with too much money and no fucking sense.

Couldn't even prosecute her for murder when I was revived and walking around within a week."

"Who revived you?"

He sighed. "My law firm. Partners didn't want the extra workload, couldn't replace my expertise. My partnership agreement had some fine print about post-mortem work arrangements. I've never asked how they did it, probably black magic or some creepy biological shit. Anyway, death made me clean up my act. I became a divorced workaholic. Picked up where I left off and kept going. Started my own firm in the late 90s, when K Street really started booming."

I'm Catholic and don't know what the Church's position is on the undead. It would probably consider Stitcher an abomination. I blurted, "Are you going to kill me?"

In the weak dashboard glow I could see the shock on his gaunt face. "No one is better qualified than a ghoul to say that a death sentence is never called for."

I nodded and stared out the window at the black tree silhouettes whipping past the nearly black sky. The blacks all blurred. "Then where are you taking me?"

"To meet the alien cannibal nerds. Before they try anything so stupid and counterproductive that they force me to rip their throats open and fuck their voice boxes with my moldy cock. Now get some sleep."

The idea of snoozing, with news of an environmental crisis sitting in my frontal lobe, while my undead abductor drove me all over hell's half acre, was ridiculous. Except that it was very late after a highly stressful night and before long the green digits of the dashboard clock swam in front of my eyes.

I woke up in the Mercedes. It was empty and parked in a rest area. It was off I-81 near Marion, VA, according to my phone's GPS. We were parked far enough back that the drone of the highway was distant through a thick median of trees. The dark leaf canopy overhead added to the gloom of a foggy morning. The blanket of moisture had obscured a sunrise and left the world murky.

I smelled coffee. A hot Styrofoam cup was in the cup holder by my elbow, along with a greasy bag of fast food breakfast. Was Stitcher messing with me?

As I drank the coffee, I spotted Stitcher behind the restroom blockhouse, pacing with his phone pinned to his ear. He gestured angrily with his free hand, then straightened his back and stared off into the distance as he let the other person get a word in.

I rubbed my eyes and got out of the car. It had been a long time since I had seen a bathroom. When I finished, Stitcher was waiting for me by the Mercedes.

"We're south of Blacksburg," I said. "You drove me all the way out here to prove that you're not lying?"

"Well, there's a shitload more to it than that," he replied. "Did you eat yet?"

At first, I didn't know what he was talking about until he motioned inside the car. "The fast food?"

He looked incredulous. "I didn't have a lot of options when I stopped at Big Bart's Fucking Gas 'N Gulp."

We got back on the highway, and I shamelessly ate the breakfast sandwich. It was delicious, and I savored every gram of saturated fat.

We drove on through the misty morning. I emailed work that I wasn't coming in and Lyle that I was fine. He hadn't risked emailing or texting me, I noticed.

To pass the time, Stitcher asked me questions about Charlie, which would have freaked me out just yesterday. But now it seemed like a pleasant diversion from the other ludicrous, terrible topic on tap.

I tried to steer the conversation away from the custody hearing. I didn't want him thinking I had a reason to desperately avoid getting into trouble. Every interaction between us felt like a protracted negotiation.

He stuck to rural roads and lightly traveled highways, headed toward Knoxville. Traffic picked up as we approached the city, but Stitcher took the exit to Jefferson City. We got caught in the early morning rush hour on the Andrew Johnson Highway until we made it to the rural stretches of the western side and into a town called New Market.

Stitcher pulled into a place called Agricultural Solutions, which was housed in a single story office building set far back from the road behind a line of pines.

He turned off the ignition. "This is where we grow the aliens. We also employ a lot of them here. But they're touchy as hell about calling them that."

I nodded and got out of the car.

A human-seeming receptionist greeted us and printed out a visitor badge for me. She had a thick Tennessee drawl. I wondered if the aliens did as well. I caught Stitcher's attention and indicated the receptionist with a questioning look.

He shook his head.

After I had a visitor badge, Stitcher ushered me past offices and cubicles. A guard scanned our barcodes before allowing us to enter the lab wing, which occupied the back half of the building.

The walls of each lab were glass. I could see everything going on just by walking down the hallway. There was a full-blown chemical lab. I didn't see any creatures with tentacles or bug eyes anywhere. Stitcher gave me a funny look as he saw me peeking and ushered me to the next one. "It's proprietary work."

At the end of the hallway was a vast lab that ran the width of the building. Along the far wall was a morgue locker. A lab worker wearing surgical scrubs and a mask opened one of the doors and pulled out a tray. Instead of a corpse, inside was a tank of liquid and something approximately the size of a squash. The worker took pictures and recorded notes on his tablet before sliding the tank back inside. The squash was hooked to a heart rate and brain wave monitor that all appeared baby-human normal.

"The hybrids are grown from seeds. At some point, the fruit-like thing becomes a womb and somehow, the baby turns mammalian," Stitcher informed me. "The alien DNA and ours complement one another during gestation."

I gasped. "That's an artificial womb. How is that possible? How do they avoid intraventricular hemorrhage?" It was a common condition that occurred for babies incubated for long periods while still developing. No machine had yet hit the sweet spot of the right blood pressure and a sufficient flow for a delicate growing fetus that needed lots of nutrients all the time. Nothing could replicate a real womb yet, at least that I knew of.

Stitcher shrugged. "Beats the shit out of me. All I know is they started with some neonatal technology and worked their way up from there. They also burned through enough fucking cash to finance a Third World country."

"What do they do when the infants are born?"

"The adult hybrids adopt them. They're all sterile anyway, so it's a good cover."

I said. "Do they marry other people? Do their spouses know the truth about these kids?"

Stitcher gave me an odd look. "No. They decided it was better to marry each other. And from what I hear, they have no libido, no romance. It's just a convenient living situation. Anyway, who's to say there's anything wrong with a loveless, sexless marriage? Certainly not the guy murdered by his wife."

"I want to talk to them," I said.

Stitcher nodded. "I figured." He made a call as we continued walking.

Stitcher knocked on an office door, labeled Dr. Donald Meers, and opened it.

Dr. Meers was in his late forties, with salt and pepper hair and reading glasses balanced on the end of his nose. He looked vaguely Asian, or maybe Native American, but honestly, I couldn't peg what his ethnicity was. Anglo-Saxon, Asian, Slavic, or a mix of them all.

He looked more or less normal, at least normal for a work-obsessed scientist. No tentacles, eyestalks, or gaping maws in his abdomen with rows of tiny shark teeth. His skin was typical. His ears, nose, eyelids and mouth seemed to be the right sizes.

His office was small but highly organized. The walls were covered in printouts from project planning software with milestones, goals, and other notes. The fake wood grain desk was devoid of any paper.

"Don, this is Dr. Elaine Cassano," Stitcher said. "Elaine, Dr. Donald Meers, lead chemist here at AgSol. Don was one of the first hybrids."

Meers smiled somewhat carefully, shook hands and offered us both a seat. "Dr. Cassano, Mr. Stitcher says you are in the loop now and that you have questions."

"Um, yes." What I really wanted was a tissue sample from him. "I want to know everything, I guess. Your dietary needs, how you were raised, where you went to school, how well you did academically."

Meers folded his hands. "I was raised in Newton, Massachusetts. I was a Westinghouse Scholar and I had near-perfect SATs. I majored in math at MIT, PhD in biochemistry from Stanford, postdoctoral work in the industry before coming here. I'm married to a chemist named Amy and we have twin boys, aged ten."

"And you eat human fat, adipose tissue, to stay alive?"

Dr. Meers nodded, smiling mildly. "Yes. There are unique enzymes in my stomach that cannot break down other fats into the appropriate compounds for brain development and nourishment. This is the only solution we have currently. We are testing artificial adipose compounds, but we are probably eight years or so away from having a production-ready version."

"Why do you work for the program that produced you?" I asked.

"The mission, Dr. Cassano. The humans who produced me only had a vague understanding of how inadequate society is to meet these challenges we face. Our research here has shown that without me and my kin, we would be even further behind than we already are."

It should have sounded arrogant, and self-serving, but his even-keeled earnestness about it wouldn't let me think that these claims were just a bunch of ego blustering. I have been well steeped in arrogant scientists for decades and didn't sense the ego that usually shone right through statements like that.

Dr. Meers continued, "Most of the brightest innovations have come from us. We are working in several different fields. Saving a world is not just a matter of mastering pollution abatement, or closing the hole in the ozone. We accelerated the development of web browsers and information networks in the 90s, massively increased battery capacity in the 2000s, lowered power requirements of computer chips in this past decade, discovered how to mass-produce algae-based jet fuel and new MS treatments that have yet to come to market. We are needed everywhere. We need more of us."

"How exactly are you better than human?" I asked, still marveling that I sounded crazy but everyone else was taking this seriously.

But Dr. Meers continued without hesitation. "Our cognitive abilities are about twenty percent greater on average. Synaptic responses, memory retention, abstract thinking are all in the top tenth of a percentile of the population in the developed world. We excel at math, science, and higher-level reasoning."

"Is there proof of this I could examine?"

Stitcher and Dr. Meers exchanged a look, waiting for the other to object. Finally Stitcher nodded and tapped a note into his phone. "I can show you some of it before we leave."

Dr. Meers continued. "And this has been proven now that my cohort has reached mid-career stage. The number of patents filed per person is two standard deviations above the mean for other highly-educated people like us."

"And to fuel your species you need the United States to have a massive and destructive obesity epidemic," I said. "So you created one."

Stitcher clenched his jaw, but didn't say anything.

Dr. Meers nodded. "At this point, yes. It's the only way to feed ourselves."

I glared at the bastard, thinking about the desperate people in that town hall back in Grand Forks. I could tell he didn't mean ill, but his nonchalance was infuriating.

Stitcher folded his arms. "Dr. Cassano is not happy that you did this."

Dr. Meers nodded. "Oh. If only our collection efforts had kept up with the production function, people wouldn't suffer as many side effects of obesity. In the mid 1990s, we predicted that liposuction visits would become common. But they never caught on as we expected. We, uh, underestimated the social acceptance of obesity and the resistance to minor surgical procedures."

"Now we are pursuing pharmacological solutions." He gave a little defeated shrug. "It's not going well. But Mr. Stitcher has reminded us that we often miss the 'important fucking consequences of our actions.'"

I laughed. Either Meers was really dense or he had a dry sense of humor. His smile suggested the latter. God, was I starting to believe this whole tale? "You couldn't stop the epidemic if you wanted to, could you?"

Dr. Meers shook his head. "The business model behind the epidemic is very strong. It's not just the food industry. Many industries have substantial investments in obesity mitigation or expansion and they are shrewd enough to repel any threat to those profits."

"Dr. Meers has earned an MBA in his off hours to get a better handle on this," Stitcher added. "I predict within a year, he'll want a damn political science degree, as well."

Dr. Meers stared at Stitcher for a long second. And then the practiced smile came back. "You're joking, but that's not a bad idea."

He looked at me. "There are many perspectives we have missed. We can build a better phone, but changing the economy, or the environment, is still somewhat beyond our reach. We are working hard to improve on this. Mr. Stitcher has been a great guide, even if he can be rough at times."

Stitcher couldn't help but smile, pulling taut the skin covering his skull. "Thanks, Donny."

Dr. Meers continued, "We think that focusing on the environment may be the best approach to controlling the obesity epidemic and stalling global climate change. Specifically, the energy production costs of unhealthy food. But changing that requires a political and marketing tool set that we haven't mastered, yet."

The phone rang and Dr. Meers peered at the number as if it were a storm brewing. "I need to take this call."

Stitcher stood and I followed suit. We shook hands with Meers and left his office.

"So what do you think of Dr. ET?" Stitcher said.

"I'd like a DNA sample," I replied.

"Not a fucking chance in hell."

"Then I need to see some proof," I retorted. "So far, all you've shown me is a strange lab and a fairly normal-seeming researcher."

Stitcher started walking. "Just come down the hall here."

CHAPTER 25

W E RELOCATED TO A CONFERENCE room at the end of the hall that had cheap wood paneling and a stack of cardboard file boxes on a round table. Stitcher closed the door and began rifling through them.

He tossed a manila envelope down in front of me. "Look at that while I dig up the rest."

There were black and white photographs inside. A blackened crater in a horizon-swallowing wheat field, wheat threshers parked nearby. Another black and white photo of men in 1960s eyeglasses circling the crater in ancient radiation suits. A yellowed page of typewritten longitude and latitude coordinates and corporate contact information. Another black and white photo of a gloved hand holding up part of a meteorite. Another photo showing tiny seeds inside the rock.

"How does the government not know about this?"

Stitcher laughed. "The government doesn't know shit unless someone fucking staples it to a tax return. The meteor was probably too small for NORAD to track. And no one screws with a wheat field on a corporate farm."

He tossed me another folder, a dossier on Dr. Meers. Photos of a jury-rigged incubator, of him as a baby sleeping in his crib in the lab, one photo for every three months of his first three years.

Several typed reports by doctors who were concerned about his weight and diet. No one knew how to fix his lack of weight gain. More reports that detailed the variety of solutions that failed. Baby formula, dairy, baby food, nothing worked.

They worried about the lack of a mother and got started on an adoption program, which was a bit tough since none of the scientists back then were women. One scientist approached his wife about adoption, and she promptly divorced him: What else would a stay-at-home wife think caused a husband to suddenly have a baby to care for?

There was another memo on experimenting with feeding little Donald Meers various animal tissues. Even bovine brain matter but no success. They were worried that the baby's brain development would be impaired. Then they tried human adipose after several rounds of heated debates about the ethics of doing so. Little Donald responded and he went on a human fat diet.

His childhood records, which Stitcher handed me, were a series of high grades, glowing psychologist reports and lots of promising signs, all with an undertone of worry about his diet. One thing kept bugging me about the file as I paged through year after year of reports, beside the fact that I was beginning to believe all of this. I couldn't put my finger on it until I reached the report on his physical at age eighteen.

He was identified as Subject Number 63.

I turned on Stitcher. "You lost sixty-two others first? You bastards."

Stitcher grimaced. "What choice did we have? Make a hybrid lab rat, first? Spend fifty years figuring it out very cautiously? The world doesn't have that kind of time."

"This is the biggest scandal I've ever heard of," I said. "Endangering the health of millions, no matter whatever noble purpose you have. Playing God to save the world but not having a clue how to do it. This makes the tobacco industry look like preschoolers! And you think I'm going to walk away from this information?"

"Yes, I do. Because you're a good person, Elaine. Good intentions with good results and some unintended consequences. Like the scientists here."

"At least sixty lives. Did you ever think of those?"

"We've raised hundreds of thousands of these beings. They are making the world a better place every damn day. Medical devices, disease treatments, better technology. You know how many lives have been saved or improved because of this program? God, you're killing me with your sanctimoniousness. You can see what we do here is valuable. If you're not fully convinced now, this should do it. I'm going to return calls to try and save your life while you read it."

He dumped what looked like a dissertation manuscript in my lap and headed out the door. The lock clicked in place behind him. *Still a prisoner,*

I thought, but realized he was also securing the roomful of boxes with trade secrets, evidence of alien life, and proof of a massive industry conspiracy.

Knowing how fast Stitcher talked, I cracked open the cover page of what was titled *Report on Project Rogers*, and tried to read as much as I could before he returned.

1964. A trio of agriculture researchers present a series of charts at an industry conference about global threats. They project pollution, climate, and toxicity into the future, and conclude that the planet will become uninhabitable even without nuclear war. The industry's own products and other externalities, like animal manure, are helping to poison the planet. Even worse, the fertilizer-heavy methods are a temporary fix to crop yields and will ultimately backfire unless something else can be developed.

After the three scientists are driven out of the industry, the leading agriculture companies decide to study the habitation issue more closely, accelerate fertilizer development, and pursue crop maximization strategies. The food industry streamlines production to maximize calorie and nutrition delivery through heavy-duty processing, just in case food shortages happen.

1968. Using Great Society grants, industry researchers are appalled to learn the effects of industrial production on the mostly poor people living near factories or who work in them. The carcinogenic and toxic exposures are correlated with a higher incidence of diseases, disabilities, low birth weight babies, and other maladies. And because of air, ground, and water pollution, the effects are spreading into wealthier communities. And these are not effects that can be cleaned up easily.

A small group located near Los Alamos Laboratory, and focusing on complexity science, has honed estimates of a habitation doomsday clock. They estimate that in less than a hundred years, by 2050, the planet will be on an unstoppable march toward desolation. Many species, including possibly humans, could be on the way to becoming extinct due to resource exhaustion. One of the key drivers of these estimates is that the rate of discovery of problems has outstripped the ability of humanity to solve them. Extrapolating this rate of problem discovery and comparing to the rate of technological development and innovation, the doomsday klatch is convinced that something drastic needs to happen to change that.

After much internal debate, industry executives decide to have agriculture expert Earl Butz approach the incoming Nixon administration with these problems, which are beyond the ability of any one industry to solve. The doomsday guys now estimate that even with the federal government on board, disaster will likely not be averted.

1969. Right as Neil Armstrong steps on the Moon, the Nixon Administration informs industry execs that the government will ready a massive change in priorities and funding to face the toxicity crisis. They will divert budget resources from NASA to overhaul health insurance, improve science education, speed cancer research, regulate pollution, and study climate change. Nixon himself even plans to cool off tensions with the Soviets and China to create the breathing room to tackle these problems, because both those nations will exceed America's contribution to toxicity in coming decades if the Cold War doesn't end soon.

The doomsday klatch knows that shifting around budget priorities will be necessary but not sufficient. They estimate that only an army of geniuses has a chance to beat the toxicity deadline. They start The Rogers Project in honor of Steve Rogers, Captain America, a soldier made better than human through science.

1971. First Project Rogers report. It includes a short history of the meteorite discovery, the DNA analysis of the seeds and attempts to grow a human-alien hybrid that converts from a seed-embryo into a mammal.

1973. A progress report on the production line. Subject 63 has been successfully adopted, but ten babies are due to be 'born' in the next six months. The memo discusses adoption rules, their special dietary needs, and the pros and cons of giving the children to families who don't know their secret. A second hybrid production line opens in Palo Alto, California.

1975. Estimated total production is 200 babies, limited only by supply of special dietary needs. Industry leaders agree to manufacture and harvest more adipose tissue that will also maximize profit margins on a variety of food product lines. Secretary of Agriculture Earl Butz has taken the lead in spearheading the 'production' of human adipose through farming and dietary policy changes at the federal level.

1979. Progress report on Subject 63. His health is poor, as he suffers from migraine headaches, random skin rashes, and allergies. A week of testing at the Tennessee facility suggests a number of tweaks to genes to improve the immune system response.

His grades are stellar, except for English literature, where he struggles with literary interpretation. His teacher has suggested that he may suffer from learning disabilities like Aspberger's Syndrome, but the Meers, his adoptive parents, decide to avoid any treatments. His social skills are subpar, but his IQ tests are in the 150s.

1982. Annual production estimate is 2,743 spread across five sites, including four in the United States and one in Brazil.

Subject 63 plays chess, the violin, and Dungeons and Dragons. The program director notes that he felt uncomfortable about the role-playing game and suggested that the Meers take it away. In response, Subject 63 invents his own role-playing game based on H.P. Lovecraft's Cthulhu Mythos, which causes even more concern, especially given the context of his purpose in life.

1984. The industry provides beginning funding for the Santa Fe Institute that takes over the complexity science work done at Los Alamos when the staff leave, including the secret doomsday clock, which itself is built on early work in complexity science.

1987. Subject 63 graduates from high school early with many honors, few friends, and no girlfriends. Annual medical tests at the Tennessee facility find that he has a zero sperm count. After much debate, Subject 63 is told of the circumstances of his birth and is intrigued rather than upset, much to the relief of his parents.

The industry quietly doubles its funding on the doomsday efforts, including Project Rogers, the Santa Fe Institute doomsday work, and agricultural innovations. The hole in the ozone and African starvation have spooked the remaining skeptical industry executives and are referred to as the Sputnik Moment. What was abstract has now become real, one executive tells his counterparts at a secret meeting in Seattle that June.

1990. The annual production estimate plateaus at 4,900 babies due to lack of parents willing to adopt and funding constraints due to industry consolidation. Donald Meers agrees to adopt twin subjects and marry a female adult subject when he earns his PhD in two years.

1994. A security breach at the Massachusetts facility leads to an OSHA investigation. Discovery of Project Rogers is barely averted due to the work of an industry lawyer named John Stitcher.

The failure of the U.S. to participate in the Rio environmental talks causes the doomsday clock to move closer to midnight. Project Rogers staff begin contemplating ways to accelerate either production or the education of their subjects, or both, since time may run out sooner than anticipated.

1996. Liposuction-induced adipose harvesting estimates are too high for the third year in a row. Project leadership discusses alternative supply methods. Industry lobbyists promote tax subsidies and insurance discounts for liposuction procedures, but the public remains wary.

The closure of the Congressional Office of Technology Assessment convinces the industry executives that the government is a lost cause in addressing the various environmental crisises, other than to accelerate the obesity epidemic and give the industry a freer hand.

2000. The industry backs both presidential candidates, feeling that it can't lose between an environmentalist and a free market corporate guy. It's just a matter of tweaking strategy depending on who wins.

2001. The Project begins using results from the Human Genome Project to improve the DNA mating that is required to make the human and alien DNA work better together. Much of the testing can be done virtually in a server farm rather than on actual embryos.

2007. The first generation of subjects have all adopted two hybrid children each. Annual production increased to 10,000 given expected adoption rate amongst future adult subjects. The Rogers Project is now 40% percent staffed by former subjects thanks to the recruiting work of Dr. Meers and his wife.

2012. The Project plans a large expansion of hybrid production. The industry wants to double the number of hybrids working in the industry due to new concerns about carcinogenic chemical contamination of the production chain. They are scared by the trans-fat near-miss and want to catch it before the public begins demanding tighter government regulation of food products.

The obesity epidemic is in full swing and the adipose harvesting is catching up. Medical waste is not a sexy topic for the press so harvesting techniques and adipose recycling have stayed under the radar of public notice. The number of teenagers receiving liposuction has quadrupled in a decade and the industry continues to lobby for more press coverage as free advertising. Once again, the industry rejects an idea from the hybrid scientists to tap into the adipose of the deceased through funeral homes.

2015. Dr. Donald Meers, AKA Subject 63, is named senior scientist at AgSol. His children enter college and begin internships at a Route 128 biotech firm outside Boston, the tip of the second generation joining the cause.

CHAPTER 26

I CLOSED THE FOLDER. IT WAS so quiet I heard a bird chirping outside the window. The door opened and I looked up at my undead captor. He tried to read my face, see what I was thinking. I had no idea myself.

I tried to cut through the fear and surprise, and focus on facts and inferences. There was too much material here to be fake. Four decades of reports and photos. A stunning collection of proprietary industry secrets. Okay, so I believed that this was all legit. The chances that it was *all* fake were too low. I'm not the type to believe that the Moon landing was staged.

Deep breath. Next, I thought about strategy. Stitcher had shown me his entire hand. What was his angle in doing that? There was no way they would just let me walk away from this and call a reporter. The other shoe hadn't dropped; I was still a captive and he must want something from me. "Now what?" I asked.

"Here's the deal," Stitcher said. "You don't tell a fucking soul about Project Rogers. You will not out us, or the true causes behind the obesity epidemic. Not a damn word. Because you risk undermining the only viable attempt to stop the environmental crisis. There's nothing even close to being as effective as Project Rogers in avoiding a habitation apocalypse. If you piss in the industry's Cheerios, the industry can take its lumps and survive. But the human race can't. Keep your piehole shut for *them*."

I opened my mouth to respond but he held up a hand. "Now, you may think the world needs to be alerted about the environmental crisis. You may even suspect that the industry is covering up the problem, or slow-walking the solutions, to protect its profit margins and business models. You may think that if only you or some other truth-teller could tell the world, we could mobilize even more resources."

I pursed my lips. "Yes. Why not?"

"Because we already have. And the world not only ignored us, the backlash set us back five years. God love him, but Al Gore and his motherfucking film did as much harm as good because it scared the piss out of your everyday asshole, convinced him that these problems were real and fucking insurmountable. The asshole, he can't handle that, so he shoots the messenger, votes the messenger out of office, and defunds the messenger's projects."

I could tell from his blazing eyes that this time, John Stitcher wasn't lying. I could imagine the kind of trouble this had given him, the messes he scrambled to fix in the aftermath, and while, even though he loved every second of fixing a mess, the larger mess left him horrified. Yes, that was it. He was scared.

Lyle and I could go public tomorrow and get dismissed as cranks for just explaining a third of this whole mess: the obesity conspiracy, or the alien cannibal nerds, or the whatever he called it—the habitation apocalypse. The last chunk would be the worst because everyone could sense that to some extent and Stitcher was right: Most people desperately didn't want to face that reality.

It was like confronting the icky truth that your parents had sex regularly, or the sobering fact that one day, you would die in pain, fear, and probably panic. The natural reaction was to angrily and violently shove these reminders aside, and to slap down whoever brought them up. He could be right that broadcasting the truth would block their ability to act on it.

But I know myself pretty well and I would just see industry secrets and scandal bottled up inside me. That made me an accessory, at least in my own mind. "You want me to live a lie," I said. Which he had to know was a non-starter for me. I still didn't see where he was headed with all of this.

"Jesus Christ, it's not a lie. Think of it as a non-disclosure agreement," he said. "The world ending is a proprietary trade secret."

I smiled. "And if I talk, I go to jail for the break-in, my career is trashed and my life is over. So, you expect me to go back to approving projects that I know are headed in the wrong direction on addressing obesity, without uttering a peep?" I shook my head.

He raised an eyebrow and shook his head violently. "Fuck that. We need your help. You could point all of these researchers in the right directions. We need a head of research—"

I belly-laughed. Couldn't help it. "After all of this, you want me to join your cabal?"

Stitcher nodded. "You know what we're doing here. You've seen what happens when these lovable shitheads are left unsupervised. I'm tired of kicking them in the nuts every six months. No one can pick apart cutting edge research like you. If you don't like the ethical or moral implications, give us alternatives. They need someone here who can blunt their illogical ideas, give them a research agenda, a vision."

"Yeah, until some corporate executive orders me to document how fast food is healthier than fruits and vegetables. And then, if I threaten to quit, it's back to threatening me with felony charges and taking my son away, right?"

Stitcher gave me a look. "No, it probably means the chemical industry assholes suck down your soul and your official cause of death will be something like an aneurysm."

I swallowed. "Oh."

"Elaine, this is how I can protect you and exploit you at the same time. We're not going to make you pimp industry marketing bullshit. We have buy-in from the CEOs all across the industry. There's no cheap-shit PR angle to this job. That's what other people do, like your baby daddy. You just save the fucking planet, that's all."

I replied, "Okay, so best case is I manage a bunch of eccentric, extraterrestrial scientists. The worst case is I become some industry stooge. Just to avoid prison and possibly having my soul eaten by assholes."

Stitcher half-smiled. "And to gain custody of your son."

It took me a second to make sure I heard that correctly. In my head, Charlie lived back in a world without undead soul eaters, an environmental crisis, and alien seed pods falling down from outer space. And then it clicked. "You brought those industry lawyers in to wreck my custody case."

Before my anger could hit second gear, the old bastard looked genuinely hurt. "I didn't. Legalistic headbutting isn't my style, is it? No, those gold-plated, pig-humping lobbyists did this on their own dime. They think they can protect the industry from more bad press by squeezing you where it hurts. You've pissed off some touchy fucking brainless motherfuckers. They will destroy your case or run you out of money, believe me. I can help you here, Elaine, but it means pulling you out of the industry's asshole for good."

"But caging them doesn't automatically win me custody. Bob won't give up until we're both bankrupt or he wins. What are you going to do, bribe the judge?" As soon as I said that, I wished I hadn't.

But Stitcher waved my joke away. "You watch too much TV. I already had Bob fired; I called his firm's partners while you were sleeping in the car."

My mouth went dry. "You had him fired?"

"Christ, Elaine, you look sad to hear it."

"He's my son's father. That's going to hurt Charlie and me, indirectly." It also upped the stakes of this offer. If I turned down Stitcher's offer, Bob would remain unemployed, I would go to jail, and Charlie would be doubly screwed.

Stitcher nodded. "I'll offer Bob a fucking simple choice: stay unemployed and probably lose any custody, or accept your generous custody offer and I may, eventually, find him a new job, if he stops being an asshole. One where he can be of more use to me. Do you want to hear the pitch? It's fucking brilliant, win-win all round, unicorns giving everyone blowjobs."

I hung my head and shook it. "No, I've heard enough." I lifted my head and looked into his twinkling, dead eyes.

Stitcher folded his hands. "So, Elaine, is this the beginning of something truly beautiful or the beginning of something truly terrible?"

CHAPTER 27

ARLY SUMMER IN THE WASHINGTON area can be wet and relatively chilly. Middle and late summer are typically dry, but during the last vestiges of spring, nature loads up the water table before that happens.

The region was into its third day of constant rain. Old Town Alexandria was flooding, the Mall was a mud pit, and the Beltway had been jammed 24/7. The Nationals hadn't played since the previous weekend. But as I pulled up to Bob's house in my new minivan, the sun broke through the storm clouds and the rain became a sun shower.

Bob's house was a former model home with a three car garage and over three thousand square feet of overpriced living space. It sat on a wooded cul-de-sac with other, smaller McMansions. Five years ago, when Bob flashed the homebuilder's brochure and his voluptuous girlfriend in front of the custody judge, I knew my case was screwed.

When I arrived, a real estate agent in a poncho was hammering a For Sale sign into the front yard. Bob wasn't selling the house: the bank had foreclosed on it and he was being evicted. He must have been living close to the line, and losing his job had sunk him.

I backed my new minivan up to the three-car garage. The door of the larger bay opened as I put the beast in park. Other parents had told me that carting a ten-year-old around required a minivan or an SUV these days. It sure came in handy to move him back to my house. I used some of the signing bonus from AgSol to buy it.

My shaggy-haired, chubby son met me the second I stepped from the van. He had a goofy grin on his face. I gave him a big warm hug right there in the sparkling rain.

"Is this yours?" he said, indicating the minivan.

"Uh-huh. I have to look like the rest of the soccer moms," I replied.

"But I don't play soccer."

"I already signed you up."

He frowned and I could see his wheels turning. Everything was changing for him. *Dad sells the house, Mom buys a new car, and I have to play soccer this summer*, he was thinking. I expected him to say something, but he stayed quiet. *Good move kid. Roll with the punches for now because you never know what's coming down the road next.*

He asked, "So, when do you start your new job?"

"After Labor Day," I said. "I'll work from home over the summer. But pretty much the whole summer is just you and me getting set up in Knoxville."

I had accepted Stitcher's offer for the position of research director at AgSol. Dr. Meers was happy to relinquish the job after the Fiesta Chip debacle. He wanted to get back to his lab work on a synthetic alternative to the adipose that kept him alive. He would transition back to the lab after his kids returned to college in August.

AgSol had offered me enough latitude that I wouldn't be a corporate drone. I had a plan to expand the number of hybrid babies born in the facilities while finding an alternative diet supplement to adipose. I was intent on stopping the industry from feeding the obesity epidemic without jeopardizing our special scientists. This would free up enough of the industry's resources to target promising research avenues. I figured I could double their return on investment in ten years.

Charlie scowled, trying to piece together our short-term future. "And you already quit your other job at The Lab?" The Lab was how he had referred to ARS for years now. When he was much younger he had dutifully memorized that Mom was a scientist and worked at The Lab, even though the terms meant nothing to him. The shorthand had stuck.

In fact, I had turned in my badge at ARS yesterday. There was no going-away party; Jeannie processed my exit paperwork with all the personal warmth of a bitter receptionist forced to delay her lunch half an hour.

Jim took me out to lunch in College Park. But even that was uncomfortable. He didn't understand why I was ditching the government for industry. He thought I was selling out to the enemy, but couldn't come out and say it.

What could I say? After what Stitcher had showed me, I knew the truth and I couldn't ignore it. AgSol was doing the wrong things for the right reasons. I could help them start doing the right things. And there was nothing else I could do from inside the government. It was truly a soul-sucking option in every sense of the word.

Charlie's belongings were piled in the three-car garage. Besides Bob's blue Corvette, a monstrous dark-green SUV, and Charlie's dusty ten-speed bike, there was little else in the cavernous space.

We loaded the minivan. These things had so much space. I even found a way for his bike to fit. He would need it a fair bit this summer.

"Is your Dad home?" I asked in a puzzled tone. Of course he was. Both cars were here. But I couldn't believe he would hide from us like this.

"Yeah," Charlie replied, leading me through the garage into the house. "He's been packing. He's been all mopey and depressed."

I nodded, taken aback by Charlie sounding so mature. When had that happened? Maybe there were times when he was more adult than either Bob or me. Especially in the last couple of months.

We walked into the giant kitchen. It was already staged, as there was a bowl of fruit standing lonely sentry on the empty granite counter top. Neither Bob nor Charlie ate fruit, I was sure.

Bob was in the two-story living room packing up family photos. He was wearing an old t-shirt and jeans, which did less to conceal his girth than the business suits I was used to seeing him in.

"Hey," he said, with a low-wattage smile I bet he used only for networking with people he found no use for. Since this was mainly for Charlie's benefit, I played along.

"You're really selling this place?"

Bob shrugged. "I don't need so much space with you not here, pal."

I was tempted to gloat. Stitcher had made sure Bob got an offer he couldn't refuse. Still, I could see the hurt in his eyes as Charlie stepped over a box to hug him.

"We're going to take off, Dad," Charlie said. "I'm all packed up."

Bob ruffled his hair. "I should've got you a haircut. Why don't you go take another look at your room and make sure you got everything."

Charlie nodded, looked at me, and headed to the staircase by the front door. He understood: Dad and Mom had to talk; best to get scarce.

"You must have friends in high places," Bob said to me once Charlie's footsteps receded up the stairs. He folded his arms.

I shrugged. He was looking for a fight and I didn't want to indulge his sour grapes. It wouldn't end well, not least because I wouldn't let him ruin this joyous day with his bullshit.

Bob shook his head and I was surprised to see he was tearing up. Then he laughed. "So, you're no longer slumming in government, Charlie says. You've finally joined the good guys."

God, he couldn't help himself. He needed to score some points or something. I wanted to tell him it didn't have to be this way, but that wouldn't have helped.

"We'll both be able to contribute more to his college fund," I replied. There was an awkward pause.

"Can you wait outside when I say goodbye to him?" Bob asked.

"Take as much time as you need," I said gently. What I thought was, *You bastard, go have just a taste of what I went through five years ago.* So, what? I'm a terrible person. I thought I had permanently destroyed my tear ducts when I had to send away my five-year-old son.

Bob smiled genuinely for once. "Thank you. And we're still sticking to the visitation schedule?"

I nodded. Charlie would stay with his dad one weekend a month and odd school days off when I had to fly to the other AgSol sites in Chicago and Palo Alto. Our arrangement was quite convenient for me, actually.

"I think Charlie is waiting on the stairs," I whispered. Louder, I said, "Take care, Bob."

He nodded and the tears welled up again. He put his hands on his hips like a superhero and nodded. I headed for the garage as he cleared his throat and called for Charlie. The sun shower continued and my minivan glistened.

Five minutes later Charlie climbed into the front passenger seat. He was a bit snuffly and his eyes were red-rimmed. I ruffled his hair and said nothing. He gave me a hug.

He looked at me, smiled sadly, and reached for the seat belt to buckle up.

"Charlie, dear, you're not big enough for the front seat."

He looked crestfallen. "I weigh enough, Dad says."

I bit my tongue. "You're too young. Your bone structure isn't ready for the front seat. Move it."

"Hey, what's this?" he said as he buckled into the second row passenger seat. He noticed the orange bathing suit with flames on the hips sitting on the seat behind me.

I grinned and looked at him in the rearview mirror. "Your swim team uniform."

"Swim team?" He held up the swimsuit in abject disgust. Then he swallowed. "Just my luck to have an *obesity scientist* for a mother."

I caught him grinning evilly at me in the rearview. Hoo-boy. Full-time mom once again. I smiled and said, "Let's go home."

Did you like it? If so, sign up for Mark's email newsletter and get a free e-book of your choice.

http://eepurl.com/YUT1X

Check out the next book in the trilogy:

THE OBESITY PANDEMIC

It's been five years since Elaine discovered the conspiracy to save the world by making Americans obese. But she and her savant researchers are under attack from within and without. A new crop of food industry executives want to shut her make the obesity epidemic a global pandemic. An unstoppable FBI agent is intent on exposing the conspiracy. Elaine has to keep the feds at bay while undermining her new corporate overlords. Running a conspiracy while raising an overeating teenager turns out to be a lot harder than she ever imagined.

AUTHOR'S NOTE:

Every American living in the early 21st century has been affected by the obesity epidemic. Most adults are overweight or obese. We all have family, friends, and coworkers who are obese, if we ourselves are not. Tens of millions have diabetes, cancer, and other diseases they probably wouldn't have had due to their weight. Childhood obesity is the latest, saddest front of the epidemic and could possibly shorten the lives of millions of our kids. This epidemic is personal for all of us.

The science fiction and fantasy community has been particularly hard-hit by the epidemic. It has shortened the lives of countless authors, editors, organizers, and fans. Despite the fact that reality of the epidemic sounds like the premise of an X-files conspiracy, it has been all but ignored by science fiction, horror, and fantasy.

But when reality becomes stranger than fiction, it's fiction's job to get weirder. Fiction gives us an safe way to understand and cope with what scares us. The book's science fiction and horror tropes are not meant to make light of obesity, but to give us some familiar fears to make it easier to face the real world ones we don't want to talk about. Plus, you know, in a world overrun with zombie fiction, good old-fashioned ghouls deserved some limelight.

—*Mark*

ACKNOWLEDGEMENTS

PATIENCE, TOLERANCE, SUPPORT
Wendy Sarney
Karenna Sarney
Jaden Sarney

ALPHA READER
Nolan Smith-Kaprosy

BETA READER
Joni Lavery

EDITING
Paula Stiles http://thesnowleopard.net/
Ellen Campbell http://thesnowleopard.net/

COVER, LAYOUT, DESIGN, AND PRODUCTION
Streetlight Graphics http://www.streetlightgraphics.com

AUTHOR INFO

Mark Sarney began writing science fiction as a geeky, contrarian kid in Rochester, NY. He created fantasy worlds while raking leaves, imagined that his elementary school was a rebel base, and gave the pilots of his Lego spaceships their own backstories. He went on to wear a Chuck E. Cheese costume, become a Washington policy wonk, find utopia, and pursue his lifelong dream of puking out words in an entertaining order.

He has been published at Daily Science Fiction.com and is the author of the Kagent trilogy. You can follow him at marksarney.com and on twitter.com/marksarney.

www.ingramcontent.com/pod-product-compliance
Lightning Source LLC
Chambersburg PA
CBHW071433260626
47170CB00008B/2701